Johnny now understood who his brother was.

Growing up, when Mack was on the international "Most Wanted" list, Johnny had sometimes wondered how he did it, how he stayed the course and steeled himself to wade through all that blood, knowing his war would never truly end, that final victory would always be beyond his grasp.

Since growing up, Johnny didn't wonder anymore.

His brother fought because he could, and knowing that he could meant that he really had no choice. If warriors were required to keep the predators at bay, Mack would be first in line to join the battle, every time. And when he fell, as all men must, there would be no doubt in the mind of anyone that he had done his best, consistently, from Day One to the bitter end.

MACK BOLAN ®
The Executioner

DON PENDLETON'S
THE EXECUTIONER®
JUDGMENT DAY

The Conspiracy Trilogy

BOOK III

A GOLD EAGLE BOOK FROM
WORLDWIDE®

TORONTO • NEW YORK • LONDON
AMSTERDAM • PARIS • SYDNEY • HAMBURG
STOCKHOLM • ATHENS • TOKYO • MILAN
MADRID • WARSAW • BUDAPEST • AUCKLAND

First edition May 2001
ISBN 0-373-64270-9

Special thanks and acknowledgment to
Michael Newton for his contribution to this work.

JUDGMENT DAY

There are times when fear is good. It must keep its watchful place at the heart's controls. There is advantage in the wisdom won from pain.

> —Aeschylus
> *The Eumenides*

It is not death or pain that is to be dreaded, but the fear of pain or death.

> —Epictetus
> *Discourses*

My enemies are terrorists who thrive upon the fear of others. Now it's time for them to taste the fear of pain and death themselves.

> —Mack Bolan

For members of the United Nations peacekeeping force
in Sierra Leone, executed by guerrillas of the
Revolutionary United Front in May 2000.
God keep.

1

This used to be Red territory, Mack Bolan thought, and at once he heard the echo of another small voice in his head, demanding his attention like a whisper in a crypt: It still may be.

The Soviet empire had fallen, shattering on impact with reality, its pieces flying off in all directions, bits of shrapnel, each demanding sovereignty and respect. Belarus was a state apart these days, and Minsk its teeming capital, but there were men at large—some of them wealthy, ruthless, powerful—who missed the bad old days and schemed to bring them back at any cost.

Minsk was another world, as foreign to Bolan as the dark side of the moon. Although he couldn't quote the statute books, he guessed there were penalties for loitering around the public streets at 8:05 a.m. with automatic weapons and explosives stashed inside his baggy overcoat. He didn't need a lawyer to advise him of the risk that he was taking on this morning when the sharp aroma of the street was one part fresh-baked bread and two parts diesel fuel.

The worst of it, to Bolan's mind: he wasn't operating on his own. The presence of two allies, one of them his brother, would have cheered him under different circumstances. Here and now, on such distinctly foreign turf, it only made him more concerned.

Three lives at risk instead of one.

And something else, he thought, but couldn't name it yet.

The target was an ethnic social club, at least on paper. It was somewhere for the sons of Chechnya to congregate, drink vodka until their vision blurred and bitch about the grave injustices they had sustained at Russian hands. Unfortunately for the neighbors on this peaceful Thursday morning, it was actually a hangout, sanctuary and nerve-center of sorts for the *Mafiya* Family run by Tolya Valerik.

Valerik had eluded Bolan for the past two weeks and change, leading him on a bloody chase across two continents, five countries and counting. Bolan hoped to end it here, although he had no reason to believe Valerik was inside the club. There would be others, though, and one of them—if squeezed correctly, with the necessary force—might put him on the Chechen mobster's tracks.

If not, then he would let their death serve as a calling card, a grim announcement of his presence on another battlefield.

It was a gamble, going in by daylight, but the club was definitely occupied. He had observed four hardmen going in since he arrived, and no doubt there were more inside, since they had found the door unlocked—and Bolan knew a morning strike would be less likely to involve civilians than a raid conducted when the club was officially open for business. Even now, there might be innocents somewhere around the premises, perhaps custodians, but he would take the chance, trusting his brother Johnny and CIA agent Able Deckard to refrain from harming any noncombatants when they made their rush.

He checked his watch again and saw that it was almost ten minutes past the hour. Time to move.

He left the alley that had sheltered him and crossed the narrow street, no traffic to dodge in this commercial neighborhood, still nearly two hours before most of the shops would open their doors for business. More good news. He hadn't seen employees or proprietors arriving yet, at any of the other places on the block. That meant less likelihood of witnesses and phone calls to the Minsk equivalent of 911. With any luck, they could be in and out before police had any reason to arrive in force.

Beneath his knee-length coat, he wore a short Kalashnikov AKSU assault rifle suspended from a makeshift shoulder sling, its curved magazine loaded with thirty rounds of 5.45 mm ammunition, full-metal jacket. Slung beneath his left armpit, secure inside a horizontal fast-draw rig, a Browning BDA 9 autoloader was the closest he had been able to come to the Berettas he favored. With fifteen 9 mm rounds in the staggered-row magazine, he reckoned it would serve for backup. Bolan's pockets sagged with spare magazines for both weapons, while three Russian-made antipersonnel grenades were clipped to his belt, out of sight.

The Executioner was dressed to kill.

The front door to the club was still unlocked, an oversight that would inevitably cost someone his life. Inside the door, a smallish foyer with another door directly opposite. Off to his left, as Bolan's eyes adjusted from the glare of sunlight to a sudden gloom, he saw a hulking lookout seated on a metal folding chair.

The guard was bald, fat-faced, slack-jawed. He obviously didn't recognize the new arrival, but it didn't seem to worry him. Perhaps he was expecting strangers, Bolan thought, which meant that there would be some kind of password, at the very least, required before he could proceed.

As if in answer to his silent thought, the bald man shifted forward on his chair, still seeming unconcerned, addressing Bolan with a voice that grated roughly on his ears.

"Where is the bathroom, please?" Bolan asked in Russian.

The bald man blinked at him, the corners of his thick lips turning downward in a scowl as he began to rise from his seat.

Too late.

A roundhouse kick slammed into the Russian's face and pitched him to his right, as Bolan registered a numbing shock between his foot and knee. The lookout may as well have had a helmet on, the way it felt to kick him in the head, and he rebounded from the nearest wall a heartbeat later, snarling incoherently, lunging for Bolan in a sudden rage that didn't leave him any time to think about a weapon.

Bolan stepped back to give himself a little room and threw another roundhouse kick, but low, this time, connecting with the hardman's knee. It cracked, the rubber leg betraying him, and Bolan was on top of him as he began to fall. He swung the pistol grip of his Kalashnikov into the toppling ogre's face, avoiding contact with the barrel, just in case the bald man's skull was hard enough to bend it out of true. Still snarling as he hit the floor, the guard was open to another kick that cracked his hyoid bone and sealed his larynx for good, his face turning blue in seconds as he thrashed and wallowed on the floor, a monstrous stranded fish.

When he lay still, the man known as the Executioner reversed directions, pushing through the second door into the cool, dark sanctuary of the club.

SOME KIND OF PROBLEM, Johnny Bolan Gray decided, thankful that at least there was no gunfire yet. He stood inside a narrow, musty-smelling corridor that stretched beyond the back door of the social club, past doors that served the toilets, kitchen and some kind of private office, to the main room of the club itself. It had required the best part of a minute for him to defeat the back door's lock with simple tools, but he was still on schedule, pausing in the hallway as he waited for the other members of his team to show.

His brother Mack and Able Deckard. Either one of them could have encountered trouble, coming in, but Johnny thought there should have been some racket—gunfire, maybe a grenade blast—if the odds were critical. Without the noise, he told himself, it's still okay.

He wouldn't think about the possibility that one or both of them might already be dead. A clean shot with a sound suppressor or perhaps an underhanded blade. His brother wasn't Superman, no matter what the tabloids used to say, before he "died" and was reborn in service to the country that had once done everything within its power to hunt him down.

Bygones.

His wristwatch told him it was time to move, whether the others were in place or not. His instinct and his military training told him to proceed as planned, and let the loose ends take care of themselves.

They had picked up three identical AKSU rifles in Grodno, as well as side arms, ammo and explosives, from a dealer Deckard knew, some kind of part-time contract agent for the Company who freelanced when he got the chance. The money they had used to buy the hardware was a "present," liberated from their enemies.

He started to think about Suzanne King, his reason for being there, then caught himself before his mind could stray, already moving out to check the doors on each side of the hallway, determined not to leave an enemy behind him as he went. Johnny found no one in the rest rooms, checking out the doorless stalls, and no one in the kitchen. When he tried the office door, he found it locked, rapped softly for admittance, just in case, prepared to kick it in, and got no answer from inside.

Dismissing his brother and Able Deckard from his mind, as much as possible, he focused on his mission, moving swiftly toward the double swing doors that marked the entrance to the main room of the Chechen social club. His nostrils had already picked up the aroma of tobacco smoke, and he could hear the hardmen talking, someone laughing at something, the laughter sounding forced, somehow unnatural.

The next few moments would demand complete and iron-clad concentration if he wanted to survive.

He used the stubby muzzle of his AKSU to push the right-hand swing door aside and shouldered back the left, no big production, nothing to distract the hardmen from their conversation as he stood there on the threshold for a moment, checking out the room. There was a wet bar to his right, a small stage for performers at the far end of the room, booths ranged along the walls and simple wooden tables in the middle of the floor. He swiftly counted heads, surprised to make it fifteen shooters at that hour of the morning.

"So," he said in English, wondering if any of the goons would understand, "I don't suppose you'd like to raise your hands and all line up against the wall?"

The conversation died, and fifteen pairs of gimlet eyes pinned Johnny where he stood, the hardmen scowling at him, as if he had broken wind in church.

"I didn't think so," Johnny added with a shrug.

There was another door directly opposite, some twenty yards away, in the direction of the street. It opened as he finished speaking, Johnny pivoting to cover it before he recognized his brother coming in, and in that instant, his attention faltering, the set began to come apart.

He had to give the hardmen credit, boxed that way and taken by complete surprise, but still responding like professionals. They broke in all directions, scattering as if the move had been rehearsed, no pattern to it, each shooter digging for a weapon underneath his jacket, shirttails, somewhere—one of them hopping on his left foot, grappling with the right, his pistol in some kind of ankle holster.

It was instant chaos, and Johnny chose the nearest target as a matter of convenience, a matter of survival, squeezing off a short burst at the hopping gunner, spinning him and dropping him as if someone had yanked the floor out from beneath his feet. By that time, his brother was firing too, and someone else, the pops of pistol fire contrasting with the rattle of the twin Kalashnikovs.

One of the Chechen shooters obviously didn't trust a semi-auto piece to do the job. He had a Czech machine pistol, the Model-61 Skorpion, and he was waving it about as if the very sight of it would cause his enemies to back away and spare his life. It might have worked in other circumstances, but the hardman didn't know who he was dealing with.

He tried his best, though; Johnny had to give him that. A

pivot to the left, and he was facing Johnny from a distance of no more than twenty feet. Call it point-blank for either of their weapons, and the gunner should have scored, but he was hasty off the mark, jerking the trigger when he should have milked it gently, foolishly trusting the Skorpion to a one-handed grip. The weapon got away from him, its muzzle climbing, veering to his left, away from the cascade of brass it was ejecting. By the time he lifted off the trigger, brought his free hand up to tame the Skorpion, it was too late. A short burst from the AKSU opened up his chest with all the efficiency of an autopsy saw, but none of the finesse. The hardman vaulted backward in a crimson spray and took one of the tables with him, which shattered as he tumbled to the floor.

Too long, Johnny thought. This was taking too damned long!

And where the hell was Able Deckard?

THE MAN FROM Langley was supposed to come in through the roof. They had an access door up there, its housing reminiscent of a chicken coop and just about as large. He wondered if the guys who handled rooftop maintenance were runts, or if the carpenters had run short of materials the day they got around to that part of the job.

Whatever.

Deckard beat the simple lock in seconds flat, then gave the stunted door a shove and found that it was bolted from inside. He knew the bolt's approximate location, from the way the door gave at the top and bottom when he shoved against it, hand and foot, but there was no way he could actually reach it to defeat the second lock.

Goddammit!

There were only two ways he could go from that point on. He could retreat and pick a ground-floor entrance, run the risk of being shot by one of his companions when they took him for a Russian mobster, or he could use force to breach the door and blow whatever edge surprise might give him. More to the point, if he announced himself by kicking in the door or shooting off the inner lock, the gunners in the club would then be ready for his two comrades, as well.

Stalemate.

Deckard wasn't going to stand there like an idiot and let the others fight alone. But if he couldn't get inside…

Deckard was stepping back to check his wristwatch in the sunlight, when a muffled rattling sound like the report of a pneumatic drill reached his ears. He couldn't tell if it was coming through the door in front of him, or through the roof beneath his feet, but either way he recognized the telltale sound of a Kalashnikov in action.

Late, for Christ's sake!

Deckard gave the door a kick and heard the wood crack, but the inner bolt held fast. He swung up the AKSU and stroked the trigger, squinting to protect his eyes as wooden splinters flew in all directions, from the door and jamb, the bolt no longer any kind of obstacle.

He had to duck his head and shoulders, going through the dwarf door, and it nearly made him stumble on the stairs inside. No light to guide him in the narrow stairwell, but for that provided by a dim bulb on the landing below. The stairwell smelled like mold and something even more unpleasant. Deckard didn't want to think about it, concentrating on the noise his entry had to have made, the possibility that hardmen would be waiting for him on the ground floor.

The sounds of combat were no longer muffled, rather amplified inside the stairwell, making Deckard's ears ring. At the bottom of the stairs, he found himself inside a kind of alcove, set back from a corridor that he supposed led from the main clubroom to the back door Johnny Gray was using as his entrance. Damn! So he would *still* be coming in behind the kid, unless…

He turned right, toward the back door, found it open as expected, and then cut hard-right into the kitchen. No one was there to challenge him, but Deckard found what he was looking for, another entrance to the clubroom for the waiters toting plates and trays at mealtime, saving them a few steps on the turnaround.

Beyond that door, all hell had broken loose. As if to prove the point, a short, disheveled stranger appeared, brandishing a satin-finish automatic pistol in one hand, the other smearing blood across his face, trying to clear his eyes as more flowed from a gash along his hairline.

Deckard shot him in the chest, a short burst, dead on target, and the impact of his bullets sent the dead man back in the direction he had come from, through the swing door. A pistol bullet drilled the upper panel of the door and struck a wall behind him, off to Deckard's left, but he couldn't tell if the shot had been a stray, or maybe a response to his dispatching of the Russian shooter.

Either way, he had to make the move.

Right now.

There was no safe-and-easy way to do it, Deckard crouching into his approach, the bullet-punctured door resisting only slightly as he shouldered it aside to scan the killing floor. His comrades both had cover, Johnny Gray behind the bar, the man whom Deckard knew as Evan Green hunched behind a table he had toppled on its side to shield him from incoming fire. It was the best that quadrant of the clubroom had to offer, but it wasn't much, already scarred by bullets, drilled completely through by more than one. If Green remained there too much longer, without help...

A couple of the hardmen were advancing on him under cover of the fire provided by their comrades, both still blissfully oblivious to Deckard's presence on their blind side. Never one to look a gift horse in the mouth, he shot them in the back, a short burst clattering from left to right and dropping both of them before they even recognized the danger on their flank. They went down without protest, like two puppets liberated by a razor drawn across their strings, at last permitted to relax.

A quick glance toward the bar caught Johnny midgrin—or was it grimace?—but the young man had his hands full with a pair of hardmen crouched behind upended tables of their own. With time and luck, Gray could reduce their cover with the automatic fire from his Kalashnikov, but time and luck were two commodities in short supply just now.

Deckard was lining up a shot to help him, drop one of the shooters, when a bullet struck the barrel of his AKSU and the weapon spun out of his grasp. Somehow, the weapon swung around and struck him on the right cheek, drawing blood before it clattered to the floor.

Was that a lucky shot, or was he up against an expert marksman? Deckard let the question ricochet inside his head, unanswered, as he drew his side arm—a Walther P-88—from the holster slung beneath his left arm. Deckard wasn't sure if his Kalashnikov had been disabled by the hit, but this was no time to be test-firing a weapon of unknown reliability.

Where was the shooter who had so effectively disarmed him? Deckard risked his life and face to answer that one, nosing out from cover cautiously, watching for any muzzle-flashes that would give away his enemy. Between tobacco smoke and cordite, seasoned with the sharp, metallic smell of fresh-spilled blood, made Deckard squint with teary eyes, but he could still see well enough to spot the shooter when he leaned out of a booth to try his luck again.

The trick wasn't recoiling from the muzzle-flash, not picturing a bullet sizzling directly toward your face. Teeth clenched against the urge to panic, Deckard found his target, squeezed off two quick shots and saw the gunner stiffen, wobbling on his perch. Another double tap, and Deckard saw his adversary slither from the booth, kissing the floor as he went down.

He scanned the slaughterhouse in search of other targets.

IF HE HAD THOUGHT about it afterward, Mack Bolan couldn't have sworn the Russian shooters were intent on killing him when they stood and made their move. They charged in his direction, both of them firing as they came, but it was possible they simply hoped to reach the exit and the street beyond, a destination that required them to pin Bolan down, at least.

They both had pistols, nothing heavy, but it wouldn't take a battery of automatic weapons, at that range, to snuff out his life like a candle flame. One well-placed slug would do it, even if the shooter scored by accident, without the luxury of lining up his shot.

Two moving targets, and the table that concealed him had begun to take on the appearance of a colander, absorbing more rounds than it managed to deflect. Bolan had been reduced to lying prone and moving lizardlike, to left or right, when he returned fire from his enemies. It was a tenuous position, and he knew it. Any moment now, the law of averages would turn against him.

Unwittingly, the two hardmen provided Bolan with the opportunity he had been waiting, hoping for. Moving between their comrades and his meager, bullet-riddled barricade, they forced upon his enemies a momentary cease-fire, no guns but their own unloading on him as they charged.

He seized the moment, pushing off with his left arm and rolling clear of cover, making target acquisition on the nearer of his enemies before the runners understood that he had moved. A rising burst from Bolan's AKSU rifle stitched the hardman from his groin to his sternum. Stopping dead, as if he had collided with some unseen barrier, the Russian staggered backward before he gave it up to gravity, crashing in a heap.

Instead of breaking for the door, the dead man's comrade veered toward Bolan, anger or a sense of duty driving him to nail the gunner who had killed his friend. The bold move might have worked if he had been a trifle more decisive when the stakes were life and death. Mindful of his desire to squeeze a prisoner for information, Bolan cut the gunner's legs from underneath him with a figure eight burst that snapped both femurs, pulped both knees. The hardman's pistol clattered out of reach as he went down.

Exposed, the Executioner kept moving, rolling, firing for effect until he emptied the Kalashnikov. By that time, he had reached another table, and he grabbed the nearest leg, upending it for cover as he pulled the empty magazine and snapped a fresh one in its place. He recognized the sound of two more AKSU rifles, knew that Deckard had arrived to join the fight and felt a new rush of adrenaline kick in.

There was a pocket of resistance in the middle of the clubroom, three or four surviving shooters who had thrown their tables over in a rough triangular arrangement, to construct a flimsy fortress. They couldn't withstand the concentrated fire of three Kalashnikovs forever, but his own team didn't have the luxury of time, when the police might even now be on their way.

Bolan reached underneath his coat, released a frag grenade from its position on his belt and used his thumb to hook the pin, discarding it. His fingers clamped the safety spoon in place until he rose to make the pitch, an almost-gentle overhand because the distance wasn't great. He didn't need to see the lethal egg in wobbling flight or watch it fall among his enemies. Before that happened, he shouted to the other members of his team.

"Fire in the hole!"

Six seconds was a lifetime on a battlefield. Two of the Russians recognized the frag grenade and scrambled for it, getting in each other's way. If only one had tried, he might have snagged it, tossed it clear in time to save them all, but as it was, the pair of them were stooped, heads nearly touching, when it went off in their faces.

In the aftermath of the explosion, there was only ringing silence in the smoky room. Bolan was cautious as he rose from cover, knowing that the blast may not have neutralized all of the gunners in the makeshift dugout. There could still be others, too, stunned into immobility by the explosion, maybe playing dead until they had a shot.

His brother rose behind the bar, Deckard emerging from a doorway that appeared to serve the kitchen.

A couple of their fallen enemies were moaning, moving, but from where he stood, it didn't seem that either one of them had long to live, nor were they in much shape to speak coherently. He turned back to the hardman he had wounded, scattering spent brass before him as he backtracked. Stepping closer, Bolan saw the soldier's slackened jaw, glazed eyes, and knew he was too late.

He checked the floor around the body, measuring the blood pool with a practiced eye. The Russian would have bled out, given time, but there wasn't sufficient blood in evidence to rank that as his cause of death. Shock killed sometimes, of course, but the expression on the dead man's face didn't resemble others he had seen, up close and personal, where shock had snuffed the spark of life.

He walked around behind the dead man, who was lying on his side, and saw the fatal wound immediately. It was tucked away behind one ear, a tidy hole, perhaps 9 mm. He wondered briefly if it was a stray round or a mercy shot from one of the dead man's associates, then let the question go. It was irrelevant in any case.

He felt the others coming up behind him as he rose. "No prisoners," he told them, just a hint of disappointment in his voice.

"We'll have to try again," Johnny said.

"Maybe try another angle," Deckard suggested. The spook was checking out his rifle, fingering a bright scar on the barrel.

"Have you got something in mind?"

"Valerik's close to home," Deckard replied. "It's not that far to Moscow, say four hundred miles. A couple hours, if he flies, or he could drive and make it in a day."

"You think that's where he's going?" Bolan asked.

"I wouldn't want to swear," the man from Langley said,

"but I can ask around. We've still got people in the neighborhood."

"People who work for you?" Johnny asked pointedly, referring to the fact that they had documented links between the Russian Mob and CIA, links Deckard had been trying to unravel when the brothers first encountered him in Amsterdam

"There'll be an element of risk," Deckard acknowledged, "but it's worth a shot."

Bolan could feel his brother watching him, placing the decision in his hands. He thought about it for another moment, listening for sirens, then he said, "Give it a shot."

"Will do," the spook replied. "And now, if you don't mind my saying so, I think it's time we hauled ass out of here."

2

"We're leaving now, today. You understand me? I won't be a sitting duck for these damned sons of bitches anymore." Tolya Valerik spoke with animation, chopping at the air in front of him with one hand, as if he were teaching a karate lesson.

"As you wish Tolya, of course," Anatoly Bogdashka replied. He was Valerik's second in command, and therefore obligated to a certain measure of agreement. More importantly, he knew the kind of violence Valerik was capable of when he entered an agitated state, the danger he posed to those around him. Cautiously, the Russian mafioso raised a hand, as if he were a schoolboy. "There is one small question…"

"Hmm? What question?" Valerik challenged him.

"Krestyanov may not think this latest problem is connected to the other troubles," Bogdashka said. "It would be helpful if we had some proof."

"What kind of proof?" Valerik asked. "The sons of bitches left no one alive, remember? Let Krestyanov and his giant go interrogate the dead if they're inclined to do so. *I* decide what is connected and what's not when the survival of my Family's at stake. If Krestyanov believes this latest incident has followed all the others by coincidence, then he's an idiot. You tell him that."

Bogdashka winced. He had expected the task of speaking to Vassily Krestyanov would be his, but he wasn't prepared to call the former chief assassin of the former KGB an idiot.

Not to his face, at least, or even on the telephone...unless, perhaps, he found Krestyanov paralyzed and dying when they met. It would be safe, in that case. Otherwise...

"Tell him this is my Family," Valerik raged, "and I have lost too many soldiers, too much property and cash to treat these sons of bitches as a minor irritation. He's not paying me—not paying us—enough to compensate for the destruction of the Family and everything we own, from Minsk to New York and Los Angeles."

It wasn't quite that bad, Bogdashka knew, but it was close. Their operations had been ravaged in Los Angeles, New York and Montreal, in Amsterdam and in Berlin. The raid in Minsk was too damned close to home, and while Bogdashka couldn't prove the same men were involved in all of the attacks, he was convinced of it himself. No other explanation fit the circumstances.

It was unbelievable. All this, because a woman named Suzanne King in the United States had hired a private investigator to find her missing brother, himself a worthless petty criminal, expunged for stealing from the Family. It was bizarre, preposterous, that such a minor incident could spark what now amounted to a global conflict, with the shock troops of their enemies still unidentified.

"You understand," he said, "Krestyanov may object."

"Let him object!" Valerik barked. "It costs him nothing to stand back and criticize. I'm not afraid of some old spy who should be out at pasture now, instead of dreaming up fantastic schemes."

Another lie, Bogdashka thought, and wondered why Valerik felt he had to keep up the pretense when it was just the two of them, alone. Valerik had grown up under communism, with the KGB a daily fact of life, and while he had elected to defy the law, make up his own rules as he went along, Bogdashka knew he felt the same uneasiness and apprehension—fear, in truth—when they were dealing with Vassily Krestyanov. The age-old fear was in his blood; it had been fed to him in infancy, mixed with his mother's milk.

Besides, it was a prima facie indication of insanity to not fear Krestyanov. The man still had some powerful connections, both within the present Russian government and on the outside. He had connections, or at least an "understanding," with the CIA. He could destroy lives on a whim, as lesser men might slaughter rats or insects.

And, of course, there was the clincher, the most telling bit of all. This time, Krestyanov was on a mission he believed in. It wasn't a simple matter of retrieving information or eliminating some specific target for a price.

This time, the former KGB colonel was playing for the world.

Tolya Valerik had become involved—correction: had involved them all, his aides and underlings—because he could obtain specific items Krestyanov required with less red tape and fewer risks than Krestyanov's associates still serving in the Russian military. If they pulled it off and made delivery, they would be rich beyond their wildest dreams.

If they didn't...

"Where shall I tell him we are going, Tolya?"

"Home." The single word so fraught with risks and possibilities.

Moscow.

Bogdashka yearned to keep his mouth shut, but he had to ask. "And if we're followed there, as well? What, then?"

He had expected Valerik's heavy-duty frown, the one that told him his boss was considering some weighty proposition: whether to make war against another Family, perhaps; whether to risk a billion rubles on investment in a brand-new territory. Bogdashka was surprised, therefore, when Valerik answered almost casually, as if the grim decision had required no thought at all.

"In that case," he replied, "we stand and fight. There will be nowhere else to go."

Not strictly true, of course. They had a world of choices, from Afghanistan to Zimbabwe, a literal A-to-Z of nations where their money would be welcome and their privacy respected—while the cash held out, at least. He knew what Valerik meant, though. It was one thing to be chased out of America, the Netherlands or Germany. They had grown up in Moscow, earned their scars and made their reputations there, spilled blood and vodka in approximately equal measure.

"I'll talk to Krestyanov," Bogdashka said.

Valerik didn't acknowledge the remark, too busy sipping vodka from a stout ceramic coffee mug. The order had been given; he assumed that Bogdashka would obey it. The acknowledgment was totally superfluous.

A question came to Bogdashka's mind, and while he knew it might be better not to speak, he couldn't keep it to himself. "You still intend to make delivery on the merchandise?" he asked.

Valerik blinked at him, as if surprised. "Of course," he said. "Why wouldn't I?"

The answer seemed so obvious to Bogdashka that he dared not put it into words. Instead, he simply shrugged and shook his head.

"We take delivery on the merchandise tomorrow," Valerik said, reminding him unnecessarily. "Another day or two, at the outside, and Krestyanov will have it—after we've confirmed the bank transfers, that is. Beyond that, it won't be our problem anymore."

Bogdashka didn't share his leader's confidence. When he thought about the problem, though, it seemed to him that many things could still go wrong, rebound against Valerik and himself, against the Family, whether they were involved directly in the game or not.

How would they function as a syndicate, for instance, if Krestyanov's judgment was mistaken and the whole damned world should be destroyed?

Instead of posing such a hopeless question, Bogdashka asked Valerik, "Would you rather fly or drive?"

Valerik blinked at him, uncomprehending. "Fly or drive?"

"To Moscow."

"Ah. The quickest way," he said, now that the question had been clarified. "It's best to fly, of course, unless we have to wait for hours to get a plane. I leave it in your hands."

As usual, Bogdashka thought, but kept it to himself. "I'll check and see before I speak to Krestyanov."

Valerik didn't insult him by reminding his second in command to alert their troops in Moscow. They would need airtight security, beginning from the moment they arrived—or sooner if they traveled overland. If they were driving, Bogdashka reckoned he should have some well-armed people meet them in Smolensk and form a convoy back to Moscow. Let the faceless sons of bitches try their antics then. Or, better yet, in Moscow, when the two of them were back on their home turf.

For just a moment, Bogdashka felt his apprehension fading, taking a back seat to anger and defiance. It had galled him, being driven out of first one city, then another, by an enemy he couldn't identify or come to grips with. Still, the run of luck that favored their opponents had to break sometime.

That didn't help the soldiers they had lost in Minsk that morning or the dozens who had gone before them, cut down as if they were amateurs caught playing a war game with professionals. It had been embarrassing, at first; as time went on, though, Bogdashka came to understand that no one in their Family was safe.

Not Valerik.

Not himself.

It was a kind of revelation, after all the battles they had been through, sometimes with the heavy odds against them. He had always known death was inevitable, never quite expected it to find him old and gray, with great-grandchildren, but this was different. In all the other battles, whether he had chosen them or someone else had forced the fight upon him, he had always known his enemies: their names, their number and their pedigree.

This time it felt like fighting ghosts.

And Bogdashka didn't like that feeling.

It made him feel as if he already had one foot in the grave.

VASSILY KRESTYANOV believed that he had dealt with every kind of human being that existed in his lifetime, either in his time with KGB, or after going private, working on his own account. He knew the different sorts of men and women he was likely to encounter in a given situation and could cope with any of them, whether it required a show of strength or a pretense of weakness, threats or flattery, seduction or intimidation. He had broken heroes in his time and coddled cowards, had inflated mice until they felt like men and tried to act accordingly. Rarely was he surprised.

This Thursday afternoon was therefore noteworthy.

Krestyanov was surprised—and troubled. He could grudgingly admit it to himself—at learning that the men who stalked Tolya Valerik had followed him from Germany to Minsk. Pursuing him from the United States to Amsterdam and then Berlin was one thing. To leave the West for Russia and her satellites was something else again. Beyond the cold war's "Redland" stigma, thinking back to when the Russian people labored under czars and Cossack tribesmen roamed the steppes at will, there was a sense of leaving the familiar world behind and passing literally "beyond the Pale."

Valerik's enemies, apparently, had no such qualms or reservations. Their persistence—not to say unmitigated gall—was what disturbed Krestyanov most of all. It told him they weren't simply rival gangsters, jealous of their territory in New York, in Montreal or Amsterdam. It told him, further, that their motivation went beyond revenge for the elimination of some two-bit criminal in the United States. Even the Gypsies and Sicilians wouldn't trek halfway around the planet to avenge a kinsman, killing scores of trained assassins in the process.

No. Tolya Valerik was the lightning rod, but Krestyanov was troubled now because he felt the nameless, faceless hunters coming closer to himself. He didn't think they were aware of his intentions yet, though it had been a near-miss in Berlin. He hadn't recognized the gunman—barely glimpsed his face, in fact—but having someone come for him *at all* warned Krestyanov that his protective buffer layers were breaking down.

How long before the faceless enemy knew everything?

Not soon enough to save themselves, he thought.

"Save who?"

The voice of Nikolai Lukasha startled Krestyanov. Despite his size, even when Lukasha wasn't in motion, when he didn't speak, Krestyanov found that it was possible to put the hulking giant out of mind completely and forget that he was even in the room. If he had ever learned the knack of passing thus unnoticed on the street, Lukasha could have been a first-rate spy instead of being relegated to the dungeons of the Lubyanka Prison where he had been placed in charge of executions and interrogations.

"Never mind," Krestyanov said, unwilling to explain his lapse. "How long until we take delivery on the merchandise?"

Krestyanov knew the answer to that question, and Lukasha *knew* he knew it. Still, it was important to him at this moment for the words to be pronounced, as if repeating them aloud would somehow guarantee success.

"Twenty-nine hours and—" Lukasha checked his ornate pocket watch against the Timex on his wrist, concerned as always with precision "—thirteen minutes."

"Are you sure?"

Lukasha understood that he was joking, even though he didn't see the humor in it. He didn't respond. It would be fourteen years next April since he first laid eyes upon the giant, and Krestyanov hadn't seen Lukasha laugh in all that time. His smiles were rare enough, the kind of once- or twice-a-year events that always startled his acquaintances, unsettled most of them, and frightened some who knew him best.

"I fear," Krestyanov said, choosing the word deliberately, "there may be some effort to divert the package or prevent us from receiving it."

"Valerik?" Lukasha made fists of his great hands and clenched them slowly, tightening until the knuckles popped.

Krestyanov shook his head. "The others," he replied. "I wish we could have stopped them in Berlin."

It was no criticism of Lukasha, since the giant had defended him—may well have saved Krestyanov's life, in fact—when they were ambushed, leaving their hotel. Lukasha didn't take offense, instead considering the problem as it lay before them now.

"We have another chance in Minsk," he said.

"It feels wrong," Krestyanov replied. "We still don't know enough about them, who they are and where they come from, what they want."

"We should have squeezed the woman," the giant suggested.

He was right, of course. One of Krestyanov's contacts in Berlin, a former Stasi officer, had traced Suzanne King and had abducted her, staking her out as bait to draw the others in. She had been questioned briefly, unproductively, the emphasis on using her to trap the men she traveled with, finish them off once and for all. It was an oversight, and it had blown up in Krestyanov's face. The enemy had liberated her, wiped out his German underlings and nearly bagged Krestyanov in the bargain.

He accepted Lukasha's rebuke without responding to it. A commander had to be able to acknowledge his mistakes, but agonizing over them was a pathetic waste of time and energy.

Vassily Krestyanov was still alive, and he would never underestimate this enemy again.

"Tolya has problems with security," Krestyanov said.

"That much is clear. It's not clear how his enemies keep track of him."

"The CIA, perhaps?"

Lukasha knew what that would mean to both of them. The obstacles and hazards they would face if their connection in the States was jeopardized.

"I hope not," Krestyanov replied, stating the obvious. "And yet..."

"I'll have to check it out. You're right, of course." He had intended to touch base with Noble Pruett, in Washington, about their latest problems in Berlin and Minsk. There was no harm in letting Lukasha believe the call was his idea. An ego stroke, deftly applied, could be more useful in the long run than a hundred threats.

"They can't stop us, Vassily."

They presumably referred to the CIA. Krestyanov, sadly, didn't share his aide's complacency. He had been very nearly stopped for good while he was waiting for an elevator in Berlin. It only took one lucky shot, and while Krestyanov was prepared to sacrifice his life if necessary for the cause, he also understood that if his enemies could get that close to him and still remain unrecognized, they also had at least some chance of interfering with the next day's delivery. And if Krestyanov couldn't get the merchandise he needed, it would mean that all his planning, all his preparation, had been wasted.

He couldn't expect to get a second opportunity, not with his nervous partners in the States.

Not with the stakes this large.

Pruett and company had psyched themselves up to the point that they were ready to proceed, permit the necessary sacrifice, but if the process was derailed, Krestyanov could expect them to retreat and reconsider, look for ways to cut their losses— and to cut their ties with him. Krestyanov could attempt to go ahead without them, but cooperation from an element within the CIA was critical to his design as it now stood. If he lost Pruett and the rest, it would be difficult, perhaps impossible, for him to carry out the *konspiratsia* as it had been initially conceived.

And if he started playing with the script, there was a chance he would also lose his critical support in Mother Russia, where it mattered most of all. His allies were determined men, but they were also realists. They wouldn't throw their lives away on some last-minute variation of the theme that had no likely prospect for success.

In short, it was imperative that nothing—no one—else jeopardize the master plan at this late date, when he was so close to the eve of Armageddon and the final victory.

When Krestyanov was finished, if he pulled it off, the order he was born to, raised with, trained to serve, would be restored. The cowards, liberals and decadent revisionists would all be swept away. Goodbye to blue jeans, heavy metal music, Pepsi-Cola and McDonald's. Generations yet unborn would honor him when they recalled the sad, humiliating Yeltsin years as a brief interlude of national hysteria.

Such periods of transient madness weren't unique to Russia; they were found throughout recorded history. The witch craze of the Middle Ages. The Crusades. The Inquisition. Alcoholic prohibition in America. The German Reich. Nations, like men, went mad from time to time, but most of them recovered, even if their madness took them to the very brink of death. Inevitably, it required a shocking sacrifice, the national equivalent of slapping a hysteric's face to shut him up.

The madness of democracy had gone on long enough in Mother Russia. It was time for her to wake, shake off her fever dream and snap back to her senses. Waking from a decade of delirium wouldn't be painless. There would certainly be casualties. Krestyanov might be one of them, but he didn't believe so.

Not if he could step in and regain control before the crucial hour.

"What time is it in the United States?" he asked Lukasha.

"Which time zone?"

"The East."

Lukasha palmed his pocket watch again and cocked his arm to check the Timex. It was like the ritual of some eccentric, slightly senile uncle. "Minus seven hours," he replied.

"Still night, then."

"Yes."

So be it. Why should Noble Pruett be allowed to sleep?

THE GODDAMNED TELEPHONE, Pruett thought, as he struggled back to consciousness from what was shaping up to be a lovely dream. It had involved his red-haired secretary and another woman whom he didn't recognize, the two of them—

"Hello!"

The only answer was the dial tone buzzing in his ear, while all the time another telephone kept ringing.

"Shit!"

He slammed down the handset and fumbled at the top drawer of his nightstand, groped inside it for the other telephone, his scrambled private line. Perhaps two dozen people in the world possessed that number, and it had to be bad news for any of them to be calling Pruett in the middle of the night.

"Hello," he said again, suppressing the desire to let off steam. Better to find out who was on the line and what they wanted first.

"You were asleep?"

Krestyanov. Wonderful. "Of course. You know what time it is?"

"Where you are," the Russian said, "it should now be 3:19 a.m."

Pruett turned bleary eyes to the alarm clock, its digital numbers glowing softly in aquamarine. "Okay," he said. "Did you want something else? Because my wakeup call's not due for—"

"It would seem we have another problem," the Russian said, interrupting him. "Or, should I say, the same problem continuing?"

"I don't know what you mean to say," Pruett replied. "It's your dime. You tell me."

"This line is perfectly secure?"

"It's cool."

"Our friend Tolya has been the victim of another incident. In Minsk this time."

"You're shitting me."

"Regrettably," Krestyanov answered, "I am not. More of his assets have been liquidated, under circumstances very similar to previous attacks."

"Same parties were involved?" he asked, and instantly regretted it.

"I can't answer that with any confidence," Krestyanov said, "since we haven't been able to identify the individuals responsible. I hoped you might be able to contribute something new in that respect."

"I'm working on it," Pruett told him.

"In your sleep?"

"Come on, Vassily, you remember how it works. You haven't been retired that long...or, have you?"

"I have never been retired," Krestyanov said.

"Okay, then, so you do remember. It's called delegation of authority, my friend. You want my chief of operations in the field, call Keane and wake him up."

It pleased him when the Russian answered in a stiff and formal tone, betraying anger. Pruett didn't often penetrate Krestyanov's armor. It was satisfying for a moment, until Pruett realized that any situation capable of rattling Vassily Krestyanov might spell disaster for them all.

"I woke you," Krestyanov was saying, "to advise you that our common problem hasn't been resolved. Rather, in fact, that it appears to be compounded, growing worse. I also note that you have still not managed to identify the individuals responsible."

"You know about Suzanne King and her PI, Johnny Gray?"

"Indeed," Krestyanov said. "And we both know that there are other men involved."

"I was thinking you could get that information from the woman," Pruett said. "A little birdie told me you bagged her in Berlin."

"Your birdie is behind the times," Krestyanov said. "My contacts in Berlin were neutralized. The woman is no longer in our hands."

Pruett knew that, as well, but he enjoyed putting the Russian on the spot. "You lost her, huh?" he said. "When you've had time to figure out how that's my fault, be sure to call me back."

"Your attitude is nonproductive," Krestyanov observed.

"My attitude?" Pruett could feel his cool evaporating. "You blame me for shit that's happening in Europe, on your watch, and you complain about my attitude?"

"You promised full cooperation."

"And you're getting it!"

"It's not enough," Krestyanov said. "I take delivery on the special merchandise tomorrow if there are no further problems. You know what that means."

"We've been all over this," Pruett said, wishing he was still asleep, his secretary and the Jane Doe making every fantasy he ever imagined come true. "You get the package over here, I'll do my part."

"Your part," Krestyanov answered, with a mocking note, "is to insure that we succeed. I hope that you haven't deceived yourself into believing that you can survive, somehow, if we should fail."

"I hear you," Pruett said. "You want a presence in the field, okay. I'm reaching out to Keane. You want him where, again? In Minsk?"

"It's too late for Minsk," the Russian said. "Tolya is going home, to Moscow. I intend to join him there and take delivery on the merchandise tomorrow, as we planned."

"Moscow." Christian Keane wouldn't like it, but it didn't

really matter what he liked, as long as he obeyed his orders to the letter. "Right. If you have any use for Keane, you'll find him at the Marco Polo Presnya. He'll register as Fletcher Christian."

"How adventurous," the colonel said. "You're sending me one man?"

"You've got two armies, as it is," Pruett replied. "What's left of Tolya's, and your own. If you start running short of men, Keane has connections, people in the area we've used before."

"Your sleepers?" Krestyanov was suddenly attentive, a spark of professional interest kindled into flame.

"They're strictly locals," Pruett told him, pleased to burst the Russian's bubble. "Believe it or not, Vassily, we found some folks who weren't all hot to trot about the Worker's Paradise."

"As we found some among your countrymen, from sea to shining sea," Krestyanov said.

"It takes all kinds," Pruett said, feeling once again how much he missed the game.

"Someday," Krestyanov said, "we should compare notes, when we have the luxury of time."

"You know I never give my people up, Vassily," Pruett replied, "unless there's something to be gained from it."

"Of course. I've always had faith in your practicality."

"So, even with this Tolya business, we're on schedule?" Pruett asked.

"I will accept no less than absolute success," Krestyanov answered.

I guess we've got it made, then, Pruett thought, and said, "Okay. Watch out for Keane, then. He will *not* attempt to get in touch with you unless he's summoned."

"I understand. I hope that it will be enough."

"Just get that package over here," Pruett said, "and the rest will take care of itself."

Which was ridiculous, of course. Nothing would take care

of itself. Pruett would have to cover all the angles, each step of the way, from that point on. The Russians or their flunkies were supposed to light the fuse, but he would have to cover them, make sure they got it right, help them negotiate whatever obstacles they might encounter on the way.

And once the fuse was lit he would be in the driver's seat.

"Your people are prepared for afterward?" Krestyanov asked him, echoing the man from Langley's private thoughts. It always pissed him off when the Russian did that.

"We're square, got all our ducks lined up," Pruett replied. "And yours?"

"I have no ducks," Krestyanov said, "but all is otherwise in readiness. You may depend on it."

"It's too bad, in a way," Pruett responded, thinking aloud.

"Too bad?"

"I guess I mean to say ironic. Think about it. We're co-operating all this time, and for what? To turn the clock back and be enemies again."

"Competitors," Krestyanov said, correcting him. "And while there may be irony, it doesn't change the fact that we're right. See what has happened to the world since Bush and Yeltsin made their peace. How many lives has the disorder cost in Germany, in Yugoslavia, in the Ukraine. The Third World is disintegrating into tribal genocide. They need us, Pruett."

"You think we'll get the Nobel Prize for this?"

"The future is our prize," the Russian said.

"Wait, let me guess—history will absolve us." Pruett quoted Fidel Castro, from his own childhood, beating Krestyanov to the punch.

"Unless one of us makes a grave mistake," the Russian said, "history will ignore us. After all, we're the men who don't exist."

The see-through men who pulled the strings.

"It doesn't piss you off, even a little bit?" Pruett asked.

"What?"

"The knowledge that we're doing all this for some half-assed politicians, so that they can take the bows? I mean, I know we'll have the power, but—"

Krestyanov interrupted him. "It's not about the power. It's about restoring proper order to the world. I thought you understood that, Pruett."

Jesus H., he was starting to believe that shit.

"Okay," the man from Langley said. "I guess we're really altruists at heart."

"We're heroes, Pruett," Krestyanov replied. "We are about to change the course of history, reverse the trend toward decadence and sloth in both our nations. Knowing that should be enough. What does it matter if our efforts go unsung? It simply proves our skill."

"I see your point," Pruett said. He had misjudged the Russian, but it didn't matter now. They were already past the point of no return, about to take a gamble that could set the world on fire. Assuming they survived, though, Pruett reckoned he would have a better handle on Krestyanov's moods and motives—something of an edge, perhaps, while they were playing chess with human lives.

"Watch out for Keane in Moscow," Pruett said. "If you need to get in touch with me, just talk to him."

The message loud and clear: Don't call my home again.

"I will," Krestyanov said, and broke the link. Another dial tone buzzed until Pruett started tapping out a number, this one with the prefix for Berlin.

He knew that Christian Keane wouldn't appreciate his new assignment, and he didn't give a damn. He wasn't being paid to like his orders, simply to obey them. Pruett listened to the telephone ring three times, answered midway through the fourth.

"Hello?"

"Are you awake?"

"Of course," Keane said. "It's almost noon, here."

"Good. Skip lunch and get your bags packed. You've got work to do."

3

Travel in Russia is simpler today than it was under the Soviet regime, but it would be a mistake to call it easy. Detailed information is still required for tourist visas, including the names of specific cities to be used on entering and leaving the country. Within Russia itself, erratic road construction and general poor maintenance make driving an ordeal, even within major cities such as Moscow and St. Petersburg where traffic regulations are honored more in the breach than the observance. Motorists in Moscow are especially aggressive, running traffic signals on a whim, veering wildly around potholes, often seeming to deliberately target pedestrians.

"It's like they never heard of Driver's Ed," Johnny remarked from the back seat, eliciting a chuckle from the spook behind the steering wheel.

"They've heard of it," Deckard replied. "They just don't give a damn. On top of that, you've got black-market driver's licenses for sale all over town. Odds are, a quarter of the drivers that you meet on any given day have never qualified to get behind the wheel."

They had flown into Moscow's main airport, Sheremetevo 2, directly from Minsk. The hasty flight meant giving up their weapons and allowing Deckard to finesse their travel papers—which had worked out well enough, from all appearances, though Bolan was uneasy, even now, with trusting Deckard's CIA connections. He had fought beside them in Berlin and Minsk, had proved himself as Bolan could have asked for, but the Company was such a murky world—particularly now, with Deckard seemingly assigned to ferret out a group of rogues who had been acting in collusion with the Russian Mafia and former agents of the KGB—that Bolan made a point of doubting all concerned.

Or *had*, at any rate, before he found that they couldn't proceed to Moscow in a timely manner without Deckard's help.

Another time, he would have called on Hal Brognola and the crew at the ultra covert Stony Man Farm to make arrangements for the trip, connections for his hardware on arrival, but that avenue was closed to Bolan at the moment and, perhaps, for good. He still hadn't been able to decipher Brognola's resistance to the present mission, his refusal to assist with anything beyond the very basic—make that nearly useless—information.

They would have to work that out between them, one way or another, but his first priority was sniffing out the Russian syndicate connection to the CIA and former KGB, disrupting and destroying it, if that was possible. If Bolan managed to survive that action, then there would be time for cleaning house back home—at Langley and at Stony Man.

In theory, Moscow boasts more than two hundred hotels, but many of those are hostels for professional delegations with such catchy titles as the Oncological Research Center Hotel. With rare exceptions, tourists visiting the Russian capital must choose their rented lodgings from two broad categories: luxury hotels, frequently managed by joint Russian-Western conglomerates, and the smaller, cheaper, ex-Soviet hotels, once operated on a shoestring budget by the state. Most of the luxury hotels stand within a fifteen-minute drive or subway ride of central Moscow, while the plain ex-Soviet hotels are generally situated farther out. Deckard had opted for a cheap place in Moscow's southwestern Arbatskaya district—the Volga, or "Vulgar," as Deckard described it—on the theory that they would draw less attention in more modest surroundings.

Their next stop, after dropping off luggage at the hotel, was a visit to a private armorer whom Deckard knew. It meant a crosstown drive of thirty minutes to a shop on Nikolskaya Ulitsa. Deckard found a nearby public parking lot with half a dozen open spaces, left them on the street before he drove into the maze and met them several minutes later, pocketing a time-stamped ticket, and they walked a long block back to reach their destination.

"Let me do the talking in the shop," Deckard advised before they reached its door. "My guy knows English pretty well, but there's no point giving him ideas."

"He knows you're CIA?" Bolan asked.

"He knows I pay in cash up front, and I don't try to talk his price down all that much. Beyond that, what he thinks, your guess would be as good as mine. He's not a contract player if that's what you're asking."

"So, he'd sell us out if someone made a decent offer?" Johnny asked.

"It hasn't happened yet," Deckard replied. "He knows if he talks too much, he wakes up dead some morning. I suspect he wants to reach a ripe old age. Instant amnesia is a form of life insurance."

"And if he asks us something?"

"I'll be speaking Russian to him," Deckard said. "He asks you any questions, just play dumb."

They paused outside the door, while Deckard offered them some final words of counsel. "We'll be going in the back room, where he keeps his stash. I think you'll be surprised at the variety. See anything you want, just point. If you have a question that won't wait, give me a whisper. Okay?"

"Let's do it," Bolan said.

Deckard's contact was a sixty-something elfin figure with a fringe of snow-white hair around a shiny landing strip atop his head. He wore a pair of wire-rimmed spectacles that seemed too large for him, or was his head too small? Bolan decided that the riddle wasn't worth his time and concentrated on the ceremony being acted out in front of him, the shopkeeper and Deckard clasping hands, conversing in rapid-fire Russian, with Deckard nodding occasionally over his shoulder, including his companions in the spiel.

A moment later they were following the old man back behind the register and through another doorway, to his storeroom, where they waited while he spun the tumblers on a combination lock that sealed a walk-in vault. When it was open, he stood back and motioned them inside to see his wares. Bolan was leery for a moment, picturing the thick door slamming shut behind them, cutting off their light and oxygen, but Deckard seemed to have no problem with it, so the brothers followed him inside.

He had been right about the arsenal's variety. The old man had a bit of everything, from semiauto pistols and revolvers, on through shotguns, rifles, SMGs and light machine guns, to a Russian M-37 light mortar, the 82 mm stovepipe, and a pair of RPG-7 grenade launchers propped up in one corner, next to a box of bulky antitank rounds.

They chose AKSUs again because the weapons were reliable, hard-hitting and untraceable to any source outside of Mother Russia. Bolan also picked out an SVD Dragunov sniper's rifle just in case he saw the opportunity for some long-distance work. They split on handguns, Johnny and Deckard going for Glocks, while Bolan was pleased to find a Beretta 92 hanging on the wall. With ammunition, extra magazines, half a case of frag grenades, and three bootleg cellular phones, their purchases filled four suitcases, the price of which was added to their tab. Deckard negotiated something in the low eight-figure range, Bolan reminding himself that they were talking rubles, not dollars. He had determined from a close-up that the guns were sound and didn't need a test fire. Twenty minutes later, they were on the street, each hauling luggage back in the direction of the parking lot. No one who passed them on the sidewalk seemed to give the three of them a second glance.

"One thing that hasn't changed in Moscow since the so-called Yeltsin Revolution," Deckard offered, "is the black economy. They're open to the West now, more or less, but still with prices through the roof. Go underground, you'll still find everything from beefsteak to bazookas if you know where to look."

"And nobody sees anything?" Johnny suggested.

"That's the ticket. The police are greased, the whole damned government is on the pad."

They reached the parking lot and stowed the baggage in the trunk, after extracting side arms surreptitiously. When they were rolling, Deckard said, "There's one more stop I have to make, a contact who can help us find out way around and spot some targets in the city."

"Lead the way," Bolan replied.

"The bad news is, he'll only deal with me—until I fill him in a bit, that is. If I show up with company, he's bound to take off like a rabbit."

Johnny leaned in from the back seat, frowning. "So, the plan is...?"

"The best thing I can think of is to drop you at the Vulgar for a little while, go meet this guy and either bring him back with me or set a four-way meet for later on. How's that?"

Bolan glanced back to find his brother watching him, and knew that Johnny would agree, however reluctantly, with whatever he decided. Bolan saw the glaring downside of the plan—the possibility that it had all been leading up to this with Deckard, somehow, moving toward the moment when he would abandon them on hostile turf and leave them to a Russian killing team—but Bolan thought the whole thing sounded too damned convoluted. Why come all the way to Moscow when he could've had them iced in Amsterdam, Berlin or Minsk?

Still, while the slightest possibility of treachery remained, he meant to cover all his bets. "Okay," he said. "We'll take the new bags up and get things sorted out. How long's this meet supposed to take?''

"An hour," Deckard answered. "Ninety minutes, tops."

"Sounds fair," the Executioner replied. "We'll see you then."

And any goons who showed up prematurely could expect a taste of Hell on Earth.

DECKARD HAD SEEN the flicker of suspicion pass between his two companions when he had suggested going off alone to meet their Moscow tour guide. It was entirely natural, what with the trouble the two of them had waded through before he joined their party unexpectedly in Amsterdam. The worst part of it was that they already knew something was funny with the Company—his Company—before he ever showed up on the scene. That boosted the suspicion factor through the roof, and Deckard reckoned he was lucky that the two grim soldiers had accepted him at all. He had been working overtime to earn their trust, and now he had another chance.

Unless it blew up in his face and got him killed.

There was an element of risk to any covert contact in the Russian capital, from hiring low-rent prostitutes to greasing cops and corporate powerhouses. Everyone in Moscow had his hand out, one way or another, and the money came from everywhere at once. A hooker might be pleased with what you paid her for an hour's labor, but she'd rip you off regardless, and consider it a "tip." The cops and politicians mostly kept their word, when they were paid to let illegal enterprises operate—and they were nearly always "honest" with the Russian Mafia, whose gunners would be pleased to clip them in a heartbeat if they tried some kind of double cross. For private operators and outsiders, though, there was a constant risk that someone whom you bought one day would turn around and sell you out the next.

Deckard had a fair degree of confidence in Rurik Pavlushka, the man he was going to meet. Unlike the weapons dealer on

Nikolskaya Ulitsa, Pavlushka *was* a contract agent for the CIA, kept on retainer, with a healthy numbered bank account in Liechtenstein. There was an outside chance that he would plant a blade in Deckard's back if someone else had raised the stakes, but the Russian had to know that retribution would be swift and sure. The Company could take him out illegally, or they could drop a ruble and report the many times Pavlushka had accepted Yankee dollars to betray the old regime. The Soviet Union might be defunct, but Russians still had little tolerance for traitors, even in the current atmosphere where all things Western were regarded as some kind of gift from God.

Deckard had telephoned ahead from Minsk to let Pavlushka know that he was coming. He had called again, once they had checked in at the Volga, and made sure that the Russian would be home when he arrived. They wouldn't meet at Pavlushka's flat, of course—that would have been too risky for both—but rather at the lake in Gorky Park.

Another public parking lot, this one patrolled by two young guards in threadbare uniforms. They weren't real cops, and they were only armed with truncheons, but they offered more security from ever-present thieves than many of the other parking lots in Moscow.

Deckard took his time-stamped ticket stub from the machine and left it on the dashboard of his rental car before he locked the vehicle and made his way toward the park and his selected meeting place with Pavlushka. He took comfort from the Glock 19 tucked underneath his belt at the small of his back, concealed by his jacket. It wasn't the best arrangement in the world for a fast draw, but he could manage in a pinch.

And if Pavlushka had betrayed him, it would hardly matter. If the meet turned out to be an ambush, he most likely wouldn't have a chance to use the Glock at all.

Deckard was thinking in Russian as he moved into the park but also striving for the proper Moscow attitude that carved its lines of doubt and resignation on so many faces, young and old. All cities took their toll on humankind, but this one claimed more than its share, with rampant poverty, inflation, unemployment, crime rates rising every day, the government that had replaced the old totalitarian regime forever on the brink of suddenly unraveling, casting the city and the nation into anarchy.

Small wonder, then, Deckard acknowledged, that some Russians lusted for the "good old days" when everyone was guaranteed a job, like it or not, programmed to think, speak, and behave like true-blue Communists. Or should that be true-*red?*

He saw the lake ahead, swans paddling on the slate-gray water, and he had no trouble spotting Pavlushka. There wasn't much of a crowd in Gorky Park, this close to sundown. It was almost change of shift, when tourists and the elderly, parents with children and young lovers holding hands, gave up the park to its nocturnal denizens: the whores and junkies, cruising gays who didn't want to risk exposure on the nightclub circuit, muggers, dips and the occasional stone psycho looking for fresh meat.

Rurik Pavlushka was a man of average height, painfully thin, with long blond hair he often wore tucked up beneath a hat, to give himself a clean-cut look. He also wore a Lenin-Trotsky-style goatee, incongruously streaked with gray that matched his ever-watchful eyes. The grapevine said that Pavlushka always traveled armed but never used a gun, preferring knives, straight razors and assorted other cutting tools if sudden violence was required. Depending on your source, he may have killed a dozen men, or none at all.

Pavlushka saw him coming, tossed a last handful of croutons to the swans and moved to intercept Deckard before he reached the lake. If there was any chance he had been followed to the meeting, the Russian was supposed to say "It looks like rain," before he walked past and left the park. If he hadn't been followed, they were free to talk.

"You're looking well," the Russian said, and Deckard felt himself relax a bit—but not entirely.

"I've been keeping busy," Deckard told him, shaking hands.

"In Minsk," Pavlushka said. "I heard."

"Heard what, exactly?" Deckard queried, frowning now.

"Nothing specific," the Russian said. "No names, of course, except for Tolya's. He was mentioned several times. He's had a run of bad luck stretching right around the world, from what I hear."

"News travels fast."

"Some news. Valerik has important friends in Moscow, but he also has determined enemies. They would be pleased, I think, if something should befall him, possibly remove him from the scene entirely, without any effort on their part."

"Both pleased and grateful, I imagine," Deckard said.

"Grateful and generous, perhaps."

"I'm not concerned with local matters," Deckard said. "If you can find a way to profit twice, by all means seize the day—as long as it doesn't present an obstacle to me or my associates."

"I understand," Pavlushka said. "You're not alone in Moscow, then?"

"I have associates," Deckard replied.

"The Company still finds Moscow intriguing, then. I'm glad."

"These men aren't from the Company." When Pavlushka offered no response to that, Deckard laid out the story he had been rehearsing since he learned that they were heading east from Minsk. "My two associates are in the private sector, but their interest coincides with mine. My whereabouts are known at Langley, but they aren't widely known. You understand?"

A gamble. There was a chance that Pavlushka's contacts within the CIA might very well include one of the rogues Deckard had been instructed to identify, expose, eliminate. If so, there was at least a fifty-fifty chance that Deckard was about to stick his head inside the lion's mouth. It finally came down to trust and what he saw in the Russian's eyes.

"You have a mole," Pavlushka offered, cutting through the smoke with one deft movement.

"That's what I'm attempting to discover," he replied. "It's apparent that someone within the Company is doing business with Valerik, also with Vassily Krestyanov and others from the KGB. As to the nature of their business, the extent of unofficial Company involvement, nothing yet has been determined."

He was watching the Russian's face the whole time that he spoke, looking for a reaction to the names he dropped, some kind of body language that would indicate involvement in or working knowledge of the Langley-Moscow link. If there was anything behind the sharp gray eyes, Pavlushka had concealed it with an actor's skill.

"This is troubling," the Russian said.

"Tell me about it. I've got bodies stretching all the way from Minsk, back to Los Angeles."

"And now the fight has come to Moscow."

"Well, Valerik's here," Deckard replied. "If Krestyanov shows up—"

"He's here, as well," Pavlushka interrupted him.

"Then, I believe it's safe to say you can expect some fireworks."

"And you come to me because…?"

"I'm out of touch with Moscow," Deckard told him honestly. "The people and the places that I need to find don't show up in your average tourist's manual."

"I see." Pavlushka thought the problem over for a moment, then announced, "I think it's time you introduced me to your friends."

BOLAN'S CELLULAR PHONE rang at half-past six o'clock and Johnny watched him snap it open, listen briefly, answering in English, "Right. Okay." He pocketed the telephone and said, "We're good to go."

The evenings were almost always cool in Moscow, and they

had decided no one would regard them as unusual or out of place if they wore overcoats. A bath towel cut in strips, lengthwise, would serve them both as shoulder harnesses to keep their AKSU automatic rifles out of sight but readily accessible.

"What's up?" Johnny asked, as he shrugged into his makeshift sling and shrugged into the coat.

"We meet him on the street, first intersection north of the hotel. He'll have the contact with him."

"You're okay with this?"

"I'll trust him that far, anyway," Bolan said. And almost as an afterthought, he palmed two frag grenades, dropping the dull green spheres into the outer pockets of his coat.

The elevator bore a crude hand-lettered sign that told them it was out of order. Passing through the Volga's lobby, they ignored the long-faced clerk behind the desk, and he returned the favor, paging through a glossy magazine with rapt attention.

On the sidewalk they turned left and headed north, walking abreast and with a yard or so of empty space between them. Johnny kept his right hand in the pocket of his overcoat, where he had sliced the lining to accommodate the AKSU's pistol grip.

Deckard was waiting at the corner with the rental car's motor idling, a goateed stranger planted in the shotgun seat. The brothers climbed in back—a demonstration of fidelity. Deckard and his companion couldn't turn and fire from where they sat before the AKSUs splattered them across the dash.

Once they were rolling, Deckard made the introductions, first name only, sticking with the "Evan Green" tag for Bolan. Pavlushka half turned in his seat to greet them both in English that was free of any noticeable Slavic accent.

"I've told Rurik what we're looking for, in general terms," Deckard said, making eye contact with Johnny in the rearview mirror. "He's familiar with Valerik's operations in the city and may have something we can use on Krestyanov."

"The men you seek are quite well known in Moscow, as

you might expect," the shotgun rider said. "They have important friends in government, on the police force, in the business world and with the press. Valerik, you already know, concerns himself primarily with sex and gambling, drugs and arms. He's not political, in the accepted sense, but he buys friends in government at every level. Anyone who moves against him openly, despite the fact that ninety-five percent of all his business is illegal, must expect retaliation from the law, as well as from Valerik's Family."

"And Krestyanov?" Bolan asked.

"He was, as you already know, a colonel in the KGB before the present system was inaugurated. He is an expert in the area of what Americans are pleased to call 'black ops,' including terrorism, counterterrorism and assassination. His associate, from the description I was given, must be Nikolai Lukasha. He was also KGB before the change, but he worked mostly from the Lubyanka, supervising executions and interrogations. He's a sadist and a murderer. Don't miss a chance to kill him if it comes your way."

"I understand the KGB connection with Valerik while the old regime was still in power," Bolan replied, "but what's the link today?"

"That, I can only speculate," Pavlushka said. "Krestyanov was and is a hard-line Communist. It may be more correct to label him a Stalinist, though he wouldn't dare describe himself as such, after the Iron Man posthumously fell from grace. His friends—the ones he sees in public, anyhow—are also KGB, or politicians who regret the course Russia has followed for the past decade."

"Which doesn't tell us squat about Valerik," Johnny said.

If the Russian was annoyed by the remark, he didn't let it show. "Krestyanov is a monster, in his way, but he would never soil himself through contact with the Mafia unless there was some profit to be made."

"You think Valerik's helping Krestyanov move cash? Some kind of laundry operation?" Bolan inquired.

"I doubt it very much," the Russian said without a second thought. "Krestyanov's friends in government and industry are fabulously wealthy in their own right. They were rich men under communism, skimming from the so-called Worker's Paradise, and they are richer still today. Some of them—some important ones, I think—are said to be in sympathy with certain groups that wish to overthrow the present government, turn back the calendar, restore the Soviet republic."

"And Valerik is on board with that?" Johnny asked. "I would have thought he'd like things just the way they are. He's raking in the rubles like there's no tomorrow, right? Why would he help a gang of old reactionaries kill the golden goose?"

"If I recall correctly," Pavlushka said, "the eggs were golden, not the goose. But you answered your own question when you mentioned Tolya making money like there's no tomorrow. If the state of our economy continues to decline, we face a nationwide collapse within a year, or two at the outside. Such a collapse could well mean civil war, perhaps a putsch to make the early coup against poor Yeltsin seem like children playing with toy soldiers in the sand. In which case, if the hard-liners emerge victorious without his help, there may indeed be no tomorrow for Valerik and his Family."

"So, you think he's just covering his bets?" Bolan asked.

Before the Russian had a chance to answer, Johnny said, "It makes no sense. Assuming that Valerik would agree to help out with this coup, expecting a reward, how does it come back to the States? Why would Valerik and Krestyanov rope in anybody from the CIA?"

"I have no answer to those questions," Pavlushka granted, "but they trouble me, as well. Krestyanov's best-known *konspiratsias* were all elaborate, convoluted, planned out to the last detail. That doesn't help, I know. Perhaps you should be asking why the CIA would deal with Krestyanov, its former adversary, or with leaders of the Russian Mafia."

"Been there, done that," Johnny replied. "We don't have squat."

"One thing we need to bear in mind," Deckard said, speaking for the first time since his contact had begun to talk, "is that the Company connection to Valerik and Krestyanov is apparently a rogue black op, without official sanction. Think of it that way. We need to work out why an outlaw clique inside the Company would want to deal with Russian gangsters and a bunch of Red revisionists."

"They need a common interest," Bolan replied. "Some end that profits all concerned."

"Agreed," the Russian said. "But if we assume that Krestyanov and company intend to overthrow the present government somehow, restoring Soviet authority, how could that benefit your country or the CIA?"

"The first mistake," Johnny suggested, "is to peg the Company and the United States as having common interests, necessarily. This wouldn't be the first time members of a covert agency put self-interest above the country they're supposed to serve. J. Edgar Hoover did it constantly, and we've had trouble with the CIA before."

Johnny expected some retort from Deckard, but their driver kept his mouth shut, concentrating on the traffic ebb and flow around them.

"Could be a variation of the Ahab syndrome," Bolan suggested.

"Come again?" Deckard was focused on the rearview now, and Bolan's reflected gaze. "I didn't catch that."

"*Moby Dick,*" Bolan said, by way of explanation. "Captain Ahab chases him around the world and sacrifices everything in the pursuit. Suppose Ahab had managed to survive their final showdown, though. What would he live for, then?"

"The past ten years," Johnny said, picking up the thread, "we've heard repeated calls for cutbacks at the CIA, a few calls for disbandment of the Company itself. Some people figure the collapse of Communism was a victory, so who needs spooks? Toss in a few embarrassing snafus where Langley called the action wrong and took more heat for screwing up, you've got an atmosphere where some on the inside might wish they had another good old cold war on their hands. Better the devil you know than some new kid on the block who keeps kicking your butt.''

"You mean, bring back the Evil Empire, and the gravy train starts rolling," Deckard said.

"That's what I mean," Johnny confirmed. "And it's a more exciting read if someone in the Red regime is linked to some incriminating action in the States, preferably something flashy, that would still stop short of all-out war. You can't play chess for long inside a burning house."

"Some kind of terrorist event?" Deckard asked.

"Well, it *is* Krestyanov's specialty," Johnny replied.

"In the United States?"

"Or here, in Russia," Bolan suggested. "Maybe both. To pull it off, the Company would need its own man at the top."

"I have to tell you," Deckard said, "that I do not believe this comes from the director."

"I was thinking someone higher up," Bolan said. He wore a troubled look that gave Johnny a moment of intense anxiety.

"Someone in office now, for instance?" Deckard asked.

"Or waiting in the wings to save the day, when it begins to fall apart," Bolan said. "It could go either way."

"We need to get on top of this and nail it down," the man from Langley said.

"My thoughts exactly," the Executioner replied.

4

The first target was simply known as Zero, an "exotic sex club," as described by Deckard's contact, with its entrance in an alley off Ulitsa Znamenka in the Arbatskaya district. Bolan asked their guide how an "exotic" sex club differed from the "normal" kind in Moscow, whereupon the Russian winked at him and said, "You'll soon see for yourself."

It was agreed that they should split into pairs. Bolan drew Pavlushka, while his brother went with Deckard, promising to follow them inside the club after a rough ten-minute interval.

The one thing Bolan hadn't counted on was how rough it would be.

An Asian woman was performing with some kind of animal when Bolan and his escort entered, guided to their table on the far side of the room by a nude hostess, Nordic looking, who wore several golden chains dependent from the rings that pierced her nipples. After they had settled in and ordered vodka neat, Bolan identified the second player in the onstage drama as a llama who had obviously lost his fear of human beings.

He tuned out the sex show and the tin-pan music, scanning the club for an appraisal of security. Without lip reading, he had no way of determining which customers were Russian Mafia and which were mere civilians with an itch that needed scratching in some place they couldn't reach. For all he knew, there could be Yanks on hand, logging a story they could tell their friends back home but only in a whisper, when the kids had gone to bed.

The ending to that story was about to take a very different turn than they supposed.

He looked around for guards, found two great slabs of beef that had to be the bouncers, both of them with ponytails, decked out in matching turtlenecks and sport coats that appeared to be at least one size too small for all the muscle packed inside. He saw no indication that the two were packing heat, but that proved nothing. They could both have pistols up their sleeves, in ankle holsters, or concealed at any one of several dozen handy points around the room.

Unbidden, Bolan's mind reeled off the first rule of engagement: When in doubt, take them out.

If there were hard-core shooters on the premises, the management was keeping it a secret, hiding them somewhere, on the off chance their services would be required. There was no reason to assume Valerik or his pals knew they had been pursued from Minsk to Moscow, but the wise mobster existed in a constant state of paranoia, knowing in his heart that he could trust no one on Earth. With Moscow in a state approximating that of Al Capone's Chicago, maybe worse, Valerik would have been an idiot to let his guard down in a place like this—which, Pavlushka had assured them, was a working gold mine for Valerik's Family.

It was time to ring the curtain down…but not before his brother and the man from Langley were in place.

They entered several moments later, hooked up with a red-haired, amply freckled hostess garbed in what appeared to be a winding sheet of plastic wrap, and trailed her to a booth near the stage. Bolan couldn't read the look on Johnny's face as he checked out the llama act, but he could make out the bribe that Deckard slipped the shrink-wrapped hostess for their ringside seat. The spook leaned into Johnny, speaking briefly through a tipsy-looking smile that nearly split his face in two, then turned his full attention to the ongoing display on animal husbandry.

Johnny, for his part, was sipping vodka, or pretending to, and checking out the hectic crowd. A microsecond's eye contact, in passing, made it clear that he was ready to proceed on Bolan's signal, bring the party to a screeching halt and see what happened next.

"They've got closed-circuit cameras," Bolan said to his companion, "ceiling-mounted, all four corners of the room."

"That's normal," Pavlushka told him. "They watch out for enemies, in case of some unpleasantness between the Families, and also for celebrities or government officials who drop in to satisfy their harmless curiosity. Suppose a member of the parliament was up for reelection and a tape should surface that depicted him in these surroundings."

"That explains your muttonchops and shades," Bolan said.

"Indeed." Pavlushka had added bushy press-on sideburns and a pair of mirrored sunglasses to his ensemble, heedless of the fact that night had fallen and was well advanced. An effort to make sure the TV cameras didn't catch his face.

"You could have tipped us off to the surveillance," Bolan said.

"For what purpose?" the Russian replied. "You're strangers to the city, and when you've finished with the task at hand, I seriously doubt that you'll be coming back. The management won't report disturbances to the police, and will deny any reports that may be filed by paying customers, after the fact. Officially, this place doesn't exist."

Which would explain the club's name, Bolan thought. He saw no profit in reminding Pavlushka that Valerik's goons would have their faces filed away on video for future reference unless they managed to destroy the tapes before they left. The Russian would have thought of that first thing, unless he was a total idiot. He had disguised himself because he had to live here after they were gone.

It was too late to fret about it, either way. They were already in, and anything they did would be on tape, unless...

He glanced across the room, caught Johnny watching him and casually raised his arms, faking a yawn and stretching like a man who'd seen enough, was tired of club-hopping and wouldn't mind returning to his rented bed. It was coincidence, of course, that Bolan's index fingers drew a bead on two of the closed-circuit cameras while he was stretching, Johnny nodding absentmindedly before he turned and spoke to Deckard, indicating that he had the watchers marked. Deckard, for his part, simply grinned as Johnny shared the news and took a slug of vodka, whistling encouragement to the distracted llama on the stage.

"You ready?" Bolan asked the man beside him, one hand sliding underneath his jacket, his fingers wrapped around the AKSU's pistol grip. For an establishment so conscious of security, the absence of metal detectors was a fatal faux pas.

"Not yet," the Russian said, quaffing his vodka rocks and signaling their naked waitress for a refill, as he rose unsteadily and spent a moment tugging at the inseam of his slacks. "I seem to need the toilet, now. Watch me, and you will know the time."

Bolan watched him moving through the crowd, feigning a drunkard's lurching gate. Was Pavlushka going to the john or not? The question led inevitably to another, more disturbing one: if he had known about the TV cameras and kept it to himself, what else was Deckard's contact holding back? Was this whole ugly scene a setup from the git-go? Had he sold them out to the Valerik Family, and was his bladder break simply a ploy to take himself out of the killing zone?

Watch me, and you will know the time.

Okay. Bolan would watch him, sure, and if it turned out that the goateed man had set them up, he would do everything within his power to take the traitor down.

RURIK PAVLUSHKA normally avoided firearms, not because he was afraid of them or inept in their use, but simply in consideration of the risks that came with owning—much less carrying—a gun in Mother Russia. When the Soviet regime held sway from 1917 until the early 1990s, it had been strictly illegal for the proletariat to own firearms for any purpose, be it sport or self-defense. Occasional exceptions were allowed for rural peasants in Siberia, who hunted caribou for meat and shared their land with hungry bears, but for the most part the fat-assed "stewards of power" who sat in the Kremlin were intent on holding a monopoly on deadly force.

Those laws remained in place after the Red regime collapsed, and while it was a point of common knowledge that black-market guns were readily available throughout the country, penalties for owning, carrying, or trafficking in arms remained severe. It meant nothing to Pavlushka that the laws were frequently ignored. He wasn't one of those who bribed police to lose their eyesight, and he knew that when his past involvement with the law was noted, being found in the possession of a gun would earn him prison time.

Edged weapons, though, were something else entirely.

Barring only swords and battle-axes, cutting instruments could be explained in any one of several dozen ways, by anyone whose IQ topped room temperature. Razors and folding knives were best, but it was also common for practitioners of varied trades to carry fishing knives and skinners, awls and hatchets, kitchen cutlery that ranged from steak and butcher knives to cleavers. All of them were tools, designed for some legitimate pursuit, and their occasional misuse by psychopaths or muggers didn't render their possession evidence of criminal intent per se.

It helped to dress the proper part and have your paperwork in order, naturally, as on the night Rurik Pavlushka had been stopped and grilled by the police about the bloodstained cleaver, boning knife and hacksaw that he carried in a greasy muslin bag. He had rehearsed his tale about working the swing shift at a slaughterhouse, located less than half a mile from where he was detained, and the patrolmen—one of them already drunk on vodka, bleary-eyed and silent while his partner did the talking—didn't bother to check Pavlushka's alibi. The other evidence of the Russian's work that night had yet to be recovered from the sewer underneath Sofiskaya Naberezhnaya, which fed into the Moskva River. No one missed the double agent or, if they did, his mourners kept their grief private.

This night, Pavlushka's hardware was less bulky—nothing but a simple six-inch balisong—and he was willing to forget his own "no firearms" rule for the duration, though he certainly didn't intend to carry any guns he might acquire outside Club Zero.

There was enough work to do, right there.

As Pavlushka moved in the direction of the men's room, doing a superb impression of a drunk unsteady on his feet, he slipped one hand into a pocket of his tailored slacks and palmed the balisong. No one in the sex club was watching Pavlushka, much less his hands, as he released the balisong's latch with his pinky, freed the keen blade with a flick of his wrist and deftly secured the two halves of the handle in place. His hand, fingers extended, hid the knife as he began to veer away from the alcove where rest rooms were marked with abstract sketches of male and female genitalia. Feigning confusion, he approached a table where an older man was drinking with what Pavlushka took to be a pair of twenty-something prostitutes, all three of them intent on making crude jokes about the llama show onstage.

When he was near enough, Pavlushka swung his hip into the old man's drinking arm, sloshing champagne across the stranger's tie and the lapels of his expensive jacket. At the same time, bending almost double, Pavlushka peered into the ample cleavage of the hooker on the old man's right, declaring, "I believe I've lost my contact lens in there."

The woman's laughter suddenly evaporated when he started digging for the nonexistent lens, assuring her that "This will only take a moment, Madam, have no fear." Behind him, he could hear the old man spluttering and pushing back his chair. A short backstep—which freed his questing hand, together with the hooker's wobbling breasts—and Pavlushka sat in the old man's lap.

"Excuse me, if you please!" he bellowed, snapping back an elbow that connected with the old man's chin. "I'm not a bloody prostitute!"

Then the bouncers had him, one on either side of Pavlushka, hauling him away in the direction of Club Zero's exit, where they might or might not have meant to thrash him, prior to pitching him outside. Pavlushka grumbled, going limp between them, playing up his drunk act to the hilt. When they had reached a point directly underneath the nearest closed-circuit surveillance camera, he knew it was time to make his move.

The noisy "drunk" was suddenly, completely sober, though his hulking captors recognized the change too late to save themselves. Pavlushka brought his full weight down upon the instep of the ponytailed gorilla to his right, the younger man releasing him in reflex action, bellowing in pain. Pavlushka silenced him forever with a lightning sweep that drew the balisong across the left side of his neck, slicing the jugular vein and the carotid artery, catching the trachea and literally cutting off his wind.

The second bouncer still had no idea of what was happening. He thought the drunk had kicked his partner in the shin, had raised a massive fist to punish that infraction, but he never had a chance to land the blow. Instead, he felt a blood-slick blade plunge deep into his armpit, bright, indescribable pain enveloping the right side of his torso. He was working up a scream when the blade struck again, this time beneath his sternum, angling toward the heart, and he was suddenly bereft of sense or sound.

Pavlushka caught the second bouncer as he fell, arms around him, underneath his jacket, feeling for the weapon big men often feel obliged to pack despite their size and strength, as if it were proof positive of their virility. He found it tucked against the bouncer's spine, an HK-4 pistol chambered in 9 mm short, the European equivalent of a Colt .380 round. He wondered, for perhaps a second, how the bouncer's thick, nail-bitten index finger even fit inside the pistol's trigger guard.

His scuffle with the bouncers had begun to draw attention, several patrons and a waitress—half her naked body painted blue, the other gold—were staring at him now, emitting exclamations as the llama and his paramour were suddenly forgotten. Pavlushka paid them no attention, didn't check to see if his companions had begun to do their part. It mattered only that he do his job, and swiftly, as he raised the pistol, thumbed back its stubby hammer, and fired a round into the nearest TV camera's lens.

THE FIRST SHOT spooked the llama and he bolted for the footlights, dumping his costar in a sweaty heap at center stage. Johnny was on his feet and moving, with the AKSU pressed against his flank, as the animal leaped into the audience and crushed a table where two red-faced macho men were swilling vodka straight, their laughter instantly transformed into expressions of dismay.

He left Deckard to take the camera nearest to their booth, behind him, braced and ready for the 3-round burst that brought it down. Johnny was off and moving toward what he had labeled Camera Three. Around him, as the audience went crazy, he watched the faces for a sign that anyone was tracking him, their hands for any kind of weapon that could bring him down.

It would be odd, he thought, if there were only two goons in the place—especially this kind of place—and Deckard's contact was the one who dropped them both. Johnny wouldn't object to leaving Club Zero without fresh blood on his hands, but if they met no further opposition, he would have to wonder if the raid had been a waste of time and energy. Why bother with a target the Valerik Family didn't bother to defend? For that matter, how would they even know Valerik really owned the club?

A few more strides and he was close enough to make the shot with confidence. He stepped into an empty booth, out of the stampede's jostling flow, and raised the AKSU until he could sight along its stubby barrel. When he had the TV camera framed in its fixed sights, he stroked the trigger twice, in semiauto fire, and watched his target's plastic housing fly apart.

Three down, and his brother was taking out the fourth eye as he turned back toward the milling center of the room. The naked "actress" on the stage was scampering for cover on her hands and knees, as if she had forgotten how to rise and walk erect. Was that a side effect of dating llamas? Johnny wondered. But he never had the chance to think it through, assuming there was anywhere to go with it.

Just then, a door on his side of the stage, where he had seen a couple of the stripped-down waitresses passed in and out, flew open to expel a troop of soldiers armed with shotguns and Kalashnikovs. There was no point in counting heads, as Johnny swung around to face them, but he noted they were all about the same size as the bouncers who had been the first to fall. They would have made a damned impressive football team, albeit with some strange ideas about offensive tactics and protective gear.

Johnny and Deckard had a slim advantage over the emerging shooters, since the late arrivals plainly had no fix on where the early shots had come from or which members of the milling crowd might be responsible. The point man had no opportunity to work it out, as Johnny slammed two 5.45 mm rounds into his chest from twenty feet and punched him backward, into a collision with the second man in line. Both gunners hit the floor, though Johnny couldn't tell if either of his shots had passed through the first man to wound his backup.

Deckard opened up then—and the whole thing went to hell. It was apparent from the sheer volume of firing, and the glimpse that Johnny managed of another flying squad, across the room, that there were easily a dozen Russian shooters on the premises. From no defense at all, Club Zero had been suddenly transformed into a miniconvention for hit men, their numbers startling Johnny more than their previous absence had done.

What did it mean? Why would Valerik send so many men to guard a live-sex show? Was he forewarned, somehow, of their arrival in Moscow? Had Deckard's Russian contact sold them out?

The questions had to wait, although in Johnny's mind, the last one had been answered when the man called Rurik knifed the bouncers, palmed a piece from one of them and took out the first surveillance camera. If he was working for the home team on this job, he could forget about that nomination as employee of the month.

A shotgun blast churned through the air a foot or so from Johnny's face, the pellets spreading, but not rapidly enough to make up for the shooter's faulty aim. The guy was racking back his pump gun's slide when Johnny shot him in the throat, followed by another round that sheared off a six-inch strip of jawbone, peeling back the hardman's ear and tatters of his scalp. There was a possibility that either wound was fatal, that close to the major arteries and organs in the neck, but all that mattered in that moment was the AKSU's knockdown power, how it kicked the soldier over on his back and pinned him there.

Alive or dead, the man was one less Johnny had to think about.

Some of the goons on the defensive line were firing bursts at random through the panicked crowd. They didn't seem to care if they hit men or women, patrons or employees, just as long as they encouraged hasty movement toward the exits. Firing at the ceiling would have had the same effect, of course, without the carnage, but from the expressions on their faces, several of the shooters got their kicks from drilling anything that moved.

Craning around the corner of the booth he'd used for cover, Johnny sighted down on one of them and gave the shotgunner a double tap that staggered him and put a sudden, dazed expression on his ruddy face. For just an instant, Johnny thought his target might be wearing Kevlar underneath his turtleneck, but then the pent up blood exploded from his ruptured heart, and Johnny watched the Russian go down like a falling oak.

Almost too late, he noticed the gunner on his target's left had glimpsed him as he fired, that soldier pivoting to unleash a long burst from his AK, raking Johnny's booth, the table and the wall above his head. He huddled in the rain of plaster dust, expecting one of the incoming rounds to drill his head or body, but the shooter emptied his rifle's magazine before he scored a hit. When Johnny risked another look, the guy was down on one knee, with his back turned, trying to insert a fresh mag into the Kalashnikov.

In Hollywood, the good guys always let their enemies shoot first, secure in the knowledge that the script wouldn't allow them to be killed or seriously injured, and they never, under any circumstances, shot a bad guy in the back.

So much for "art."

Astounded by the hardman's negligence, Johnny lined up the shot and drilled three holes between his shoulder blades before the gunner could reload his weapon. The first round's impact wrenched his shoulders back, as if he were about to fling his arms above his head, perhaps burst into song, and then the others put him facedown on the carpet in a creeping pool of crimson.

Good. How many left to go?

Killing instead of counting, Johnny got down to business, squeezing off hot rounds at human targets on the firing line.

HE DIDN'T recognize the hardmen who were charging from the club's back room, but Able Deckard knew their type on sight and understood that they weren't in any mood for conversation. That was fine, of course, since he had nothing to say to hit men from the Russian Mafia, so Deckard let his stubby AKSU do the talking, squeezing off short bursts of automatic fire as his opponents ducked and dived for any cover they could find.

One of them didn't make it, stitched across his left side by a burst of 5.45 mm rounds as he was turning back in the direction he had come from, maybe thinking better of the banzai-charge approach. It was too late for him to reconsider, though, and Deckard watched him go down in a heap, his own Kalashnikov whirling away from spastic fingers, slithering across the floor.

Toward Deckard.

Luck of the draw, he thought, already calculating that it wouldn't hurt to have a backup weapon larger than his side arm, with the odds arrayed against them. Crouching, ducking forward, Deckard snagged the liberated AK by its muzzle, dragging it behind him as he duck-walked backward, toward the partial cover of the booth that he had occupied with Johnny Gray a few short moments earlier.

Thinking of Johnny then, he glanced to his right and caught a glimpse of his companion, popping semiauto rounds in the direction of two gunners who had flipped over a table, hoping it would cover them. From what he saw, it wasn't working out, but Deckard had no time to focus on the action over there, as he was busy dodging the incoming rounds from other guns, their users bent on nailing him before he had a chance to cause more problems for their team.

Too late for that, as well. Deckard already had one of them spotted. The guy was big and mean, like all of his companions on the hit team, but they needed small and sly to make the flanking move reality. The shooter stood out like a wart hog at a garden party, and his last few seconds on the planet were about what any wart hog could expect if he was caught trespassing in polite society. A short burst from Deckard's AKSU gave the gunner a crude lobotomy, dropping him in a rumpled heap.

Most of the paying crowd had cleared the field of fire by now, and those who lingered were in no shape to be going anywhere. Deckard had seen a number of them fall, and knew that no rounds from his weapon could be traced to any dead or wounded innocents, if it should ever come to that. Of course, if it *did* come to that, the man from Langley guessed he might be dead, himself, with prosecution ranked among the least of his concerns.

Right now, his first priority was getting out of the club with his life and limbs intact, while seeing to it that his comrades did the same. Crouching beneath the table in his booth, he could see none of them just now, but from the racket in the clubroom, he could tell that two of them, at least, were still alive and carrying the battle to their enemies.

Either that, or the Russian goons were hopelessly confused and dueling furiously with one another.

Time to stir the pot and see what surfaced.

Reaching underneath his jacket, Deckard found the single frag grenade that he had carried on their outing, in addition to the AKSU and his Glock. Besides, he told himself, one charge should do it, if strategically applied. He didn't plan to wipe the Russian shooters out with his grenade, but he could scatter some of them—with any luck, set the survivors running for their lives—and thus provide fresh targets for his comrades and himself.

Countdown.

He pulled the pin, waited perhaps two seconds, lining up his pitch, and then released the safety spoon before he tossed the green egg underhand toward the middle of the room, where four or five of Valerik's beefy gunmen had collected in a knot, facing in all directions, like some tiny Russian simulation of the standoff at the Alamo.

Meet Santa Ana, boys, he thought, and ducked back under-cover as the doomsday clock ran down.

Bull's-eye!

He bowled a strike or would have, if the shooter facing him hadn't seen the frag grenade en route and called a warning to his comrades. Even then, two of them didn't make it, hesitating while the others scattered, banging into chairs and tables in their haste to put ground zero well behind them. One of those who lingered opened fire on the grenade with his Kalashnikov and missed it by at least three feet in his excitement, while the other dropped his shotgun, hunkered down and clasped both arms above his head.

The duck-and-cover syndrome. Great.

It didn't save him when the frag grenade went off, but Deckard had no interest in the shooters who had managed to absorb the blast head-on. His targets were the runners, those still capable of fighting back, and from the swift converging fire, he knew his three companions felt the same.

Deckard had framed one runner in his sights, when suddenly a burst of AK fire from someone else's weapon nailed the goon, slugs sending ripples through his tailored jacket as the big man staggered, stumbled, going down. Deckard held off and swung around to find another moving target, nailed this one with three or four rounds of his own before a burst from somewhere else took off the left side of his skull.

How many left? Deckard was scanning for another target when he realized that there was no more movement on the battlefield. No, wait! That wasn't right. He had some character with shades and puffy sideburns moving toward the very center of the action, sweeping with a pistol held in front of him. Deckard was sighting on the shooter's chest, when he saw through Rurik Pavlushka's not-so-suave disguise and took his finger off the AKSU's trigger.

"Are we done?" he asked of no one in particular.

"Looks like," Johnny said, from somewhere to his right. "But keep an eye out."

"Moving," Bolan called before he rose from cover, taking time to feed his AK a fresh magazine. The man pocketed the empty, whether for reuse or to avoid leaving his fingerprints behind, Deckard couldn't have said.

"You figure someone called for backup?" Deckard asked, again with no specific member of the team in mind to answer him.

"It stands to reason," Johnny replied, now visible, as he emerged from his concealment, three booths farther down the bullet-scarred west wall.

"Then I suggest we move," Deckard said, "and adjourn to more congenial surroundings for the postgame party."

"We're just getting started," Bolan reminded him.

"That's cool," Deckard replied. "I think we'll have Valerik's full attention after this."

5

"If I can be of any further service, sir," the bellhop said, fawning, rubbing his bony hands together as if he were washing them, "please do not hesitate to ask. A woman, possibly? Or...something else?"

"I'll settle for some privacy," Christian Keane replied, making no secret of his weariness or his bad temper. When the bellhop made no move to exit, Keane fished in a pocket of his slacks, palmed several coins—God only knew what they were worth today; ten cents or something, but to hell with it—and dumped them in the porter's outstretched palm. Before the guy could count his take and register displeasure, Keane had steered him toward the open door and through it, closing it behind him with sufficient force to make the brass chain dance.

Screw Moscow, anyway. And screw how Pruett would predictably react, once he received the bills Keane would generate for a suite at the Sovetskiy, a classic kick-ass palace on Leningradskiy Prospekt that ate up the rubles as if they were going out of style. The bill was going on his brand-new plastic, in the name of "Fletcher Christian"—that was Pruett for you, showing off his literary crap again—and anyone who tried to tap his check for reimbursement in the next pay period was looking at a world of hurt.

The summons from Berlin to Moscow had been bad enough, when Keane expected to be going home. The thought of holing up in some ex-Soviet flophouse and living on cold sandwiches for the duration was simply too much to bear. Keane would obey his orders, go where he was told, but if his cover didn't call for him to emulate a homeless loser, he would damned well go in style.

Keane had no clear idea of what he was supposed to do in Moscow, which compounded his dislike of the assignment. In their brief and cryptic conversation, Pruett had referred to "panic management," adding a quasi-sarcastic remark about "moral support." In fact, Keane couldn't think of any other kind to offer, being one man on his own—a foreigner, at that—unarmed in Moscow, with some fourteen million people thronging the greater metropolitan area. He spoke and read the language, reckoned he could pass at least a casual inspection, but he still felt like a pawn, and that disturbed him, even though he knew the rules by which the game was played.

This whole damned thing was meant to boost him up the ladder with the Company. That wasn't Pruett's goal, of course. His boss was rather deeply into "patriotic insurrection" at the moment, dreaming up one grandstand play after another, but Christian Keane was a practical man as well as a patriot. He would die for his country, of course, provided there was absolutely no way to avoid it, but if given any kind of choice at all he much preferred to live.

And that meant living well.

Why walk, when he could ride? Why take the streetcar, when a limo was available?

Why change the world if it meant trading down and settling for a lifestyle that was worse than what he had before?

The good news, on this pitiful assignment, was that Keane wasn't required to seek out their Russian allies. It was enough for him to sit and wait at the Sovetskiy, standing by in case Valerik or Krestyanov suddenly decided that they couldn't live another moment without asking his advice. They both knew where to find him, had his code name memorized, but Keane believed it was unlikely either one would call on him. What could he do for them, in point of fact, besides delivering complaints to Langley in their stead? Krestyanov already maintained his own pipeline to Noble Pruett, and it wouldn't please him to be cut off from the man in charge, left dealing with a mere subordinate, however prized. As for Valerik, there had been a strict no-contact rule as far as Pruett was concerned. Pruett wasn't prepared to soil his hands directly.

That's what aides were for.

And so, Keane waited.

He was waiting for a call he hoped would never come.

Three days, Pruett had told him on the scrambled line. He was to give it three days. If nothing happened, he could go home. "Home" meaning Langley, where he could look forward to debriefing by the boss, even if he never saw or heard from any of their Russian contacts.

Hurry up and wait.

There was as much of that in the clandestine services as in the military, or in any other line of work. He could recall some cop who had once described the average policeman's job as ninety-eight percent boredom and two percent blind panic. In the cloak-and-dagger trade, Keane reckoned it was more like sixty-five percent boredom, thirty percent anticipation and five percent excitement—which, of course, could also equal panic, if you lost control and let the good times get away from you.

To hell with it.

He picked up the in-room directory of television offerings and scowled at what he saw. If programming was any guide to public interest, Muscovites were seemingly obsessed with news, soccer and cooking programs, in that order. There were also several Western dramas, purchased from their networks in the U.K. or the States and dubbed in Russian, but he didn't feel like catching up with the old gang on "Hill Street Blues" or "Dr. Who." That left some adult movies on pay-per-view, and Keane decided that the best thing he could do was get some sleep.

He was emerging from the shower—long on heat but short on water pressure—reaching for a bath towel when he heard the telephone. How long had it been ringing? Keane was fumbling with the towel, trying to don it like a kilt, when he remembered that the caller couldn't see him. Not unless the room was wired for fiber-optic cameras. In which case, he decided, why not ditch the towel and make his watchers envious?

He picked up on the fourth ring or the fortieth, not really caring which it was. "Hello?"

"Would this be Mr. Fletcher Christian, please?"

"It might. Who's asking?"

"Uncle Joseph," the caller replied, with no inkling of the humor Pruett had to have had in mind, choosing a recognition signal with a whiff of Stalin to it.

"Ah," Keane said. "You're well, I trust?" His end of the exchange. Whatever followed would determine whether Keane was bound for Dreamland or the Moscow streets.

"There is a matter that requires attention," the voice answered. "I hope that you will meet me for a cocktail, if you have no other pressing plans."

Bye-bye, Dreamland.

"Just tell me where and when," Keane said, proud of the way he kept the irritation from his voice.

"Shall we say fifteen minutes? I will meet you in the lobby."

Meaning Pruett had to have faxed his photograph ahead, or it was someone Keane had worked with previously, maybe on Valerik's operation in the States. Whatever, he now wished he had taken time to purchase a black-market gun before he settled into the hotel.

Relax. They wanted advice, maybe another pair of eyes. If he needed hardware, it was their job to provide it.

Right. Unless the only hardware in the crowd was meant for him.

Keane shrugged off the morbid thought as he dressed. Same clothes that he had traveled in, and never mind if someone didn't like the way he smelled after the long flight from Berlin.

Whatever waited for him in the Moscow night, Keane wouldn't know until he hit the street.

Let's get it done, he thought, and closed the door behind him with the sound of grim finality.

NIKOLAI LUKASHA felt at home in Moscow. He was still a giant in a world of stunted drones, but here, at least, he shared the kinship of a common heritage, a purely Russian bent toward suffering. It mattered not that Lukasha himself had been the instrument of suffering and death in many cases. These were still his people, even if he couldn't walk the grimy streets without experiencing an urge to grind them underfoot.

His mission, at the moment, was to meet with someone from Tolya Valerik's so-called Family—though not the yellow rat himself, in hiding since the last unpleasantness in Minsk—and make arrangements for delivery of the merchandise Vassily Krestyanov required to finalize their master plan. The package was supposed to be available that afternoon, their early plans for an exchange on neutral ground discarded after Valerik suddenly attracted the attention of an unknown man or men who had pursued him from Los Angeles to Minsk—and now, according to the latest news reports, to Moscow proper.

Lukasha didn't enjoy his contacts with the Russian Mafia, though he was wise enough to recognize their usefulness and cynical enough to use whomever was available to suit his purposes. This day, his irritation stemmed more from the fact that he was forced to travel and collaborate with an American, some kind of functionary from the CIA whom Krestyanov had summoned to the Russian capital to witness the delivery of their crucial package.

Fletcher Christian he was called, Krestyanov smirking when he spoke the name, as if it ought to have some meaning to Lukasha, something of an inside joke. In point of fact, Lukasha didn't care what the American was called as long as he kept quiet and didn't butt into matters that he didn't understand.

The man spoke fluent Russian with the barest trace of an American inflection, but his linguistic skill was wasted, since he kept his mouth shut on their drive through downtown Moscow, heading for the park on Prospekt Mira where they were supposed to find a mouthpiece for Valerik's syndicate and hear the final plans for the delivery. Why the American had been invited—or commanded to appear—was still a mystery to Lukasha, but he didn't allow such trivia to tax his mind.

Krestyanov had his reasons. That was all Lukasha had to know.

The park on Prospekt Mira wasn't large, nothing compared to Gorky Park, Sad Tsdra or Mandelshtama Park. It featured botanical gardens and a small man-made lake, neither of which Lukasha came to enjoy. He had been sent to retrieve certain information, and retrieve it he would, regardless of the risk or cost. If the American tried to obstruct him somehow, friend or not, then Lukasha would deal with him accordingly.

The Russian saw structures of the park before they reached it, greenhouses and such, for the exotic species that couldn't survive in Moscow's weather, even during relatively balmy spring.

Lukasha had been something of a hothouse specimen himself, in childhood, ridiculed by one-time playmates when he started to outgrow them, swiftly and inexorably leaving them behind. He stayed at home as much as possible, and when the others started to harass him, making fun, Lukasha took advantage of his special gift, fought back with vicious strength that soon encouraged school yard bullies to avoid him as they would a nest of vipers.

Their chauffeur drove once around the park, as he had been instructed, Lukasha and Fletcher Christian silently examining the meeting place, both men alert to any indications of a sting or ambush. Both of them were conscious that their actions on this Thursday evening put them one step closer to a major violation of assorted laws. If they were captured—more particularly, if the two of them were caught together—it would damage, maybe doom, Krestyanov's master plan. They might face prison time; even if they weren't incarcerated, the American would certainly be deported with prejudice, his CIA link very likely revealed.

In short, disaster.

That was why Lukasha had a loaded AK-47 on the floor, vying for space with his enormous shoes. He also carried two handguns, and their chauffeur was armed. Lukasha hadn't frisked the Yank. If there was trouble, he would simply have to take care of himself.

When the Russian had satisfied himself that there were no policemen, soldiers or assassins lurking in the park on Prospekt Mira, he gave orders and their driver instantly obeyed, veering across two lanes of traffic into the deserted parking lot. No other vehicle pursued them or slowed as if to note where they were going. If they had a tail, the watchers were discreet, professional.

"With me," Lukasha told the stoic American before he got out of the car. It was a sweet relief to stretch his legs again. Lukasha felt like yawning, but he swallowed it and pinched his own thigh viciously, unseen by the American, to make himself alert.

Pain had a wide variety of uses, even when inflicted on one's self.

"With me," he said again in the darkened parking lot before leading the way into the park, leaving the four-lane traffic and its noise behind them, moving toward the lake.

"With you, it is," Fletcher Christian said, falling into step.

Three men were waiting for them at the north end of the lake, two of them obviously muscle, their eyes alert, their faces new to Lukasha. He recognized the man who stood between them as the chief lieutenant of Valerik's operation, Anatoly Bogdashka. They didn't shake hands, exchanging nods and murmured almost-pleasantries instead.

"Who's this one?" Bogdashka asked the giant, staring hard at the American.

"A friend from the United States," the hulk replied. "Vassily asked him to attend our meeting, since the merchandise will ultimately be delivered to his territory."

Bogdashka spent another moment staring at the stranger, squinting in the dark, as if sheer concentration would enable him to see through flesh and bone, pluck thoughts from the *Amerikanski*'s mind.

When he was either satisfied or amply frustrated, Bogdashka turned to Lukasha again and said, "We have the merchandise."

"It's here? In Moscow?" the giant asked.

"Soon. The colonel will be pleased, I think, to learn that we can make delivery tonight, ahead of schedule."

"He will be relieved," Lukasha said, "if the delivery is made on time, and the equipment is in working order."

"Let him be prepared for great relief, then," Bogdashka said with an annoying note of sarcasm. "Shall we say midnight, at the zoo?"

"You will be informed if that is satisfactory," Lukasha said. "The normal number?"

"Yes."

Without another word, the giant turned and walked away, leaving his stoic American companion to catch up.

Midnight.

The colonel would be pleased, indeed.

ZHENYA ROMOCHKA clamped his cigar with yellow teeth, then removed it from his thin-lipped mouth. "Why has this trouble come to Moscow?" he demanded, leaning forward as he dropped his voice an octave even though he was alone with Krestyanov inside the sealed cocoon of his official vehicle, a black Zis limousine.

"It's nothing that concerns us," Krestyanov replied with what he hoped was just the right degree of candor, flavored with dismissive scorn.

"Nothing?" Romochka's tone and his expression were incredulous. "These bastards raid a sex club in the city where, unfortunately, some members of my own damned party have been known to gather and amuse themselves. They killed at least two dozen people—half of those, I might add, drawn from the elite of Moscow, one the mistress of a man who has contributed a minor fortune to my own political campaigns— and you suggest that it does not *concern* us? I, for one, am now officially concerned, Vassily!"

Krestyanov knew he had to proceed with caution, since his agitated colleague was a key member of Parliament, a powerhouse within the ruling party, and the man who would be ruler of the new USSR—with Krestyanov's assistance, naturally—once they had carried out the last stage of their *konspiratsia*, deposed the weak-kneed traitors now in office and restored the working mechanism of the People's State. It wouldn't serve Krestyanov's purpose now to mock Romochka's fear, make light of his concerns. They had to retain a certain unanimity of purpose, the colonel aware that even as he paved the politician's road to power, he was building up a man who might one day become his mortal enemy.

"I mean to say that it shouldn't affect our plans," Krestyanov said, his tone conciliatory, verging on apologetic, but without patronizing. "I have news for you," he said.

"More news?" Romochka didn't seem encouraged by the prospect.

"Good news, this time," Krestyanov said. "By midnight, we should have possession of the instrument that will deliver us from treason. Two days hence, the target will have been acquired. Nothing can stop us now."

"Nothing but arrogance, perhaps," the politician said. "I still don't trust the CIA. Suppose they're simply scheming to expose us, and they spring a trap. What, then?"

"You know I've made allowances for that," Krestyanov said. "Our friends at Langley share our interest, and they must proceed as planned, in any case. They and their sponsor have been fully compromised. If they attempt what the Americans would call a double cross, their words of treason and their faces will be spread around the planet from Calcutta to Cape Cod. Their actions, if exposed, would mean disgrace and life imprisonment, if not a death sentence.''

"You've thought of everything," Romochka said, his eyes narrowing. "My mentor, Gorbachev, once told me I should beware of any man who thinks of everything."

"Your mentor Gorbachev betrayed the people's revolution with détente and glasnost," Krestyanov reminded him, his voice a chisel scraping stone. "He is as much responsible as Yeltsin for the downfall of the Soviet republics."

"True enough," Romochka said, "but he wasn't without some wisdom, all the same. You scheme too much for your own good sometimes, Vassily."

"It's my job," the former colonel of the KGB replied.

"It may undo you sometime, all the same."

The warning, plainly stated, didn't trouble Krestyanov. As long as he knew how the politician felt, what he was thinking, then Romochka had no hope of sneaking up on him, to stab him in the back.

"I've been considering America," Romochka said a moment later, as if he had never threatened Krestyanov.

"In what respect?" the colonel asked.

"I think about their possible reaction to the incident. If NATO should become involved…"

"NATO will not become involved," Krestyanov promised him, not for the first time, striving for a tone of utmost confidence. "The incident will seem to be a product of America's own terrorists, the fringe we hear so much about. We have been shielded, insulated from exposure in this matter."

"Still…"

"There is no reason for you to be concerned. Our risk lies here, at home."

"I have considered that, as well."

"Our allies are in place and ready to perform their roles,"

Krestyanov said. "When the Americans react, once they begin to make the proper noises, then it will be time for us to strike."

"What of the People?"

"They crave leadership. You've told me so, yourself."

"And what if I am wrong?"

"The strongman of the new USSR wouldn't ask such a question," Krestyanov informed him, a rebuke without the normal sugarcoating that Romochka normally expected. "If you mean to lead, then you must be a leader. Failing that, it would be best for you to step aside."

Romochka blinked at that, a trace of angry color rising in his doughy cheeks, but he recovered swiftly. "You are right, Vassily. We need men of iron to lead the revolution."

"Iron is soft," Krestyanov said. "I would prefer a man of steel."

"And you shall have one," Romochka replied. "I will not betray the people or our cause."

Krestyanov never ceased to marvel at the ancient rhetoric of communism, how it clung to every movement that the Party made, despite three-quarters of a century in practice that had proved so much of it mistaken or an outright lie. Whatever Marx and Engels once intended "the People" had no power to speak of in any functioning Communist state, and they never would. Lenin's revolution of 1917 had replaced one Russian aristocracy—the czar and his extended family—with another: the elite of the Communist Party. The early Bolshevik promise of "power to the people" had no more impact on real-world politics than when it was repeated, decades later, in the puerile lyrics of a John Lennon song.

Successful rulers told the People what they wished to hear at crucial moments, and ignored those campaign promises that undermined the strength and order of the State. If necessary, they removed the velvet gloves, revealing fists of steel.

All hail the proletariat, as long as it was in its proper place and working diligently for the masters who preserved it from its countless enemies. Russia would need another enemy, in order to regain her unity of purpose, her determination, strength and pride.

Krestyanov had that covered.

He had thought of everything.

"KEEP THAT DAMNED thing away from me!" Anatoly Bogdashka commanded, scowling as one of his soldiers hastened to move the ordinary-looking suitcase several paces farther west. Still unsatisfied, Bogdashka snapped, "No! Put it back in the trunk for Christ's sake."

He was behaving foolishly, he knew, perhaps even jeopardizing his image in front of the men, but at the moment Bogdashka didn't care. He had been briefed about the merchandise, the suitcase lined in foam rubber to cradle it, with lead to keep any stray radiation from escaping, and he didn't give a damn about that, either.

Courage was one thing, and balls were another. Bogdashka couldn't be a real man if *his* balls lit up in the dark—or if they shriveled up like raisins, either, come to think of it.

Objectively, he knew the warhead in the suitcase—one of many salvaged from an old MIRV rocket after the collapse, the rocket itself one of hundreds, maybe thousands that were up for grabs—was perfectly safe in its present state. It couldn't be set off by any means except a primary explosion, not with heat or hammers, point-blank gunfire, nothing. It was also certified as safe to handle, with a lead skin of its own, besides the extra insulation built into the suitcase. He absorbed more radiation on a daily basis from his wristwatch and his television set, Bogdashka had been told.

And none of it meant anything.

He thought of radiation sickness, as it was depicted in the motion pictures he had seen, with running sores and bloody, toothless gums, hair falling out, eyes clouded over from within, and vowed that he would never die that way. Not if he had to put a pistol in his mouth. And he wouldn't expose himself promiscuously to the "safe" warhead he was assigned to transport, not for all the rubles, yen, or U.S. dollars in the world.

Once it was locked inside the limo's trunk, Bogdashka felt a little better. He began to picture silent beams of radiation pulsing from inside the car, all aimed directly at his groin, but with an effort he dismissed the thought and focused on the job at hand.

Delivery.

Someone, most probably the giant with some soldiers, would be coming for the suitcase in another…what? Three minutes, by his Rolex watch. They were free to open it, inspect the merchandise if they were so inclined, although Bogdashka would be standing well back from the bag if they appeared inclined to do so. Then, before they were allowed to leave and take it with them, someone on the pickup team would verify the transfer of Valerik's payment to a numbered bank account in Switzerland. Laptop time, as it had been explained to him, since no one was on duty at Swiss banks, this hour of the night. Bogdashka didn't "do" computers, understood them only vaguely, but the man who stood beside him with a vague smile on his face—perhaps at Anatoly's little sideshow with the warhead—was supposed to be an expert, who could verify the transfer had gone through.

If it wasn't confirmed and verified, the suitcase and its contents would remain in Bogdashka's custody. There would be hell to pay in that event, he realized, and that was something that he understood completely. It wasn't for nothing that he wore a Skorpion machine pistol buckled to his left side in a heavy shoulder rig, while his four soldiers were armed with AK-74 assault rifles.

If it came to killing, he was ready, but he also knew that it would mean defeat. This handoff was the object of the whole protracted exercise. If anything went wrong, it meant the best part of a year was wasted; all the soldiers they had lost in recent days would have died in vain.

Bogdashka cared about such things in only abstract terms,

and in the most distracted sense. He focused on himself, primarily, and knew there would be brutal repercussions if the handoff failed, and more specifically if that failure was deemed to be his fault. That could not happen under any circumstances, and Bogdashka was determined to prevent it at all costs.

"Headlights," one of his soldiers said a beat before Bogdashka picked them out himself, approaching from the far end of the narrow access road. They were five miles outside of Moscow, more or less assured of privacy, unlikely to be interrupted by police patrol cars passing by.

"Get out the bag," Bogdashka ordered, feeling foolish now for having stowed it only moments earlier. One thing about his rank within the Family, at least: he knew none of the other men would mention it in front of him or laugh about it openly, where they were likely to be overheard.

Not if they wanted to survive.

The trunk lid slammed, one of his soldiers coming back with the suitcase. "That's far enough, right there," Bogdashka said, and stopped him in his tracks. To cover for his phobia, he added, "We don't want it too exposed in case something goes wrong."

The soldier shrugged and laid down his burden, uninterested in explanations. He, like all the rest, was focused on the lights of the approaching vehicle, his right hand clutching at the pistol grip of his Kalashnikov.

Bogdashka recognized the giant when he stepped out of the car. How could he not? The other three were strangers to him, and he was content to let it stay that way. He had no interest in Vassily Krestyanov's associates in the spy game, unless there was some profit to be made from them.

As there would be this night.

"Is that the merchandise?" The giant's voice sounded as if it had been piped up from the bottom of a well.

"It is," Bogdashka told him. "Feel free to examine it."

"We will."

Bogdashka stood his ground, cringing inside but hiding it well, as one of the giant's companions stepped forward to open the suitcase, peering closely at the object it contained. When he was satisfied, the stranger closed the suitcase, nodded to his master and stepped back to join the others.

"So," Bogdashka said. "You are prepared to verify the transfer?"

The giant nodded, and the same man who had opened the suitcase walked back to their car, retrieved a portable computer from the rear compartment and approached Bogdashka's limousine.

"Show him," the mobster said, and nodded to the man who stood beside him, hoping it would look like delegation of authority to a subordinate, instead of simple ignorance.

The giant's man opened his laptop on the limo's hood and switched it on. A moment later, he was tapping keys, while Bogdashka's man watched every move he made, nodding along as if for someone else's benefit. When it was done, Bogdashka's techie got his own computer from the limousine, logged on and spent a moment peering at the screen before he said, "It's done. The transfer is confirmed, in full."

"The merchandise is yours," Bogdashka told the giant, feeling suddenly magnanimous. "I hope it serves you well."

"There is no doubt of that," Lukasha said, and turned back toward his vehicle, as one of his companions grabbed the bag.

Bogdashka felt himself relaxing as the taillights of the giant's car began to dwindle, finally winked out. He gave them just a moment longer to get clear, before he told his troops, "All right, let's go."

It had been simple, tidy, neat.

The world ends with a whimper, after all, he thought, and smiled for the first time that day.

6

"I don't like these delays," Johnny said, punctuating the remark by racking the slide on his Glock to chamber a round from the fresh magazine.

"We're cool," Deckard replied, wiping down his own Glock with a chamois. "He just has to tap some more contacts before we play another round."

"He" being Rurik, the goateed Russian who had helped them close Club Zero for remodeling. He had performed his duties well enough on that excursion, but the man was still a stranger, still connected to the CIA, and very possibly the Russian underworld, as well. Informers had those kinds of contacts—hell, they couldn't operate without them—but it still made Bolan nervous as they sat in the hotel room, waiting for the chirp of Deckard's cellular phone to announce that the Russian had returned.

It would be just as easy Bolan knew, and Johnny sensed as well, for Deckard's contact to betray them, send a team of shooters in his place to wipe them out.

But why, when he had helped them on one raid, already?

Working Moscow was a problem, since no one ever really knew the players, or how many different, even hostile, factions they were trying to appease.

Instead of voicing his suspicions, Bolan simply said, "I hope it doesn't take him too much longer. We don't have a lot of time to spare."

"Rurik won't dick around any longer than necessary,"

Deckard replied. "He has to pull some strings without getting tied up in knots, if you get my drift."

"I hear you," Bolan stated, but he was still unhappy with the wait. He wanted to be out and moving, doing something, carrying the battle to his enemies. The longer they delayed, the more time their intended targets had to fortify positions, call for reinforcements from the hinterlands, or possibly evacuate the city altogether.

"I've been wondering," Deckard said, shifting subjects, "about what happens when we're finished here. I mean, when we go home."

He was assuming all of them would make it home, but Bolan didn't feel inclined to point that out. The three of them had ample problems on their plate as it was, without injecting a strain of negative thinking.

"I had in mind to ask you the same thing," Bolan replied. "From what I see, you still don't have a thing to help identify the rogues you're looking for inside the Company."

"I'm not the only one involved," Deckard said. "There's a team at Langley, going over everything with microscopes. It's down on paper as an audit by the Senate Oversight Committee, but they're really our guys. The equivalent of Internal Affairs, I guess you'd say."

"They watch the watchmen," Johnny stated.

"Essentially. They obviously don't have perfect records, or there never would have been an Aldrich Ames, but once they have a lead to chase, they don't give up. They'll ultimately find whatever's there to see."

"And if there's nothing," Bolan said, "what, then?"

"There has to be," Deckard answered with an air of confidence that didn't quite ring true. "If this was being run outside the shop entirely, as a private thing, there'd be no access to the necessary funds, support and personnel. It's covered somehow, but it's there. I'd stake my life on that."

"You have," Johnny reminded him without a trace of mirth.

"I guess that's right." The man from Langley turned to Bolan now. "We haven't talked about it, and I'm figuring you'd rather not, but for the record, I don't buy you chasing this halfway around the world on your own dime to help a friend. Smart money says that you're connected, somehow." Deckard raised an open hand, anticipating the denial. "I'm not asking, mind you. I don't need to know, and I don't want to know, okay? I'm satisfied that you're not with the Company, but if your guys have some connection to my guys...well, you see where I'm going, right? I mean, it could be that we get back home and find out we're all screwed."

It was the last thing Bolan wanted to consider, heaping more doubt on the problem of his rift with Hal Brognola and the team at Stony Man Farm. He had attacked the problem mentally from every angle he could think of, and there was still no satisfactory answer to the questions that nagged at his mind. Why had Brognola—and, by extension, Barbara Price—refused to cooperate on this mission beyond providing the bare minimum of background information? Why had the big Fed repeatedly implored Bolan to let it drop, move on to something else? If the unthinkable had happened, and Brognola had crossed over to the other side, how should—how could—the Executioner respond?

Bolan had never killed a trusted friend, and he had vowed to never kill a cop, regardless of the circumstances. If it turned out Brognola was dirty, bent somehow, what could he do about it?

He felt Deckard watching him and waiting for an answer. Bolan frowned as he replied, "I can't believe it goes that far, that deep. There wouldn't be a rogue hunt at the Company if your superiors were compromised. My end's completely separate. I'll do what's necessary, and we'll let it go at that."

"I hear you," Deckard said. "It's just—" He hesitated, staring at the pistol in his hands. "I'd like to think there's something left worth fighting for, you know? That it's not all a bunch of rotten shit with nothing but a bunch of black hats trying to get one up on each other for the payoff. Hey, I know stuff happens, but I try to keep it in perspective. I do not believe there were a hundred different plots to murder JFK or twenty different snipers in the plaza. Am I making any sense at all?''

"You'd like to think the system works more often than it fails," Bolan replied, "and I believe it does. As long as you have human beings on the job, you'll have to deal with human problems—greed, fear, hatred, jealousy, insanity, the whole nine yards. Sometimes you have to fumigate, but you don't burn a house to get the roaches out."

"You've obviously never been to my apartment," Deckard answered, stretching for a grin that didn't quite come through. He gave it up and said, "Sometimes, it just feels like the roaches *built* the house."

"They had a hand in it," the Executioner replied. "They've always been there, and they always will unless machines take over. Then we'll have to worry about who designed and programmed the machines."

"You're telling me it never ends."

"It hasn't yet," Bolan said. "Maybe that's some kind of white-hat victory, you stop and think about it. All the wheels keep turning. Life goes on."

For some, he added silently. There was no need to state the obvious.

"So, you're a soldier and philosopher," Deckard said, managing the smile this time. "How's that work out?"

"A soldier needs to understand the principles he's fighting for," Bolan answered. "If you just let someone aim you like a weapon, take down anything that moves in front of you, you're nothing but a zombie. You've surrendered your humanity."

"It keeps things simple, though," Deckard replied.

"As long as you don't come out of the trance one day and wonder what it is you've done."

"Last time I checked, the military wasn't big on independent thinking in the ranks. First thing they told me, as a boot, was that you've got three ways of doing things—the right way, wrong way and the Army way.''

''I don't fault discipline,'' the Executioner replied. ''In combat, it's essential. But the Military Code of Conduct also recognizes that there comes a time when soldiers have to draw a line. You know the drill on war crimes and illegal orders. There's a difference between surrendering your will to storm an enemy position and collaborating in atrocities. If that's philosophy, I guess I've got one.''

''But you don't care all that much about the law, per se, from what I've seen,'' the spook remarked.

''Some predators exist outside the law,'' Bolan said. ''Ask them, if you get the chance, and most of them will tell you that themselves. They make the rules up as they go along, and never mind what's written in the Constitution or the statute books. It gives them an advantage that the rules can't overcome in many cases. I judge every situation by the adversaries and objectives. When the letter of the law won't work, I find another way.''

''It doesn't bother you?'' Deckard inquired. ''I mean, I'm obviously not in any place to criticize. We're in this together, right or wrong...but sometimes when I'm on assignment, even when there's no wet work involved, I have to wonder if there's any difference between me and the assholes I'm supposed to be protecting. You ever feel that way?''

Bolan replied without a trace of hesitation, ''Not at all. The predators condemn themselves. I play by their rules, so they've got no grounds for crying foul, but I'm still playing by *my* principles. We have an obligation to prevent atrocities by any means at our disposal, whether it's negotiation or a surgical preemptive strike.''

''Is that what we've been doing?'' Deckard asked him. ''Surgery?''

''It isn't always tidy,'' Bolan answered. ''But sometimes, neatness doesn't count.''

"You mean the operation was successful, but the patient died?"

"Some patients *need* to die," Johnny said, holstering his Glock.

"You guys have got some bedside manner," Deckard said, smiling. "I'll give you that."

"You ought to see the HMO we work for," Johnny wise-cracked, switching on a grin. Bolan could tell from Johnny's aspect, though, that he was thinking about something, maybe Suzanne King, waiting for him back in Switzerland, unable to go home alone.

"I may sign up," Deckard said, "if they're taking applications."

Bolan offered no response to that, and Johnny also let it go. It may have been a joke, but either way, he wasn't dropping any hints that might lead Deckard back to Stony Man.

For all he knew, when this was over, the Farm might no longer exist.

RURIK PAVLUSHKA hated cruising Gorky Park. It wasn't the embarrassment, because he felt none. There was no more stigma, in his view, to feigning homosexuality than in pretending to deal weapons, drugs, or any other form of contraband in Moscow. Not that being gay was criminal in modern Russia, the repressive legislation of the Soviet regime regarding homosexuality as "decadent" and "counterrevolutionary" had been repealed nearly a decade earlier, but old habits died hard, and Moscow's gay community was still "in the closet" to a large degree, kept there by prejudice that could rebound against known homosexuals in forms that ranged from loss of jobs to physical assault.

As luck would have it, being driven to the shadows for three-quarters of a century had turned gays into outlaws, of a sort, and made them cognizant of certain information, certain contacts.

This night, in Gorky Park, Pavlushka was supposed to meet

a drag queen called Alexei, who spent his days working for the Ministry of Health, his nights engaged in exploration of a world most Muscovites would never glimpse. Alexei was particularly useful when it came to leads on various narcotics labs and operations, since his ministry shared responsibility for curbing drug addiction with the Ministry of Justice. Through some quirk of legislation, maybe borrowed from the West, where such diverse topics as alcohol, tobacco and firearms were lumped together under the control of a single agency, the Ministry of Health also had partial jurisdiction over certain weapons violations and sundry accidents, including the nuclear variety. It made sense to Pavlushka—well, as much as anything made sense in Moscow—on the theory that it was unhealthy to be shot, blown up with hand grenades, or dosed with radiation that would rot your body from the inside out.

Rurik Pavlushka wore no special costume for his nighttime trips to Gorky Park. Though Moscow had its share of flaming queens, they played their wilder dress-up games in private, for the most part, or in certain nightclubs that were sparsely advertised. Cross-dressers like Alexei, who went out in public wearing drag, tended to be conservative and tried to ''pass'' among their fellow Muscovites, rather than sporting feathers, sequins, fright wigs. Most of them, Pavlushka reflected as he moved through brooding darkness, pulled it off with fair success. On balance, they were normally more feminine in aspect than the women athletes Moscow sent to the Olympic Games or many of the housewives one encountered waiting in the endless lines at grocery shops.

Gorky Park extended for nearly three hundred acres along the Moskva River. It was roughly one-third the size of New York's Central Park, and it offered similar features: hiking paths, man-made lakes, an outdoor theater with seating for ten thousand. Not surprisingly, by night it also shared the urban problems of its larger cousin in New York—purse snatchers, muggers, rapists, street gangs clashing over turf, drug addicts and their dealers, hookers and their pimps.

Pavlushka didn't fear the park, as did so many Muscovites, including some policemen he could name. He had enough self-confidence to know he would prevail in any normal confrontation, one-on-one or even two-on-two, as long as there were no firearms involved. If he was too badly outnumbered, Pavlushka's also had the common sense to cut and run, survive to fight another day.

As always, he was armed this night, but not with firearms. He had ditched the pistol taken from the bouncer at Club Zero as they were leaving, pitched it from the moving car a few blocks from the scene. Police might find it, but they would discover none of Pavlushka's fingerprints; more likely, some street thug would come along and claim the weapon for himself, facing a rude surprise if he was captured with it later and ballistics tests performed.

Pavlushka had the balisong, his favorite, and a straight razor that he carried in the left-hand pocket of his jacket. He was ambidextrous and could wield both blades at once, with murderous effect, or he could choose the one that fit his needs for any given situation. If he lost both weapons, somehow, there was yet another, this one a wicked double-edged push dagger, serving double duty as the buckle of Pavlushka's belt.

He felt like an American Boy Scout, always prepared.

Male prostitutes occasionally hit on Pavlushka as he navigated through the darkness toward the largest of the park's three man-made lakes, and he rebuffed each in turn with a shake of his head and a soft-spoken *"Nyet."* They posed no threat to him and took rejection in their stride, knowing full well that other customers would come along before the night was over.

The Russian hoped that he wouldn't be forced to kill again this night. It didn't trouble him in any moral sense, particularly when the men he killed were violent criminals themselves, but sudden death was almost always inconvenient, and Pavlushka had other plans. It was information he wanted, not blood. With any luck at all, he could get one without the other.

As for what the three Americans would do with any information he obtained, what Pavlushka would himself be called upon to do before their business in Moscow was finished, he could only speculate. If the raid on Club Zero was a preview of coming attractions, then he knew there would be blood enough to go around for all concerned.

Rurik Pavlushka only hoped that none of it was his.

He found Alexei trolling near the lake, as usual. Alexei saw him coming, flounced across the grass to meet him, moving with a stride distinctly feminine. His makeup was subdued, the wig he wore a stylish pageboy, nothing in the way of flashy jewelry to entice a mugger.

"Rurik!" Such enthusiasm, every time they met. It had to have been the money talking. "It's so good to see you!"

Alexei took his hand, the left one, Pavlushka having warned him once before about his need to keep the right hand unencumbered. They appeared to be a couple, this way, if one didn't look too closely, and Pavlushka didn't feel his masculinity imperiled by the contact. It was no more part of him than any of the false names he affected in his trade, or the occasional disguise.

"You have something to tell me," Pavlushka said, not asking. He already knew that much, Alexei having said so on the telephone.

"You asked about Valerik, yes?"

"That's right." The same old song and dance, as if they hadn't played this scene a dozen times.

"This is a bit unusual," Alexei said. "Not what you might expect."

"I've given up expecting anything," Pavlushka told him. He wasn't about to plead for information, but he was prepared to give Alexei's slender hand a painful squeeze and go from there, if the transvestite started playing games.

"It isn't drugs, this time," Alexei said. "I thought you might be hoping for a drug lab, like the last time."

"Anything at all," Pavlushka replied, still casual, but feeling tension in the muscles of his left arm now, preparing for the crunch.

"You understand I don't know who this article is meant for, what he means to do with it?"

"From the beginning, please, Alexei."

"I'm just nervous. You know how it is."

"Best have it done with quickly, then."

"You want to get away from me."

"I have no end of things to do." Pavlushka allowed the sharp edge of his mounting irritation to be heard. "You want your money, I want information. I have no time to play games."

"It may be that we're all running out of time."

"For God's sake, spit it out!"

Alexei grimaced, as if he had heard that phrase employed before, in even more unpleasant circumstances. All the better then, to make him focus.

"As you wish," he sniffed. "I'm told Valerik has obtained some kind of bomb. A nuke, I mean. It's not unheard-of since the great collapse, you know."

"I've heard. You wouldn't know what he intends to do with this device, by any chance?"

"What does he ever do but trade? I mean, he's not a terrorist, for heaven's sake. Valerik is a businessman. It's who he sells the damned thing to that worries me."

"Who's the customer?" Pavlushka asked.

"I've no idea, I swear," Alexei said. "I only know about the bomb because I have a special friend attached to the…um, let us say, another ministry."

Most likely Justice or Intelligence, Pavlushka thought, not really interested. Alexei's source meant nothing to him if the man had no more information to reveal.

"About this bomb…"

"It may have been a warhead, if that makes a difference," Alexei said. "Anyway, I don't have details. It may only be a rumor, but my friend was certainly convinced."

"There's been no move against Valerik, though?"

Alexei shrugged. "No evidence for an arrest, apparently. It almost makes you miss the old days, eh?"

Not quite, Pavlushka thought. "If there was no description of the bomb or warhead, then I don't supposed you'd know about its size."

"Oh, size," Alexei said, and fanned his free hand in the air before his face. "It's overrated, don't you think? But yes, there was some mention of a suitcase, if I'm not mistaken. That would make it fairly small, I think."

"You're right about the size, Alexei," Pavlushka said. "It hardly matters."

Not with nukes, at any rate. A suitcase nuke could easily destroy the heart of any major city on the planet.

"Here's your money, then," Pavlushka said, freeing his hand to palm the wad of bills. "We'll have our stroll another time, all right?"

JOHNNY WAS SITTING in the corner, with his back against the wall, when Deckard answered Pavlushka's knock and let the Russian in. His man had called ahead to let them know that he was on his way, and even leaning toward acceptance of the Russian as a bona fide ally, Johnny remained on the defensive. Moscow was too strange, too alien for him to think about relaxing during their sojourn.

The Russian came in looking worried, which concerned Johnny. He barely knew the man, but Pavlushka had impressed him as unflappable during their brief acquaintance, most particularly when he knifed the two gorillas at Club Zero. He had been out scrounging information on new targets since that strike, and from the grim expression on his face, Johnny was betting that he had bad news to share.

The Russian produced a flask from somewhere underneath his coat and offered it around, no takers, before tossing off a swallow for himself. Thus fortified, he sat on a corner of the bed and started speaking in the same near-flawless English he had used the first time they had met.

"I have discovered something," he informed them, "which may help you, or may simply make things worse. There is a chance that it's unrelated to your business in the city, but I fear that is not the case."

"We're listening," Deckard replied, hunched forward in his straight-backed wooden chair. Bolan occupied a stool, to Johnny's left, positioned so they would have had the door pinned in a cross fire if a hostile visitor had blundered through in Pavlushka's place.

"It seems, according to the information I've discovered, that Valerik has obtained a bomb or warhead of the nuclear variety." Johnny could feel the chill start down his spine, the short hairs stirring on his nape as Pavlushka spoke. "Such things, regrettably, are not unknown in Russia since the Soviet collapse. Deactivated stockpiles have gone missing in Belarus, in Kazakhstan, the Ukraine. The government suppresses news of this as much as possible. Who wants the world to know that there are doomsday weapons unaccounted for? And some of them have been recovered. Others, it is said, may have been sold in China or the Middle East, perhaps to terrorists."

If so, none of the stolen nukes had yet been used, but it was every Western leader's nightmare, some fringe dweller with a nuke that he could transport in a pickup truck, or maybe even in a backpack, parking it somewhere in Tel Aviv, in London, maybe even in New York or Washington, D.C. Procedures were in place to deal with such a crisis, but they mostly focused on its aftermath—the cleanup and mass burials.

It stood to reason, after all, that if a band of diehard terrorists obtained a nuke by one means or another, they would use it. Any kind of blackmail or coercion scheme was far more risky than a simple detonation without warning, and the modern terrorists appeared much more adept at killing than at bargaining. There had been no heads-up call before the World Trade Center blast, in Oklahoma City, in Omagh, Northern

Ireland, or in any of the other recent terrorist "events" that kept on making headlines from around the war-torn globe.

It almost seemed that terrorism in the classic sense, of issuing demands and deadlines to the enemy, had suddenly become passé. What mattered to the new breed of extremist was a body count, and nothing stacked up the corpses—or turned them into drifting dunes of ash—quite like a nuke.

"We know about the leaks," Deckard replied. "That's someone else's problem. Right now, all I care about is this one package."

"Certainly," the Russian said. "I understand."

"I don't suppose there's any word on when Valerik got his hands on this alleged warhead?"

"Nothing specific," Pavlushka said. "I would assume it is a recent acquisition, since it hasn't been disposed of yet. Such things are not retained for long, with all the risks involved."

"You're sure he hasn't moved it yet?" Bolan asked.

The Russian shrugged. "I offer only what my source has told me. As to firsthand knowledge of the object, I have none."

"Okay," Deckard said, "but you think he would have moved it if he'd had it more than…what? A week or two?"

"Much less, I think," the Russian replied. "The penalty for trafficking in such devices is equivalent to treason. That means death, effectively without appeal. Tolya has friends in government, of course, but none who would assist him if he were condemned on such a charge."

"So, he'd unload it right away, you're saying."

"It is customary in such dealings, so I have been told, to make arrangements in advance, but not to take delivery until the details of the transfer are arranged. Of course…" The Russian hesitated, frowning to himself.

"Go on," Deckard urged.

"I'm thinking the information could have reached my source belatedly," Pavlushka replied. "He's not connected to Valerik's Family, but rather to a ministry of government. It wouldn't be unusual to learn about a nuclear transaction only after it's occurred.''

"So, we could be too late," Deckard stated.

"For the sale, perhaps," the Russian said. "But maybe not to intercept the package, if you knew Valerik's customer."

"Maybe we do," Bolan said, three faces swiveling in his direction.

"Are you thinking Krestyanov?" Deckard asked.

"It's the name that comes to mind."

"He's definitely doing business with Valerik," Johnny said. "You nailed that down, yourself. Besides, what other suspects do we have?"

"Okay, let's grant that," Deckard said. "What's Krestyanov's objective? How does it connect with any of their action in the States?"

"We're looking for a common thread," Bolan said. "What binds rogue operators in the Company to members of the Russian syndicate—or more particularly, to the former KGB? Assume Valerik is a handyman, some kind of gofer valued for his acquisition talents on the shady side. Delete his broader goals from the equation. Focus on Krestyanov and your rogues."

"You want to give me a hint?" Deckard asked.

"When you boil it down," Bolan said, "I only see one thing they have in common."

It came to Johnny in a flash. "Nostalgia," he suggested.

"Come again?" The frown on Deckard's face was almost comical.

"Krestyanov got the boot when KGB went belly-up," Bolan said. "He does all right in private life, financially, but he's a zealot, right? It's hard to shift those gears and make a mercenary of a zealot."

"And you're thinking...?"

"Maybe someone in the Company feels likewise," Johnny said. "Maybe they miss the bad old days, when they could use the Evil Empire to unlock appropriations, get the green

light for all kinds of operations in the field. Suppose they plan
on turning back the clock."

The man from Langley blinked. "They'd need a trigger
incident," he said.

"Most likely more than one," Bolan offered, "but they
have to start someplace."

"The States, you think?"

Bolan shrugged at that. "We haven't got the data for a call
like that," he said. "My guess, they'd need a string of incidents to make it work."

"Or maybe not," Johnny replied, nearly trembling as the
pieces started falling into place.

"How's that?"

"The restoration of a Communist regime in Russia would
be all the incident it takes to bring the cold war back to Washington. You've got a faction on the Hill that doesn't think it
ever really ended, as things stand today. Put Reds back in the
Kremlin, a reactionary group would pick up all the votes it
need in Congress, just like that. You couldn't run for President
or any other office on a platform of conciliation. Talk about
a time warp, you'd be back in 1962, with everything except
the missiles in Havana."

"What you're thinking now could start a damned world
war," Deckard said.

"Not if it was lined up in advance and everybody plays his
cards according to the script," Bolan said. "You'd have the
saber rattling, probably another arms race, but these guys don't
want to push the button. What's the point in turning back the
calendar if you blow everyone away? Nobody wins that kind
of game. But if they start off talking tough and bring it to a
draw, it pays off all around."

"But first, they need the trigger incident," Johnny said.

"Right."

"So, all we have to do is find the nuke and/or the target

and make sure nobody lights the fuse?'' Deckard asked. ''Hell, I thought this job was going to be tough.''

''We've got one place to start,'' Bolan said, and Johnny knew the name before his brother spoke it. ''Krestyanov.''

7

The intercom in Barbara Price's private quarters always made a soft metallic click before a voice came through, thereby alerting her, allowing to focus. It was nearly always business when Aaron Kurtzman or anybody else called her in her quarters, where she went to simply be alone. It could be anything from a mechanical malfunction or a glitch in scheduling to a red-flagged alert from Hal Brognola, in Washington.

She was accustomed to the unexpected, but her heart still skipped a beat when she heard the duty officer announce, "Ms. Price, we have a call from Striker on line three. ID's confirmed, ma'am. He won't speak to anyone but you."

"I'm on my way," she told the flat wall-mounted speaker, pulling up the jumpsuit zipper she had lowered to her waist for comfort's sake, secure from shifty eyes. There were no telephones in private quarters at Stony Man Farm, since every room was linked by intercom. Communication with the outside world was handled via modem in the Farm's computer lab; by satellite, through dish antennas mounted on the roof and in the yard; by radio, on any one of several hundred channels; and by telephone, from sundry offices and conference rooms. All land-line calls passed through a central switchboard, theoretically diminishing the risk of leakage, and the calls were taped, archived for future reference, purged only on direct commands from Brognola, or when a minimum of three executives agreed the tapes were no longer required for any reasons of security. At that point, they would be magnetically erased and then recycled to the switchboard.

Waste not, want not.

Price had no reason to believe that anyone would eavesdrop on her conversation with the man called Striker, though a trace on all incoming calls was automatic at the Farm. The last confirmed location on the man had been Berlin, but Price had a notion that he would be moving eastward. She looked forward to the trace results, to see if she was right.

Inside the office closest to her quarters, the mission controller lifted the receiver on a plain black telephone and pressed the lighted button numbered three. "Hello?"

"I need to know which side you're on," he said without preamble, skipping the amenities.

"You have to ask me that?" It hurt more than it angered her, but there was anger, too.

"These days, considering the freeze and all," he said, "I think I do."

"Well, damn you, then," she responded. "I'm where I've always been."

"I didn't ask you for a job description," Bolan said.

"Now, listen—"

"No, you listen," he said, interrupting her. "Since day one on this thing, Hal's tried to call me off, and when that didn't work he froze me out. You helped him with the minimal disclosure game. Want to deny it?"

Price hesitated, felt the burning in her cheeks and found she didn't want to lie. "I'm not denying it," she said.

"So, what's the game. We're getting short. I need to know."

She hesitated for a moment, felt precious time slipping through her fingers, maybe one last chance. "I honestly don't know," she said at last. "I asked him for an overview of what was going on, and all I got were cryptic references to national security." She thought about the tape recording every word they spoke. To hell with it. "It isn't like he's frightened, more like he's carrying twice the usual weight on his shoulders and can't set it down, can't share it with anyone.''

"It's about to get worse," Bolan told her. His voice sounded clear and strong, as if he were calling from an extension in the next room, instead of God knew where, halfway around the world. "How much do you want to know?"

"I want it all," she answered without hesitation. "Whether I can move on it, well, that's another story. But I want to know."

"Okay," he said, and laid it out for her. "Tolya Valerik deals in weapons, right along with drugs and sex and whatever else the traffic will bear."

"I took that for granted," Price said.

"The latest item on his auction block is some kind of nuke. They're saying 'warhead,' but it's obviously portable. It could fit in your basic suitcase for all I know."

"They're out there," Price told him, knowing it for years, and still unable to suppress the sudden chill. "It would be much more useful if we knew the customer, and where the merchandise was going."

"I've got the *who,* but *where*'s still up for grabs."

"I'm listening," she stated, trusting her memory, ignoring the coffee mug bristling with pens a few inches away from her elbow.

"You're taping this?" he asked, knowing the answer in advance.

"Of course." No point in lying, since he knew the Farm's security by heart.

"Okay. The buyer is a Russian named Vassily Krestyanov. He's former KGB, a colonel, forcibly retired since the collapse. He's worked the private sector ever since, but word is that he still has powerful connections in the government, reactionary types who wouldn't mind the cold war coming back to play an encore for another hundred years of so."

"What's Mr. KGB want with a pocket nuke?" she asked.

"His special field of operation for the *Komitet* was terrorism, counterterrorism and counterintelligence. He's tried toppling governments before and may have pulled it off for all I know.''

"You have a certain government in mind?" she asked, not liking the direction this was taking.

"Here's the bad news."

"And I suppose the rest of this was good?" she interrupted him.

Bolan ignored her, pushing on. "You know that we've been working on a link between the Company and the Valerik Family."

For once, the *we* excluded Price, and that knowledge stung her like an open-handed blow across the face. She closed her eyes and said, "I know."

"Okay," he said, oblivious to the flesh wound he had inflicted. "Now we know the game's a threesome, with Vassily Krestyanov. I can't give you chapter and verse on the motive, but we know for sure that Krestyanov has contacts with the Company, aside from any echoes that Valerik passes on. In fact, I'm leaning toward Krestyanov as the architect, Valerik and his people helping out on the construction crew."

"Constructing what, exactly."

"We were thinking it might be a time machine," he said.

That damned exclusionary *we*, again. Instead of letting it distract her, Price forged ahead. "You've lost me, Striker. Where does H. G. Wells fit into this?"

"Figure of speech," Bolan replied. "We know that Krestyanov and some of his associates are mourning for the change in Russia's form of government. They'd love to hit the Rewind button, play back everything from 1989 or so through 1992, but with a happy ending for the Soviet regime."

"Makes sense to me," she told him, meaning it, "but I don't see the Company's percentage in rewriting history. I mean, we won that round, if you'll recall. When was the last time that you heard a winner asking for a rematch?"

"That depends on the rewards or spoils of victory," he said.

"In sports you get the medals, the endorsements, the big bucks. You go to Disneyland. In the defense or cloak-and-dagger business, maybe you get budget cuts and layoffs, the important people start ignoring you. Maybe they put you out to pasture with a pension if you're lucky. Otherwise, you wind up watching neighbors kill each other in Armenia."

"You're saying someone in the Company has thrown in with Krestyanov, and they want to bring the cold war back?"

"The first part's definite," Bolan replied. "The motive's educated guesswork, based on what we know about Krestyanov and his pals, plus what's been happening with Langley since the Soviets dropped off the screen."

"Which brings us back full-circle to the nuke," she said. "You're figuring some kind of incident?"

"What else? Unfortunately, if we don't move soon, it could end up on either side of the Atlantic."

Price didn't know if he was asking, but she answered the unspoken question, anyway. "I don't know whether we can get a fix on Mr. KGB in time to do any good." She hesitated, adding in a softer voice, "I don't know if I'll be allowed to try."

"Don't sweat it," Bolan said. "We're working on some angles here, and if we miss it, there'll be no way we can track the package, anyhow. Consider this a friendly heads-up, just in case it's coming your way."

Friendly, right. The goddamned kiss of death. "Well, I appreciate it," Price said. "Will you be calling Hal?"

"No time," Bolan replied. "I have to move. Take care."

Not "See you," or "I'll catch you later." Not even *"Hasta la vista,* baby."

Price's eyes were brimming as she cradled the receiver, quickly lifted it again and tapped the button for an outside line.

"YOU SAY THIS pocket nuke is earmarked for a one-time Mr. Big out of Dzerzhinsky Square...what was his name, again?"

"Krestyanov," Barbara Price reminded him. "Vassily Krestyanov. And no, I didn't say it. Striker said it. Last I heard, we still considered him a source of proven credibility."

Brognola felt her anger crackling through the line and understood where it was coming from. Price and the Executioner were more than just comrades in arms. On various occasions, when he visited the Farm between assignments, they had wound up in each other's arms. So be it. There was nothing Brognola could do about it.

"Striker's credible, no doubt," he said. "But if I'm hearing you correctly, all he gave you was a name. No targets, nothing that could be mistaken for a deadline."

"No, sir."

"So, what we've got, then, is a credible threat against some unknown target, somewhere in the Western world."

"I'd say we have a good deal more than that," she said.

"You mean the plot? A has-been Russian spy joins forces with the CIA to resurrect the cold war? I don't think that story line will fly in Hollywood."

"Which brings us back to Striker's credibility," Price challenged him.

"We both know there's a world of difference between reporting factual events—the transfer of a nuclear device, for instance—and projecting what some total stranger plans to do with it. As far as a domestic link, we can't name any suspects at the Company. The only homegrown spooks we've managed to identify so far are dead, and one of them was freelance, could have been reporting to Valerik or this Krestyanov, instead of Langley."

"You believe that?" Price asked.

"I'm telling you what someone else will say to me if I try bucking this upstairs. That's right before they tell me not to let the screen door slap my ass on the way out."

"We're going to ignore this." Price didn't pose it as a question. When she spoke, her voice was flat, devoid of affect, as if she were reciting a loathsome fait accompli, refusing to admit that it disgusted her.

"I didn't say that," Brognola replied, wishing that he could see her face. Where in the hell were all those TV-telephones that were predicted for the future, back when he was coming up through school?

"What, then?" Price's knife-edged voice recalled him to here-and-now reality.

"What else?" he said. "We try to find Krestyanov and/or this alleged device. If we can do that, put full-time surveillance on him and/or it. But carefully, remember."

"I pulled his file," the mission controller said. "I know what he can do."

"Associates?"

"No shortage there," she said, "mostly in Eastern Europe and the former Soviet republics, but he has connections all around the world. They tend to be left-wing or revolutionary, but he buys officials and policemen, too, regardless of their politics."

"That's business for you," the big Fed replied. "Nothing on Langley, I presume."

"Clean as a whistle," Price said, "so far. We're hacking into databases at the moment, but I don't expect to find this operation neatly indexed under 'Things to Do.'"

"You take for granted that there's an operation to be found," Brognola said.

"I'm running with the only ball we have. Without it, I'm just sitting on my hands and killing time."

"All right," Brognola said. "I know that I don't have to say this, but I'm going to, regardless. You be extra careful when you're eavesdropping on Langley. I don't want the echo of a whisper getting back to anyone but me."

"I understand."

"I *know* you understand. Do you *agree?*"

"Of course." That cutting edge was there again. Brognola had a sudden urge to check his throat for open wounds. One thing about Price, though: he never had to fret about knives in the back. If and when she made a move against him, she would do it eye-to-eye and toe-to-toe.

"While you're checking out Langley, Job One is still to watch this Krestyanov and any of his comrades you can tag, with emphasis on tracking down the nuke."

"Yes, sir. And if we find it?"

"We'll decide that, if and when. I'm not convinced it's headed our way, yet. If it turns up in someone else's yard, we'll let them handle it."

"Assuming they can handle it."

"Assuming that, of course. But for the moment, let's not borrow trouble, shall we?"

"Right," she answered, sounding unconvinced. "I'd best get on it, then."

The click was followed by a droning hum until he cradled the receiver. Price was steaming and she didn't mind Brognola knowing it, though she had stopped short of the line that separated concern from open insubordination. She was good at that, and the big Fed admired her skill.

Most of the time.

Right now, he was concerned about her instinct—which was always good and seldom short of excellent. Her motives for accepting Bolan's judgment might be multifaceted, but so was Brognola's. It was impossible to wholly separate their friendship—should he make that former friendship after what had happened in the past two weeks?—from an assessment of the Executioner's integrity, his insight, his performance on the job.

The blood-red bottom line was this: he knew there had to be compelling reasons for the Executioner to speak in terms of a conspiracy that could, if it misfired at any point along the chain, potentially destroy the world. And that, in turn, left Brognola to wonder whether he had been deceived.

More to the point, he wondered if it was already too late in the game for him to draw new cards.

"ARE WE SECURE?" Christian Keane asked.

"We are. Proceed."

There was no need to check the scrambler. Noble Pruett knew it was engaged and fully functional, and he abhorred the wasted of time involved in double-checking certainties. He didn't need to walk outside and toast his retinas to know the sun was shining overhead.

"Okay, so here's what's happening," Keane told him, sounding as if he were calling from the dark side of the moon instead of Moscow. He could pick out cheap equipment every time. In Keane's experience, the Soviets had never spent a ruble more than absolutely necessary on domestic maintenance, and their successors rarely had been wading in red ink since the collapse. Assuming that they knew equipment was outmoded or defective and they gave a rodent's rosy rectum, they could ill afford repairs.

"There were no problems at the transfer," Keane informed him. "Our associate received the package several hours early, if you can believe it, and the vendor has been paid. No fireworks, no apparent animosity on anybody's part. Now, if I'm finished here—"

"You're not," Pruett said, interrupting Keane before he started another rant about his burning yen to get back home. "I need you in the neighborhood until the package is delivered to its final destination," he explained.

"When you say 'in the neighborhood,' you mean…?"

"I mean removed by a safe distance from ground zero, naturally. We wouldn't want you setting any Geiger counters off."

"What's the schedule look like?" Keane inquired. "I couldn't get the time of day from Krestyanov if I was running late for triple-bypass surgery."

"Our friend's a cautious man."

"Our so-called friend is one backstabbing mother—"

"We can trust him," Pruett interrupted again, "for the limited duration of our partnership. Beyond that, we shall have to watch him carefully, of course…but that's the point. Agreed?"

"If you say so."

"I do, indeed. We trust each other to a point, as able adversaries have throughout recorded history. But only to a point."

"Whatever," Keane replied. "It's not my call."

"But you have a suggestion, anyway." There was no need to phrase the statement as a question. Pruett knew his hand-picked underlings as well as—and often better than—they knew themselves. His unrestricted access to the smallest details of their lives, including incidents that some had managed to persuade themselves were mere "false memories," let him predict with an impressive accuracy how each man and woman under him was likely to respond in any given situation, from selecting lunch to fighting for survival on the firing line.

"Well, if you're asking me…"

"Assume I am." As if I needed your opinion, Pruett thought, keeping the low blow to himself.

"Well, I was thinking," Keane replied, "that we may just be passing up a golden opportunity."

"Said golden moment being…?"

"An unprecedented window of opportunity," Keane said. "We're talking instant chaos when the shit comes down. A good, decisive move at the right time could put us in the driver's seat. It doesn't have to be a race, you know. It could just be a victory parade."

Not bad. And not that far removed from some of Pruett's own ideas.

"I'll have to think about that, Christian," he replied. "We have some time, yet, to decide. Meanwhile, stay focused and remember why you're over there."

"Will do." Some of the eagerness had faded from Keane's tone, as Pruett hoped. He wanted the man calm, collected and obedient. The last thing Pruett needed was an aide-de-camp who started thinking for himself.

Perish the thought.

Perish the *man,* if he couldn't be readily controlled.

"You'll stay in touch with Krestyanov and his associates, as they've requested," Pruett said.

"The freak show, right."

"Keep your opinions to yourself, Christian. These men are sensitive by nature, unforgiving by design."

"Don't worry, I'm not stepping on their toes."

"See that you don't. And stay in touch."

Pruett hung up before his chief lieutenant could respond to that with any further questions or concerns. He had enough to think about already, without coddling Keane. The man was a professional, for God's sake. He should act that way.

As far as Keane's suggestion of a change in game plans, maybe a preemptive strike, Pruett had pondered such a course from the beginning—and was wise enough to know that Krestyanov would have expected nothing less. It was a suicidal pipe dream, since the Russians, those with whom Krestyanov was allied in his endeavor, would be well prepared for any such eventuality. And since their ranks weren't confined to politicians, but included ranking military officers as well, Pruett assumed they would've the muscle needed to defend themselves from any sudden or aggressive moves.

Enough, perhaps, to set the world on fire and ruin it for everyone. Assuming anyone survived.

No, Pruett decided, it was better to proceed according to the plan they had devised, and perilous to deviate.

There were times when Pruett regretted being blessed with such an active imagination. This was one of those times.

He could imagine various catastrophes that might arise from someone getting greedy or unduly arrogant, trying to push the envelope and grab more than his share. That, he reflected, was the basic problem with the first cold war. It had been launched by men on both sides who believed that they could win, and both sides pushed their luck until the human race had nearly been incinerated more than once. It took the Missiles of October to persuade both factions that a stalemate was acceptable, even desirable. The next two decades had been splendid for the military and intelligence communities of East and West alike, until an aging has-been actor out of Hollywood had managed to persuade American's electorate that he would look good in the White House. Once installed, his Messianic fervor fastened on the concept that he was imbued with God's own strength to bring down the Evil Empire.

And he had pulled it off, with some unwitting aid from the corrupt and fatally myopic Soviets.

The actor's error—one of them, at any rate—had been his inability to grasp the value of a global stalemate. He never understood that cold war was good business. By the time he vacated the Oval Office, still adored by millions of pathetic sheep, he left rampant inflation, a skyrocketing national debt and a global balance of power whose foundation had been deeply undermined, already teetering toward collapse.

It was time to recapture the balance, and Noble Pruett was doing his part as best he could.

"IT STILL sounds dangerous."

The sound of Hargus Webber's voice impressed its owner so much that he made a daily ritual of talking to himself in private, reeling off dramatic monologues on any subject from the cost of foreign aid to gun control and the decline of morals in the fashion industry. The latter topic was a favorite, in fact, and while he absolutely doted on those skimpy outfits spawned on Paris runways, Webber would denounce them publicly as long as he had breath to spare.

This day, though, he was more concerned about the prospect of annihilation, being transformed into one of those stark shadows etched in stone that had been found among the smoking ruins of Hiroshima.

"It's not a problem," Noble Pruett told him, sipping lemonade and offering the bare suggestion of a reassuring smile.

"These people know their business, Senator. They don't want to inherit rubble, any more than we do."

"But they're still Reds, Mr. Pruett. We agree on that, I think?"

"Of course, sir."

"You would do well to recall what Cleo Skousen said, back in the fifties." Pruett wore a blank expression, so Webber thoughtfully supplied the punch line. "You can trust the Communists," he said, pausing for effect, "to *be* Communists."

"I see."

"You disagree?"

"I know these men—their leader, anyway—and while he is indeed a Marxist-Leninist, I can assure you that he never strays far from enlightened self-interest. He won't betray himself. More to the point, he won't allow the men who serve him to betray his cause."

"And it's the cause that worries me," Webber remarked, snipping the blunt end of a seven-inch cigar with his gold-plated clippers. "We've discussed all this, I know, but sometimes it still seems to me we're giving up too much. The Warsaw Pact is shattered, Eastern Europe has been liberated after half a century of despotism. Cuba has been neutralized, for all intents and purposes, without the Russian teat to suckle on."

"You're right, we have been through this, Senator, and my response is still the same. You may consider Eastern Europe and the Balkans 'free,' but at what price in chaos, civil war and genocide? We've been reviled and ridiculed for our half-hearted policies in Bosnia and Kosovo. What's next, peace-keeping troops in the Ukraine, with U.S. soldiers taking orders from the secretary general of the United Nations?"

"Well—"

"And what about the Far East?" Pruett challenged him. "I know you hate the way your opposition spent the best part of a decade kissing China's ass and selling military secrets to Beijing. Two factors have historically restrained Beijing from stretching out its tentacles since 1949—our nuclear deterrent force, and Russia's dagger, aimed at China's back. With Moscow neutralized and Chinese technicians working overtime on ICBM guidance systems that we let them have for peanuts, who's to say you won't wake up some morning with a red-hot fortune cookie in your lap.''

''I didn't say—''

But Pruett wasn't finished yet. ''And let us not forget the clincher while we're at it, Senator. Without the threat of a renewed cold war with Moscow, your prospects for nomination and election to the White House rank somewhere behind the governor of Mississippi's.''

Webber pinned the man from Langley with his well-rehearsed, most disapproving glare. ''As I attempted to explain, before the sermon, I am still committed to our plan. I simply think we should be extra-careful dealing with a group of men whose mentor vowed he would bury us, not forty years ago.''

''Pure showmanship,'' Pruett replied dismissively. ''You've made enough stump speeches that you recognize a touch of melodrama, Senator.''

It irritated Webber that the spy could take his measure so easily—and so accurately—on relatively short acquaintance. At the onset of their give-and-take relationship, Webber had worried that he might have lost his touch, become transparent to the common man. Transparency was nearly always fatal in the nonstop gladiator contest that was Washington, but Pruett ultimately reassured him on that score. Webber could still deceive the common man or woman.

But Noble Pruett was no common man.

''It profits neither of us,'' Webber said, his voice a trifle stiff, ''if something should go wrong and we inherit leadership of a nuclear wasteland. Can we agree on that much?''

''Your fears are groundless, Senator. I'm telling you, Krestyanov has his people well under control. None of them want to die. None of them want to ride around a desert waste in football gear like something from *The Road Warrior,* all right? World War III is *not* on the menu."

"No hidden agendas?"

"No, Hargus," Pruett replied, using his first name for once, either to charm or humble him. Webber wasn't sure which, and he didn't give a damn. "The cold war was all about hidden agendas, am I right? We bring that back, we get the whole nine yards…but with an understanding at the top. It's a game. Krestyanov's people know you're not about to push the button and blow up the stadium, right? You know the same about them, and more to the point, they know you know."

"And afterward? What happens then?"

"Excuse me, Senator?"

"I'm asking you what happens afterward," Webber repeated. "Somewhere down the road, suppose someone forgets about the deal, or maybe never heard of it. Suppose some head case comes along who doesn't give a shit. What happens after?"

"'Somewhere down the road.'" Pruett repeated Webber's phrase, as if he wanted to explore its texture, maybe taste it, roll the words around and find out what they felt like on his tongue. His eyes were briefly fixed on some point over Webber's head, perhaps one of the paintings on the study wall behind him. When they came back into focus, they were hard and glinted with a cruel amusement.

"Somewhere down the road?" he said again. "You're how old, Senator? I do believe it's fifty-nine, month after next. You'll start campaigning right away, of course, with Company assistance, but elections aren't until next fall. That makes you sixty, right? If you behave yourself in public and keep all eyes focused on the Russkies, you should have no problem with a second term, which makes you sixty-eight before you have to leave the Oval Office. I assume you'll have a handpicked protégé on tap to follow in your footsteps, while our friends in Moscow—each of whom are several years younger, by the way—stir up enough anxiety around election time to make your boy a shoo-in. Two terms for Junior, and you're seventy-six, assuming that you're still alive. What road was it you were concerned about, again?''

The senator was properly offended. "Listen to me, Mr. Pruett. If you think I'm doing this solely—even primarily—to feather my own nest, then you're sadly mistaken. I explained my motivations in our first discussion—order for the world at large, an end to pointless genocide and insurrection, an effective, managed peace—and you pretended to agree with me.''

"There was no pretense, Senator. I do agree with you, on all those points. We're in complete agreement, and I hope you will forgive me if I seemed too—let's say flippant?—there, a moment earlier. I simply don't presume to think we can control the course of history throughout all time to come. We're laying a foundation here, my friend. We're working on a sturdy house. We're not responsible for who moves in ten years or fifty years after we're gone. Agreed?''

"Well, if you put it that way…''

"It's the only way," Pruett said, sipping at his lemonade. "We're patriots, not prophets. Not magicians. Those who follow after us must bear responsibility for their own lives.''

"And what if history decides that we were wrong?" Webber asked.

Noble Pruett shrugged. "By that time, Senator, we'll both be history. Don't borrow trouble for yourself. You're about to become an American savior. Relax and enjoy it, already.''

8

Cleaning his weapons once more while he waited, Johnny Bolan Gray made sure that he didn't fieldstrip the AKSU and his Glock at the same time. The lion's share of Johnny's consciousness had come to terms with trusting CIA agent Able Deckard and his Russian contact, but he still wasn't about to leave himself defenseless for a moment, just in case he might be wrong.

They were waiting for word from another of Pavlushka's connections in Moscow, hoping for a lead on Krestyanov or on his doomsday package, whichever was spotted first. It seemed to Johnny that the nuke would be well hidden if, as he suspected, it hadn't been spirited away from Moscow instantly. So far, they didn't have a clue where it was going, which city on Earth Krestyanov might have chosen for his target. If his brother and Deckard were correct in their supposition, and the nuke's explosion was intended to set off a chain reaction that would ultimately reinstate a new, improved cold war, the target could be found in either East or West, depending on the fine print of the script. He thought the Third World nations could be pretty well excluded from the hit list, since a blast touched off in any one of them—including mighty China—would do nothing to promote reimposition of a Soviet regime in Moscow.

Johnny saw the problem breaking down in either one of two worst-case scenarios. Script A would call for detonation of the nuke at some point in the West, most likely in the States, a kind of catastrophic Reichstag fire that would unite Americans of all political persuasions to confront a common enemy. The link to Russia couldn't be too obvious or too official, or else the Congress would immediately vote for war and missiles would be flying toward Red Square before the Russian president had time to go on CNN and swear that he was innocent. With the U.S. recovering, rearming, rattling every saber it could find, the hard-core Reds in Moscow and its former satellites should have no difficulty selling their program of strong defense in Parliament, or to a frightened public.

Script B provided for a detonation in the East, with giant Russia offering a perfect target. Nothing critical like Moscow, mind you, but perhaps a town of decent size that Russia's up-and-coming commissars would never miss. Conversely, Johnny thought, the plotters might decide to set it off in one of the former Soviet republics, preferably in one most likely to resist the second coming of the Evil Empire. Either way, it seemed unlikely that the blast would be attributed to American sabotage. There was simply no motive, for one thing, and blaming the United States would mandate retaliation in kind, thus touching off a global war the Russians were, at least for the present, in no shape to win. An alternate scenario—and the more likely one, in Johnny's view—would blame some dissident or other for the blast, focus on lax security and all the other problems Russia had confronted in the decade since the fall of Communism, and suggest a return to the Soviet state as a cure for all Russia's ills. That move, in turn, would trigger a predictable reaction in the States, retired anti-Communists dusting off their pamphlets and speeches, taking their sheets and John Birch Society caps out of mothballs.

Either way you smacked the ball, to right or left, it quickly bounced back to the far side of the court. And it would keep on bouncing, Johnny figured, East to West and back again, through the inauguration of a new arms race, new brush-fire wars and efforts at "containment," until the first decade of the twenty-first century resembled the 1950s or the "Red Scare" years that followed World War II.

Unless, of course, they somehow managed to prevent the bomb from going off. A bomb they couldn't find, earmarked for the destruction of a target they couldn't identify without cooperation from their highest-ranking enemies.

He didn't like their odds.

Unfortunately, there was no Plan B.

He finished reassembling the Kalashnikov, reloaded it, a sharp metallic click as he jacked a round into the firing chamber, put the rifle's safety on and placed it on the bed, where he could reach it instantly if someone crashed the party. Switching to the side arm, he unloaded it and stripped it down, taking a chamois and a little can of gun oil from the nightstand.

Johnny knew his way around most standard military hardware, though he couldn't claim to be an expert armorer, like his brother. He didn't build his guns from scratch or manufacture special loads of ammunition in a spare bedroom converted to a miniarsenal. When it came down to shooting, Johnny knew the drill and he wasn't afraid of spilling blood, although he took no pleasure in it.

That was one trait that he did share with his brother.

Growing up, when his brother was on the international "Most Wanted" list, Johnny had sometimes wondered how he did it, how he stayed the course and steeled himself to wade through all that blood, knowing his war would never truly end, that final victory would always be beyond his grasp.

Since growing up, he didn't wonder anymore.

His brother fought because he could, and knowing that he could meant that he really had no choice. If warriors were required to keep the predators at bay, his brother would be first in line to join the battle every time. And when he fell, as all men had to, there would be no doubt in the mind of anyone that he had done his best, consistently, from Day One to the bitter end.

He caught himself before the morbid train of thought could carry him away and concentrated on the pistol, oiling its component parts and reassembling them, another click as he primed the Glock for battle. Now, if they could only hear—

The chirp of Deckard's cellular phone made him blink involuntarily. He turned to face the man from Langley, watching Deckard palm the phone and flip it open, speaking quietly into the mouthpiece. Russian. Just a word or two, before he broke it off.

"Okay," he told the room at large. "We're on."

"IT SEEMS A SHAME, of course," Zhenya Romochka said before he sipped his glass of Starka. The liquor was a heady mixture of vodka, brandy and port, with an infusion of apple and pear leaves, aged in oaken casks to earn the title of "old vodka." It was strong enough to knock a novice drinker on his rear, or leave a veteran craving more.

"A shame, of course," Vassily Krestyanov replied. "But sacrifice is necessary for the cause, and Russians love their martyrs. Yes?"

Romochka waved a hand and noted that his upper lip was tingling now, preparing to go numb. It was his first benchmark for any Starka binge, a welcome sign indeed.

"I understand the need," he said with all sincerity. In truth, he didn't care about the death of several thousand workers, peasants and what-have-you. Russia's greatest resource was, had always been, her people, their proclivity for breeding through disaster and good times alike. Although, in fairness to the men and women who were marked for death, good times for anyone outside of the elite had never been enduring or widespread in all of Russian history.

"It could be worse for them," Romochka added, and again he was sincere. He knew that several million peasants had been starved to death, some of the feverish survivors driven to the point of cannibalism, when Stalin had revamped the nation's failing agriculture system in the 1930s. Thousands more—or was it tens of thousands?—had been executed in his successive purges, weeding out the traitors from his government. Those who came after him had given less work to the firing squads, but they had spilled enough blood in the cellars of the famous Lubyanka Prison, worked enough opponents to an early grave in the gulag, that they could surely also qualify as epic murderers.

Why should Romochka fear to take on that mantle himself?

"Where is the package now?" he asked, trying to make the question casual. "Has it been transferred out of Moscow yet?"

"Tonight," Krestyanov told him. "Nikolai will supervise the shipment personally. I have made arrangements for the best security available."

"I hope so," Romochka said. "It's one thing to incinerate St. Petersburg, and quite another to be caught at it, before the instrument is even set in place."

"You worry over nothing, Zhenya," Krestyanov replied.

"On the contrary, Vassily, I worry over everything that threatens my career, much less my life. If these slick bastards who keep running rings around your hoodlum friends should intercept the package, for example, who's to say that no one from the transport team would speak a name to save himself?"

"I vouch for Nikolai," Krestyanov said. "He'll die before he lets himself be taken into custody. None of the others knows your name. For that, the state must come to me."

The politician sipped his Starka, savoring the burn, and held Krestyanov's gaze. The colonel didn't blink, nor even seem to breathe. "All right, then," Romochka said at last. "I trust you well enough." And pray to Lenin's ghost, he thought, that it is not my downfall.

"And so you should," Krestyanov told him, blinking now, and putting on a smile of sorts. "We're both in this together, after all."

"For Russia," Romochka said, raising his glass as if to make a toast. It got no further than his lips, however, and he took another deep pull on the Starka.

"For the Revolution," Krestyanov replied.

Zhenya Romochka nearly laughed aloud at that, but drowned the impulse with another hearty swig of vodka. He had long since recognized—as Krestyanov had to also understand—that being Communist in modern Russia, almost ninety years since Lenin and his cohorts manned the barricades, had nothing to do with revolution or the precious proletariat. The politician had been schooled in mouthing platitudes about The People while he fortified the state against its enemies. And in the process, he had done quite well himself.

He meant to do quite well again, and very soon.

"The day after tomorrow, you said?" he asked Krestyanov, looking forward to their deadline for St. Petersburg.

"Or Monday at the latest," the colonel said. "Sunday would be preferable, I think. Besides the impact of the blast itself, we also emphasize once more the impotence of God for those who use Him as a crutch."

"Hear, hear."

Another slug of Starka, as Romochka pictured the Cathedral of Transfiguration in St. Petersburg. The structure was magnificent, albeit in a maudlin, superstitious sort of way, selected almost as a lark, nearly a year before, when he and Krestyanov were shopping for potential targets. Romochka had approved the choice, based on the irony alone. What better place to plant the bomb that would transfigure Mother Russia for at least a century to come?

Their scapegoats for the act of savage terrorism were a handful of pathetic dissidents who called themselves the Sword of Victory and Truth. Romochka wasn't sure exactly what they stood for, and he didn't care. They were available, sufficiently outspoken, with a record of arrests for vandalism and assaulting officers. The devastation of St. Petersburg would be a quantum leap for members of the Sword, but Krestyanov had forged a paper trail that would incriminate them, with a witness plucked from the Ukraine who would denounce them in return for grants of personal immunity and a substantial payment to his brand-new Swiss account. Unknown to the witness, the final payment would amount to only twenty-five or thirty rubles for a bullet, plus a headline that would name their witness as the final martyr to the Sword of Victory and Truth.

It was a perfect plan—or had been, until someone started shooting up the streets of Moscow, vanishing like ghosts beyond the reach of the police and Mafia alike.

"I simply want it to go well," Romochka said.

"As do we all," Krestyanov answered, through teeth so white Romochka thought they had to be false. "As do we all."

"HE COULDN'T GET a fix on where they've got it stashed in Moscow," Deckard said, recounting Pavlushka's telephone report. "It may be just as well, all things considered. If we tried to take it in the city and they have it armed, it could be a hot time in the old Kremlin tonight."

"But Rurik's positive about the transport route?" The question came from Evan Green, as he still called himself. The guy was cautious to a fault, and Deckard couldn't blame him. It was how a soldier stayed alive.

"They're heading overland, through Tver' and Novorod, to reach St. Petersburg," he said. "The main transport's a Zis sedan, new model, black. They'll have two escorts, no description on the other cars available, but Rurik got the main ride's license number."

"All that information," Johnny remarked, "but he can't find out where they stashed the bomb?"

"Apples and oranges," Deckard said. "His source is some guy who's connected to Valerik's Family, but on the fringe. They're not involved in storage, once they hand off the package, but Krestyanov arranged with them for transportation to St. Petersburg."

"How do we know this convoy has the bomb?" Mack Bolan asked. "If it's Valerik's transport, he could just as easily be moving drugs or weapons, anything at all."

"Because it's not Valerik's convoy," Deckard said. "His men aren't even riding shotgun, this time out. He just supplied the wheels."

"Krestyanov's people couldn't find a car?" Johnny inquired.

Deckard responded with a shrug, hiding his irritation. "If you want my guess, the colonel went back to Valerik for his ride so he'd be covered, just in case there's any problem on the road. The way he works, he'll make sure that there's something in the car to link the bomb with Tolya or to someone else, if it gets intercepted."

"One more question," Bolan said. "How do we know for sure it's Krestyanov moving the merchandise, and not Valerik?"

"That's the easy part," Deckard replied. "He's put his circus act in charge, to make sure it arrives on time, intact."

"The big guy you were telling us about?" Johnny inquired.

"My buddy Nikolai Lukasha," Deckard said. "Goddamn, I still can't figure how I missed all seven feet of him back in Berlin."

"Looks like you'll get another chance."

"In case something goes wrong," Bolan said, "do we have any kind of fix on what their target may be in St. Petersburg?"

"That's negative," Deckard answered, showing his displeasure with a frown. "If we don't nail them on the road, we're screwed."

"You don't have anybody in St. Petersburg?"

"The Company has people there, without a doubt," Deckard replied, "but they're unknown to my immediate superiors, and they don't feel secure enough to ask around—"

"Until you have an ID on the rogues," Bolan finished for him.

"Right."

"Okay, then. I suppose we'd better not screw up."

"It wasn't on my list of things to do," Johnny said.

"Is there some kind of estimate on strength for this convoy?" Green asked.

"Nothing concrete," Deckard said. "I figure they can squeeze six shooters, maybe seven, in the Zis if they decide to trust their cargo in the trunk. Two escort vehicles, you could be looking at another four to eight men, minimum. Say twelve or fifteen guns would be a ballpark estimate. This kind of load, if it was me, I'd carry all the men and hardware I could manage."

"Rurik's going with us?" Johnny asked.

"Affirmative. He's waiting for us at a rest stop north of town. That gives us two cars if it turns into a chase."

"We need to watch that if we can," Bolan said. "A running firefight multiplies the hazards exponentially. If one of them can reach the bomb, they might decide to arm and detonate it, if it looks like they won't get away. Even a crash or hit from a stray round may compromise the payload. Crack it open, you can get a lethal does of radiation even if it doesn't blow."

"So, what we need is something quick and clean," Deckard stated.

"Right."

"Regardless of the traffic, and in spite of escorts that we may not recognize."

"That's right."

"I can't say that I like this much," the man from Langley told his two comrades.

"I can't say that I blame you," Bolan replied. "If there's another option here, I'd love to hear it."

"Nope. The way it looks, we either take them on the road or let them go."

"The road it is," Johnny said.

They spent the next few moments triple-checking weapons, ammunition magazines, the pins on antipersonnel grenades. Evan Green had the sniper's rifle packed with his Kalashnikov, in case he saw the opportunity for some long-distance work.

That seemed unlikely to Deckard, but he didn't care to second-guess a stone professional.

Not when the guy was on his side, at any rate.

He checked his watch and marked the time.

"Okay," he said, "we'd better roll."

"WHY MUST WE follow them, Tolya? Why should we care what happens to the bomb, as long as we've been paid?"

Bogdashka had a point, of course. They had no stake in what became of the Ukrainian device once it had left their hands, and yet...

Tolya Valerik harbored dark suspicions that Krestyanov may have lied to him when he was sketching out his plan for the device. It was supposed to go off somewhere in "the West," which could be Europe or America, for all Valerik knew or cared. But something nagged at him, a small voice in his mind, just audible above the sound of seven million U.S. dollars riffling into his bank account.

What if the bomb didn't go to the West, for reasons only Krestyanov could fathom? What if it were used in Russia, or in one of the allied republics? What if Krestyanov required a scapegoat for the tragedy and tried to pin it on Valerik's Family somehow, another crime against humanity by the demented Russian Mafia?

Valerik had no reason to believe this was the case, but years of living on the razor's edge between a fat life and a sudden death had honed his paranoia almost to the point of prophecy. Valerik fancied he could read another man the way most people read a billboard, pick out a man's secrets and turn them to his own advantage. Granted, Krestyanov had decades of experience at hiding his emotions, thoughts, desires, but he was still a mortal man. Valerik didn't know what kind of double-cross the colonel had in mind, but he would bet a fair chunk of his brand-new fortune that Krestyanov had been lying to him all along.

"How many men?" Bogdashka asked.

"Two carloads should be adequate," Valerik said. "Make sure they are not seen, unless they need to intercept the package and retrieve it."

"How will they know when it's time?"

"They'll know," Valerik replied. "If it goes anywhere besides an airfield or a seaport, leaving Russia, they will know that we have been betrayed."

"And then you want it back?" Bogdashka's face wore an incredulous expression.

"To dispose of it, by one means or another," Valerik said. "Who knows, perhaps we'll have a chance to sell it twice. One of the Arab countries, possibly, where we can rest assured it will be safe."

"Krestyanov won't forgive that kind of action," Bogdashka stated.

"If he's betrayed us, he's as good as dead already," Valerik replied. "Who cares about forgiveness from a traitor rotting in the ground?"

"You know it will not be a simple thing to deal with Krestyanov," Bogdashka cautioned him.

"I love a challenge, Anatoly. But enough about what happens after. Let us focus on the work at hand."

It would have been extremely difficult, perhaps impossible, to track the warhead, but for one mistake that Krestyanov had made. Ironically, it was the same act that had tipped Valerik's vague suspicion into a near-certainty that he and his had been betrayed. Krestyanov had arranged for Valerik to supply a vehicle for transportation of the bomb from Moscow to the embarkation point, from which it would—allegedly—be leaving Russia. And Valerik, while accepting the assignment and the cash, had instantly begun to ask himself why would a well-connected colonel with the former KGB need help to find himself a car in Moscow?

It was silly, when he thought about it. Krestyanov had people on his payroll who could steal a hundred cars, repaint them, change the license plates and have them standing ready by this time tomorrow. With a phone call, he could probably arrange to be escorted by police, perhaps by military guards. Why order up a car from Valerik, then...unless, of course, Krestyanov meant for the vehicle to be traced.

That part of it was simple, the mobster realized. A Geiger counter would reveal to searchers if the package had been present in the car. Toss in a fingerprint or two, planted if need be, and the finger of suspicion would be aimed at one of Valerik's men. Krestyanov wasn't fool enough to place Valerik at the very scene. Life didn't work that way. It was enough to single out one of his lowly soldiers, let the aftermath of tragedy produce a witch-hunt fever that would carry on from there.

But Krestyanov had made two critical mistakes. First, he had underestimated Valerik's personal suspicion, his ability to keep it under wraps. And second, by demanding the delivery of a car, he told them were to find the package, how to follow it from Moscow to its final destination. It would be a relatively simple game of hide-and-seek, except that lives and empires would be riding on the line.

"And we're to intervene in any one of three scenarios," Bogdashka said.

"What three?" Valerik was suddenly confused and didn't like the feeling.

"First, of course, as you have said, if they attempt to place the bomb on Russian soil," Bogdashka said. "Second, if we are seen and they attempt to shake us off."

"Best not to let them see you," Valerik said. "And number three?"

"If someone else should try to intercept the package. Unless, of course, you'd rather that we let it pass to strangers."

"No!" Valerik scowled at the idea. "If they are interfered with, and it seems to you that Krestyanov's own people can't protect the merchandise, of course you must prevent its being taken from their clumsy hands."

"At any cost?" Bogdashka asked.

"At any cost," Valerik said, "short of exploding it yourself or bringing notice to the Family."

"I understand."

"Best to be on about your business, then, my friend. We've little time to spare, and none at all to waste."

Valerik watched him go and wondered whether he would ever see his friend, his second in command, again. It was a hazard of command, but other matters took priority.

The Family had to be preserved. He had to survive.

Bogdashka and his soldiers would take care of it.

The Russian godfather had every confidence.

"I WAS THINKING," Able Deckard said, "that we should have some coverage from the media."

Bolan was riding shotgun as they motored north through Moscow, toward the outskirts, in the brown four-door sedan. The statement startled him, but it was Johnny who reacted first.

"You're kidding, right?"

"I don't mean for the main event," the man from Langley clarified. "But afterward. Before the fallout settles, so to speak. If I know Krestyanov and company, they'll have spin doctors standing by to cover them, whatever happens. They'll be counting on confusion, panic, and the first voice with an explanation could turn out to be the next great oracle."

"Makes sense," Bolan said, as he watched the streets slide past his window. "What's your plan?"

"Rurik knows people at the major papers, radio, TV," Deckard replied. "What can I tell you? He's a man of many parts."

"I hope they're all on our side," Johnny muttered, from the back.

"Don't sweat it," Deckard said. "He lost his father to the gulag and two brothers in Afghanistan. He hates the Reds worse than J. Edgar Hoover ever did."

Deckard dodged a weaving taxi, coming back to his original

idea. "So, anyway, these friends of Rurik's will receive a story—hell, for all I know, some of them may have it already—running down the link between Valerik, Krestyanov and the illegal traffic in your basic decommissioned nukes. It would have gotten buried in the old days, but these Moscow newsies since the shift have learned a thing or three about investigative journalism. Granted, they still write about the day a giant alien was seen in Volgograd, but hey, nobody's perfect, right? For what we need, the tabloid splash may be a better angle, anyway."

"It won't stop Krestyanov from laying down his own smoke screen," Bolan said.

"True enough," Deckard replied. "But our side will have evidence, if all goes well. I mean, there'll be the bomb, the cars, some dead guys for the press to try to name. Unless it all goes boom, that is."

"If it goes boom," Bolan said, "we won't care what's in the morning paper, one way or the other."

"There's a reassuring thought," Johnny said from the rear, but he was smiling as he spoke. Whatever reservations Johnny may have had from time to time about his brother's endless war, the kid was always game.

Bolan hoped that he wasn't about to *die* game.

He had considered grounding Johnny, telling him to wait behind at the hotel—or, better yet, to head back for Berlin and meet Suzanne—but he had known the kid would never go for it. If they left Johnny stranded at the curb, he would have commandeered another car before the brown sedan was out of sight. Excluding Johnny from the daily course of Bolan's war was one thing, after all, the kid did have a life, but once Johnny was on the job, he hung on like a pit bull.

"So, when does our side start the spin?" Bolan asked.

"They've been tipped off what to look for," Deckard replied, "in general terms. They obviously know a nuke's involved, but all they've heard about from us, so far, is smuggling. If it blows, they'll start from there, I guess, and follow where it leads. If we come out on top, they'll take the outline of the story we supplied and dress it up to suit themselves. Whatever, if there's no news flash by midnight, they've been cleared to run it as a lead tomorrow morning.''

''I don't mean to be a killjoy,'' Johnny said, ''but are you sure that none of Rurik's contacts in the press are doubling? Even if they're straight—with him, I mean—what's stopping one of them from running to Valerik, maybe even Krestyanov, to get a pithy quote? That happens, you can kiss surprise goodbye.''

''Which would explain,'' Deckard said, smiling for the rear-view mirror, ''why they weren't told anything about the hit itself. Worst-case scenario, one of them drops a ruble to Valerik or the colonel, and they think their cover's blown. Shit happens. No one in the media knows anything that could alert the heavies to a hit in progress.''

''They could scrub it anyway,'' Johnny said.

''Wouldn't matter,'' Deckard told him. ''Once we've got the target in our sights, it won't make any difference if they turn around or keep on going. They'll be ours.''

Bolan agreed with Deckard on that point, at least in theory. Once he had the convoy spotted, he would stick to it like flypaper and do his best to neutralize the deadly cargo it conveyed, but he wasn't oblivious to the attendant risks. Aside from maybe setting off the nuke or breaching its container, there were countless other things that could go wrong, from flats and engine failure to the kind of lucky shooting by their adversaries that would take them out and leave the Russians free to plant their bomb.

Bolan was conscious of the possibilities, but he refused to dwell on them. Defeatist thinking ranked among a combat soldier's most persistent enemies, and Bolan froze it out. He had enough to do without surrendering to self-indulgent visions of his own demise.

The Executioner was on a roll, and it could only end in death.

9

Nikolai Lukasha was uncomfortable in the Zis sedan, but he could live with it. What troubled him the most was head room, forcing him to slouch in a position that would have his muscles cramping long before they reached St. Petersburg. In normal circumstances, he would have been seated in the front and pushed his seat back all the way, to hell with comfort for the men behind him, but he had selected the back seat this time, with younger men packed in on either side of him, and he would have to suffer for his choice.

The reason for his choice of seating was that Lukasha anticipated trouble—looking on the bleak side was a major facet of his work with Krestyanov—and if it came, the giant reckoned it would come upon them from behind. Pursuit from Moscow, he decided, was more likely than a roadblock on the highway leading north. Of course, if they were followed and their shadows had authority, there could be helicopters, even armored vehicles lying in wait for them, somewhere ahead.

Lukasha didn't think so, though. The bastards who had terrorized Tolya Valerik for the best part of two weeks were obviously from the private sector, or there would have been a show of uniforms by now, official paperwork in triplicate. Likewise, the man who had attempted to kill him in Berlin. He might be working for some government or other, but if it had been official business, he wouldn't have been alone, and Lukasha most probably wouldn't have given him the slip.

With that in mind, Lukasha wanted to be near the broad

rear window of the Zis sedan, where he could turn, however awkwardly, considering the space available, and use his AK-47 to its best effect. His flankers would do likewise, and they might—coincidentally, of course—stop any bullets fired at the giant from left or right.

It was the best that he could do, together with the escort vehicles, but he still hoped they reached St. Petersburg without a fight. He wouldn't tell Krestyanov that, could hardly bear confessing to himself, but he would be relieved—damn near ecstatic, truth be told—to get rid of the lethal package that resided in the auto's trunk.

Goodbye, St. Petersburg. Hello, fond Soviet Republic.

Lukasha couldn't see the escort vehicles, but that meant nothing. One of them was on the road ahead, perhaps a mile or two in front of them, where it would note any apparent ambush and report back via two-way radio. The other was behind them somewhere, watching out for tails and ready to close up, respond immediately, if they were attacked or stopped for any reason on the highway.

Lukasha would have been happier with five or six escorts, say thirty men instead of the fourteen they had, but Krestyanov had been afraid more vehicles would attract attention, thus increasing risk. Besides, he thought, if fourteen men couldn't protect one suitcase on the open road from Moscow to St. Petersburg, the mission had to be hopeless.

All of them, including drivers, were equipped with automatic weapons and side arms, some of the guards wearing two pistols, as if they had been transported from America's Wild West. The soldiers in the lead car also carried an RPG-7, in case they needed to blast their way through some kind of roadblock, while the team in the pursuit vehicle had a CIS-40GL, a single-shot 40 mm grenade launcher manufactured in Singapore, complete with a satchel of smoke and high-explosive rounds.

It was enough, Lukasha told himself. Please let it be enough, he added in what could have been mistaken for a silent prayer.

Lukasha had no open fear of death, per se. There had been times when he was growing up—and growing, ever growing—that he might have welcomed it, to end the taunts and insults from his peers. This day, however, riding with one of the world's most deadly weapons only inches from his backside, Lukasha was determined to live.

How else could he enjoy the blessings of a Soviet Union restored?

"There's trouble" the man seated beside Lukasha said. He wore foam-padded earphones, tuned to pick up any comments from the escort vehicles. A microphone no thicker than a pencil curved around one side of his clean-shaven face, permitting him to relay orders back to either car, at need.

"What trouble?" the giant demanded.

"They're not sure." The young man hesitated, listening, his head tilted as if that would somehow help him listen or interpret what he heard. "Two cars behind us, closing fast. No way to tell if they're together, and it may not be connected to—"

"Stay with them!" Lukasha snapped, interrupting, and the young man instantly repeated his command to their comrades in the pursuit car. Out ahead of them, the message and his order would have jolted nerves inside the point car, too.

"Get ready, everyone," Lukasha told the five men packed into the Zis sedan around him. His Kalashnikov was cocked and locked already. Now he flicked off the safety and held the rifle in a firm two-handed grip. Their tinted windows would prevent the occupants of other passing vehicles from noticing the weapons on display, and should prevent their enemies—if these were enemies approaching from the rear—from noting that Lukasha and his troops were on alert.

"They're closing," the young man with the headphones said. "Just a hundred meters, now."

In seconds, Lukasha would have to choose between a wait-and-see approach, or a preemptive strike. The vehicles approaching from their rear might signify no more than drunks, commuters in a rush, or rowdy youths joyriding for the hell of it. If he should stop the trailing cars with gunfire, it was very possible that some neutral civilian would observe the shooting and report it to police, with a description of his car, perhaps even the license number. That, in turn, would mean a hunt along the highway, covering the whole four hundred miles between St. Petersburg and Moscow.

But only if Nikolai allowed potential enemies too close and didn't fire.

"Be ready," he repeated.

And the young man with the headphones echoed, "Fifty meters. Closing."

Lukasha twisted in his seat and waited for his first glimpse of the hunters. Any second now...

"I'D LIKE IT better if we knew for sure which cars were riding shotgun," Johnny said to no one in particular.

Bolan shared his brother's concern. The highway wasn't jammed, by any means, but there were half a dozen cars in sight at any given moment, and the great majority of them carried multiple passengers, most of them male, as if the concept of a ride-share program had been drafted into law, car pooling made compulsory. None of the cars they passed, or which passed them, were readily identifiable as crew wagons. None cruised along with hardware showing, radio antennas bristling from the trunk and fenders. There was nothing in the faces of the other motorists that would betray their purpose; virtually without exception, they were grim, bored-looking, seeming vaguely angry at the world.

Deckard's associate, the goateed Russian, was a hundred yards or so in front of them, driving an old MG that looked as if it had survived a series of collisions with larger, heavier cars, its bodywork a motley camouflage of primer gray and putty. He was driving with the ragtop down, although the day was cool and threatened rain, wind whipping tangles in his curly salt-and-pepper hair.

When it came down to shooting, Bolan knew, the open car would give Pavlushka something of an advantage, but the extra combat stretch was balanced by the fact that he would have no steel around him, nothing to deflect or even slow incoming rounds.

A burst of static crackled from the walkie-talkie lying on the seat between Deckard and Bolan. Pavlushka's voice, distorted by the cheap receiver and a rush of wind, told them in English, "There! I see it! Up ahead, a Zis sedan. The license number is...another moment...yes! We have it!"

"Rock and roll," Deckard said, as he stood on the accelerator.

Bolan grabbed the walkie-talkie, thumbing down the button to transmit. "Can you pick out the escorts?"

"No," the tinny voice came back. "Not yet. I trust them to find me."

"Well, he's got nerve," Johnny said from the rear. He sat hunched forward, with the AKSU ready in his lap.

"There's Rurik," Deckard said, a moment later, pointing through the windshield toward a zooming, weaving, gray-brown vehicle in front of them. "And there's our payload."

There was nothing noteworthy about the boxy Zis sedan, which was presumably the reason it had been selected in the first place. Its black paint job was standard for the make and model. The blacked-out windows, also fairly common, based on what he had observed in Minsk and Moscow, might conceal a firing squad, but they probably weren't bulletproof. The Zis sedan, in fact, didn't resemble any armor-plated car Bolan had ever seen. There might be hidden gun ports, but he would have bet against it, meaning that the shooters had to expose themselves in order to fire.

"Get ready," Deckard cautioned, as he barreled in behind the Zis and the MG. "Contact in ten...nine...eight..."

In front of them, the MG braked, then swerved, accelerating suddenly to swing around behind the Zis and pull up on the starboard side. Bolan was watching as the right-rear window powered down, too smoothly for a hand crank, and the stubby muzzle of an automatic weapon poked out through the opening.

"They made him!" Bolan said, flinching as bullets started slamming into the MG.

OH, GREAT, Christian Keane thought. I'm in a frigging action movie now. Where's Arnold-frigging-Schwarzenegger when you need him?

He had trailed Lukasha's three-car caravan from Moscow in a nondescript Toyota compact, hanging back enough to keep the escorts in the chase car from deciding that he was a threat. So far, they either hadn't spotted him or else had satisfied themselves that he was just another traveler, coincidentally northbound, no threat to them or their employer in the Zis sedan.

And now they had their hands full on the road ahead of him, as bloody hell broke loose.

Keane had been hoping for an uneventful, even boring trip. He'd kept his fingers crossed, thinking that drowsiness—the dreaded "turnpike trance"—would be his greatest hazard on the drive up to St. Petersburg. The Walther P-5 automatic pistol on the seat beside him, hidden underneath a folded newspaper, was just supposed to sit there, keep him company throughout the lonely ride, and not be heard from if his luck held out.

So much for luck.

Keane saw the MG coming up behind him, passing on his left, and while the driver's face meant nothing to him, there was something in his attitude, hunched forward, leaning to his right, lips moving, that suggested madness—or, worse yet, a two-way radio. Such instruments weren't routine in Russia, though possession of them was no longer banned by law. The average Russian couldn't afford one, and had no desire to speak to anyone while he was driving, even if he could. The wealthy had their cellular phones, and they didn't drive ancient

British sports cars that resembled rejects from a demolition derby. A two-way radio meant cops, soldiers...or maybe something worse.

The second car, a plain sedan, swept past him moments later, prompting Keane to pick up speed, though cautiously. The escort vehicle, still well in front of him, had fallen in behind the other two. Its crew didn't appear to notice the Toyota gaining from behind.

What is this shit? Keane wondered, knowing in his heart that it couldn't be good, and that whatever happened, he was hopelessly outgunned. He wasn't being paid to intervene, of course. In fact, he had been told to keep his distance, strictly speaking, but he also knew that failure here, derailment of the master plan, could well mean hell to pay at home.

"Stay cool," he told himself, unconscious of the fact that he had spoken. "Watch for openings. Do what you can."

And stay alive.

The bottom line for any mission.

Keane heard the automatic fire, most likely a Kalashnikov, as he was coming up behind the other vehicles, still trying not to draw attention from the shooters in the trailing escort car. One hint that he was part of what was happening ahead, and they would blast him off the road without a second thought. Keane thought there was a chance he could avoid them, if he drove completely off the road and risked disabling his car, but there was no way he could duel on equal terms with four men and the AKs, SMGs, or whatever they had between them, to protect the mother lode. Likewise, he had no way of telling them that he was on their side, for all intents and purposes— as if they would believe him in the middle of a firefight, anyway.

He had an off-and-on view of the Zis sedan now, Nikolai Lukasha and his soldiers firing at the MG and the second car, which had their own vehicle flanked. The solitary driver in the old sports car was popping rounds off from what looked to be a Skorpion machine pistol, some of his bullets missing, others knocking shiny divots in the black sedan's paint job. No hits on flesh and bone, as far as Keane could tell. At least, the starboard gunners in the Zis were firing back in concert, two or three guns spitting at the MG simultaneously.

On the other side of the sedan, an equal number were unloading on the second chase car, but their opposition there was better armed, more numerous, a tad more cautious when it came to driving through a free-fire zone. Keane counted two men in the brown pursuit car, plus the driver, both of them armed with Kalashnikovs and firing measured bursts through open windows, peppering Lukasha's ride, while taking relatively few hits on their own.

That was about to change, he saw, as the giant's rear escort came in hard and fast behind the chase car on the left and rammed into the brown car's bumper, jolting those inside, spoiling their aim and forcing them closer to the Zis sedan. Another moment, and Lukasha's men would have the raiders in a sandwich, where they could—

The brown sedan's rear window suddenly exploded, raining glass and bullets on the hood and windshield of the car that had it boxed in from behind. Keane saw the escort vehicle begin to swerve, then slew broadside before he had to slam on his brakes, cranking hard-left on his steering wheel in self-defense. He just had time to mouth a string of Anglo-Saxon oaths before his compact left the pavement, briefly losing contact with the ground, and sailed into a grassy field beside the highway.

THE CHASE CAR car seemed to come out of nowhere, rolling up behind them and slamming into their ride before Deckard could register the image in his rearview mirror, much less give a warning. Johnny was leaning halfway out his open window, squeezing off another burst from his Kalashnikov at the Zis sedan, when the impact pitched him from his seat. He wound up kneeling on the narrow strip of floorboard just behind his brother's seat, a sharp pain tinged with numbness flaring in his neck.

He checked for blood, thinking a bullet may have found him, but his fingers came back dry, no crimson smears. Cursing, he lurched across the seat and cleared out half the brown sedan's rear window with a burst from his AKSU. A couple of his bullets dinged the chase car's hood, but they were hanging in there, shooters craning out on either side to take their best shot on the fly.

"You wanna get them off our ass?" Deckard said, sounding strangely calm, all things considered.

"That's the plan," Johnny replied, raking the speeding escort with another burst of automatic fire.

His first rounds clipped the gunner hanging from the right-hand side of the pursuit vehicle, slapped the automatic weapon from his hands and sheared off half his face in a wet burst of crimson. Tracking on, still firing for effect, he blew out the windshield and had a glimpse of snarling, screaming faces, one of them behind the steering wheel, before the chase car swerved on smoking tires and swung around broadside. The last rounds from his AKSU's magazine punched through the driver's door and made his target twitch before the chase car came to rest.

Behind it, other vehicles were braking, swerving, drivers leaning on their horns in panic. Drawing back to feed his weapon a fresh magazine, he still had time to register a flash of shiny paint and chrome, one of the other drivers losing it and veering off the highway, churning dirt and weeds across an open field. Good luck, Johnny thought, and he meant it, but he had to focus on the task at hand.

"We're clear, for now," he called to his brother and Deckard, turning back to get a clean shot at the Zis sedan. He had a queasy feeling in his stomach, firing at the car that they believed to have a nuke inside, but there appeared to be no viable alternative. The other side had started shooting first, and backing off would simply guarantee their clean escape.

And if they lost the warhead, it was Magic Mushroom time.

He caught a fleeting glimpse of Pavlushka—or, at least, the primer-mottled tail of his MG—before the gutsy Russian made another rush to keep pace with the speeding crew wagon. What he could see of the old sports car had been bullet-scarred and shot to hell, but it was still in motion, keeping up the pace. The rattle of a lighter automatic weapon, clearly not an AK, told Johnny that Pavlushka still had ammo for his Skorpion, and he was bent on scoring if he could.

"Now, what the hell's this shit!" Deckard exclaimed.

His tone made Johnny swivel to the front, in time to see another car speeding directly toward them, scattering the northbound traffic as it raced along the wrong side of the highway.

"My best guess," he said, "you're looking at the second escort."

"Fucker thinks he's Jimmy Dean," Deckard replied, eyes on the road. "He wants a chicken run, I'll give it to him."

When it happened, everything seemed to go down at once. A burst from Bolan's AKSU shredded the left-rear rubber on the Zis sedan, and it began to fishtail, swerving back and forth erratically across three lanes. The driver of the point car, speeding southward, saw the hit and nudged his wheel enough to keep from smashing head-on into his own comrades in the middle of the highway. Veering slightly to the left, still pouring on the gas, there was no time for him to compensate for the MG that suddenly appeared before him on a dead collision course. There was no time to brake, to scream, to pray.

The point car met the bullet-pocked MG with a resounding crash, and Johnny caught a glimpse of Pavlushka, airborne, tumbling like a world-class gymnast, with the Skorpion still tightly clutched in his right hand, before he hit the point car's windshield and smashed through, into the driver's lap.

It got a little hectic after that, as Deckard struck the Zis sedan broadside and both cars spun away from each other, rubber smoking as they tumbled off in opposite directions, coming gratefully to rest some thirty yards apart.

DECKARD CLAWED at the latch on his door, as the battered sedan came to rest. Dust swirled across the hood in front of him—or was it smoke? He could smell something burning, but it took a moment for him to remember the collision, Pavlushka's MG smashing nose-to-nose with Nikolai Lukasha's second escort vehicle.

Lukasha.

Deckard found his AKSU on the floorboard, scooped it up and took it with him as he stumbled from the car and dropped into a crouch. Across the wreckage-littered highway, he still heard the sharp, staccato sounds of automatic fire, but there were clearly fewer weapons joining in the contest now, than there had been a few short moments earlier.

There was a shuffling thump behind him, and he glanced that way as Evan Green bailed out the driver's side, bringing his AK and the duffel bag that held the Dragunov. Beyond him, hunkered down behind the left-rear fender, Johnny Gray was waiting for an opportunity to fire another burst in the direction of the damaged Zis sedan.

How badly damaged? Deckard didn't even know for sure if his car would be fit to drive, assuming that he ever got another chance to try it. As for Lukasha's, he hoped the giant would be stranded, left afoot when the police began arriving, as they had to before much longer. Even in a country where communications breakdowns were routine, this kind of shooting match and six- or eight-car pileup would attract the uniforms.

They were, he realized, already running out of time.

He risked a look across the hood of their rental car, and someone in or crouched behind the Zis squeezed off a burst of automatic fire that sprayed his face with pebbled safety glass from the windshield. Stung without bleeding, he dropped back out of sight and duck-walked toward the front of the car, looking for an angle that would let him return fire without being fully exposed.

How many guns against them? Deckard still had no clear fix on numbers, and he couldn't say how many of the home team were disabled, either in the crash with the MG or in the early stages of the firefight. From the hits his rental car was taking, Deckard knew there had to be several shooters still alive and kicking, any one of whom could take him down with one clean shot.

But that game went both ways.

The Zis sedan possessed no armor; that was obvious from all the holes and shiny metal showing where the jet-black paint had chipped away on impact, vacant windows where the glass had crumbled under fire. That could be good or bad, depending on the point of view. It meant his enemies were vulnerable— just as he was, crouching on the shoulder of the highway, trusting in the rental car's engine block to stop a hot round coming through to nail him—but it also meant that any stray round pumped into the Zis might find its cargo and unleash a cloud of deadly radiation.

Somehow, though he couldn't imagine any way to pull it off before the law arrived, they had to neutralize the Russian goons, retrieve the nuke and get the hell away from there before things got worse.

Right.

Lead by example, someone once had told him, though he couldn't quite remember who it was. Some guy sitting in a comfy office miles behind the lines, most likely.

Deckard was moving when he heard a sound distinct and separate from rifle fire. It was the kind of squeaky sound that metal hinges made, sometimes, when they needed oiling. Like a car door opening, perhaps...or maybe someone opening the trunk.

He chanced another look and saw the giant, Lukasha, standing behind the Zis, all six foot nine of him, as if he were impervious to bullets. And the trunk was open, dammit, with Lukasha reaching in for something that he wanted there.

Deckard saw the shiny metal suitcase being lifted clear. He recognized that this could be his one best chance—perhaps his only chance—to score that bag, together with the deadly secret locked inside.

It was a short step, after that, from thought to action. Deckard lunged from cover without warning his partners. He came out firing from the shoulder, not the hip, careful to aim as best he could while running, so he wouldn't hit the metal case.

Lukasha took the first round in his upper arm, the impact spinning him, facing directly toward his enemy. That put the metal suitcase in between them, shielding most of Lukasha except his face and long, long legs. The head shot was a risk he didn't want to take, and Deckard was already lowering his AKSU's muzzle, firing into the giant's kneecaps, when something struck him in the side and staggered him.

Goddammit!

Deckard couldn't tell if he had cursed aloud or not, and didn't care. He concentrated on the giant with the suitcase, saw a couple of his rounds strike home, blood spouting from Lukasha's thighs, the big man folding, going down. A heartbeat later, Deckard saw his target's free hand rising, wrapped around a pistol that seemed toylike in his grasp, but there was nothing make-believe about the bullets it was spitting into Deckard from a range of less than thirty feet.

Somebody else cut loose on him, some goon behind the Zis sedan, his AK hacking gobs of flesh and muscle from the lurching zombie on the highway. Deckard just had time to mutter, "Fuck it," squeezing off a last short burst that opened Nikolai Lukasha's skull, before the pavement rushed to meet him and the world went black.

Two DOWN, their forces cut by half, and Bolan estimated that the Russian shooters still had them outnumbered two- or three-to-one. He heard a distant siren wailing now, still miles away but coming fast in their direction, and he knew that Johnny heard it, too. Whatever they were hoping to accomplish had to be done within the next few moments, leaving time for them to flee the scene—assuming they could find a working vehicle.

The shiny metal suitcase was his first priority. Krestyanov's hulking second in command had died defending it, while Deckard gave his life trying to fetch it for their side. It had to be the nuke, and even though he saw how small it was—a megaton or two, at most—his mind still offered up the grim, unbidden scenes of devastation it would cause. A "small" nuke detonated in a major city could slay thousands, maybe tens of thousands as the fallout spread. It could be years before ground zero would be fit for occupancy without radiation suits and bottled oxygen.

Get the case, already.

Bolan was considering the safest way to pull that off, fully aware that dying on the blacktop next to Deckard would do nothing for their cause. He was considering the impact that a frag grenade might have, if he could lob it well behind the bullet-pocked sedan, when he was suddenly distracted by a blur of motion from his right, at the periphery of vision, moving rapidly into the target zone.

He turned in that direction, saw a man he didn't recognize— dark hair, a sport coat, turtleneck, dark slacks, some kind of dress shoes smeared with mud—advancing on the Zis sedan with long, swift strides. The runner didn't glance at Bolan, didn't seem to care what happened on the far side of the highway. He was focused on the fallen giant and the shiny metal suitcase that lay balanced on his chest.

One of the goons behind the Zis woke up to what was happening and shouted something, angry Russian, harsh and guttural, as he moved out to intercept the new arrival. Bolan held his fire, uncertain what was going on and hoping to find out. The runner clearly wasn't recognized or welcomed by the convoy escorts, one of them—presumably the man who'd shouted—standing and leveling an AK at the stranger's face.

The new kid on the firing line was faster. Bolan hadn't seen the pistol in his hand, but now he saw it, heard it, as the double tap took down the rifleman before he had a chance to fire. That done, the runner snagged the shiny suitcase with his left hand, yanking twice to free it from the dead hulk's grasp and started running back in the direction he had come from.

Bolan was swiveling to drop him—hoping that he proved to be an enemy, but unwilling to delay and take the chance— when one of the surviving troops behind the black sedan unloaded with a long burst toward their rental, chipping paint and chrome, filling the air with angry hornets that could take a man's head off if he let them. Bolan ducked back under cover, the survival instinct winning out, and when he looked again, the well-dressed runner had already vanished with his suitcase full of death.

"Too late," he told his brother. "We need to get out of here, ASAP." A glance back toward the south, toward Moscow, showed him some kind of small, foreign car lurching through a U-turn, heading out to meet the sound of sirens.

"Any thoughts?" his brother asked.

"Grenades," the Executioner replied.

They each palmed two, released the pins and held the spoons, wound up and pitched on Bolan's signal. They had four eggs in the air before their adversaries registered the fact that no one was returning fire. A moment later, when the frag grenades went off like giant firecrackers, the screams of dying men were smothered by a gust of superheated air from hell and blown away.

"I'll try the engine," Johnny told him, lunging for the driver's seat. Incredibly, he started on the second try, and Bolan piled in on the right. Wind whipped his hair and face as they got rolling, and he knew that they would have to ditch the bullet-riddled car first chance they got, but at the moment, the priority was putting space between themselves and the police.

"So, what's the plan?" his brother asked when they had covered several windy miles.

"I wish I knew," Bolan replied. "I swear to God, I wish I knew."

"It's me," the familiar voice said.

"Of course it is," Pruett replied. "I've been expecting you."

There was a hesitation on the other end, before Keane asked, suspiciously, "What have you heard?"

The first, faint sound of an alarm bell jangled in the back of Pruett's mind. It didn't sound like Keane, exactly. Not the voice, per se—the special monitor incorporated with the scrambler on his private line confirmed the voice print five by five—but rather something in the attitude. There was a certain nervousness, a hesitancy that was altogether alien where Keane was concerned.

"I've heard nothing at all," Pruett replied, "but it's still early yet. If you have something I should know, by all means, share."

"There's been an unexpected change in plans."

"And that would be...?"

"The shipment won't be going to St. Petersburg," his aide replied.

"I'm listening." It seemed to Pruett that the office temperature had plummeted. It could have been a meat locker, with the pervasive, sudden chill he felt.

"Somebody jumped the transport," Keane informed him. "Twenty, maybe twenty-five miles north of Moscow."

"Somebody?"

"I didn't catch their names," Keane said, regaining some of his traditional acidity. "It was a pretty rowdy scene."

"Our interlopers from the States, perhaps?"

Keane took a moment, finally responding, "There's no way for me to answer that. I never heard them speak. It could have been some Russian thing. Krestyanov's people should be able to find out, though, from the stiffs."

"Excuse me?"

"They've got bodies, this time. Two of them, at least. I saw one of their shooters take a header through a windshield, and another one got capped trying to grab the merchandise."

"What about Krestyanov's people?"

"They took a beating," Keane replied. "Vassily's number two, big Nikolai, went down for sure. I saw his brains. Some others, too. A few of them were still alive and fighting when I split, though."

"And the merchandise?" Pruett felt silly using euphemisms, but it was a deeply ingrained habit and he couldn't shake it, even talking on his line, where full security was guaranteed. There was always the chance, however infinitesimal, of an interception—or deliberate betrayal—at the other end.

"Well, that was mainly why I called," Keane said.

"I'm listening."

"Vassily's boys don't have it anymore."

Pruett imagined he could feel the Earth tilt on its axis, hear the polar ice floes shatter into frozen shrapnel, see his world imploding, rushing toward the sun.

"I see." What else was there to say?

"From where I sat, it looked like they were bound to get their asses kicked. After the big guy bit the dust, especially." The nervous tone was back in Keane's voice. What was he working up to, beating so cautiously around the bush?

"Christian."

"I'm here."

"What happened to the package?"

"Well, I didn't think you'd want the hijackers to have it,

and Vassily's boys were getting dusted left and right. I started thinking what would happen if they fought it to a draw and everybody bought the farm, or they were still there fighting when the cavalry showed up.''

"Christian." Showing his own impatience now.

"So, what I did," Keane said, "was take a chance. I took the weight off, so to speak."

Pruett was silent for a moment, trying to decide on the appropriate reaction. A part of him was stunned at Keane's audacity, and yet relieved that he had prevented both police and unknown enemies from capturing the bomb. Another part was furious at Keane for jeopardizing his—and Pruett's—bastion of deniability. And yet another part of Pruett was oppressed by fear, so nebulous that he couldn't have confidently named its object. Was he frightened of what Krestyanov would say and do when he found out that one of Pruett's people had the bomb? Was it his fear of Keane's exposure and arrest, inevitably leading back to him, that raised the gooseflesh on his arms?

"Where is the package now?" he asked.

"I'm hauling it around," Keane said. "Trunk of my car. Should be all right there for a while, unless the Russian traffic cops have Geiger counters in their squad cars."

"Listen carefully. I need to know who saw you take the package. Can you tell me that, Christian?"

"One of Vassily's boys," Keane said, "but he's not talking much these days."

"Just one?"

"I'm pretty sure," the field agent replied. "His buddies had their hands full when I made my move. I smoked the only one who tried to stop me."

They would never tell Krestyanov that, of course. Keane didn't need to hear it said aloud. The danger to them both was obvious. As for the other risk...

"All right," Pruett said. "What about the other side. Could they have seen you?"

That made Keane hesitate again. Pruett could picture him, head tilted slightly to one side, his eyes closed perhaps, trying to reconstruct the scene. His answer, when it came, was honest to a fault and brought no comfort.

"I can't say for sure," Keane said. "The shit was flying thick and fast. When I glanced over at their ride, it seemed like they were busy keeping out of sight."

"But someone could have seen you."

"Yeah," Keane said. "It's possible. How would they know me, though? American or Russian, that's the long shot of all time."

But long shots had been known to pay, most commonly when Pruett bet against them. "They don't need your name, Christian. They could describe you if they saw your face. There might be cameras we don't know about."

"Oh, please. This isn't La-La land, and I'm not Rodney King. Who ever heard of Russian motorists with minicams?"

"I wasn't thinking of the Russians, necessarily," Pruett said.

"Oh." That silenced Keane for a beat, but when he spoke again, his voice still broadcast confidence. "I can't see any of the raiders taking time to shoot home movies, with the shit-storm they were dodging. Anyway, I'm heading out of Russia as we speak."

"What?"

"You heard me," Keane replied. "I take for granted that our friend will want his package back, but I'm not leaving it in some bus station locker, and I'm not about to make the hand-off in his own backyard. I want some neutral ground, if nothing else, to make sure that I walk away."

If nothing else. The implication was that Keane would almost certainly come up with something else, before the drop was made. A little bonus for himself, perhaps? If Keane jeopardized the operation for another paycheck, Pruett vowed the he would gut the little prick, himself.

"I see," the man from Langley said. "What did you have in mind, as far as neutral ground?"

"It's funny you should ask that," Keane said. "I was just thinking…"

"PARIS? What's in Paris?"

It was all Vassily Krestyanov could do to keep from ranting incoherently, ripping his telephone out of the wall and flinging it across the room. Such tantrums would accomplish nothing, though, and there was so much to be done, his head was virtually spinning.

"Neutral ground," Noble Pruett said, speaking on the scrambled line from somewhere in the States, perhaps Virginia, or even from the nation's capital. One thing was certain: he wouldn't have dared to make the transatlantic call from Langley.

"I see." The icy calm that made Krestyanov legendary in his field was thankful returning, calming him. "What does this person want?"

"I didn't ask him," Pruett answered, "and it doesn't matter. He's on board, and I'll take care of it. He's my responsibility."

"I'm glad you recognize that, Noble," Krestyanov replied.

"Don't worry. He's afraid of being taken out by some of your enthusiastic troops. Can't say I blame him, from the sound of things."

"You side with him, then?"

"Did I say that? Jesus, you and your conclusion jumping. You should really take care of that before it gets you into trouble." Having intercepted and returned the threat, he felt renewed and fully in control. "My guess would be your people want the package back, correct?"

"You know the answer," Krestyanov replied, his anger seething just below the surface. "What do you suggest?"

"A simple hand-off in the heart of Paris. That's as public as it gets, and no one will waste a second glance on our folks."

"I'll be there," Krestyanov informed him. "And I look forward to seeing you."

"Now, just a minute—"

"We're supposed to be partners, remember?" he stated, cutting off Pruett. "Now, one of your subordinates has stolen the most crucial object of my quest. His crime must be atoned for. It's your responsibility."

"But—"

"I require a gesture of good faith. It's nonnegotiable." He pictured Pruett sitting at a desk, watching his dreams of power slither through his hands.

"All right, the hell with it. I'll be there."

"Where is your man now?" A long shot, but Krestyanov had to try. Pruett would have been doubly suspicious if he didn't ask.

"Beats me," the man from Langley said. "We traced his last call to Velikiye Luki if that helps. That's about—"

"Forty miles from the border or Belarus. Thank you, yes. I know. How long ago was that?"

"A couple hours," Pruett said. "If I know Keane, he's well beyond your reach by now."

That nearly wrung a laugh from Krestyanov, but he controlled himself. No one on Earth was well beyond his reach, but he admitted that the bastard thief's escape from Russia complicated things. An international pursuit was costly, time-consuming and often fruitless.

"Paris, then," he said to Pruett, still resolved to intercept the package if he could, before it got that far. He needed Lukasha, goddammit! Trust the giant to be dead, just when Krestyanov needed him the most.

"Yeah, right." Pruett already sounded distant, doubtless thinking of the orders he had to issue, all the work that had to be done or delegated to subordinates before he left for France.

"No more mistakes," Krestyanov said again. "And no more interference."

"Hey, I'm not the one who hit your convoy," Pruett testily reminded him. "If Christian hadn't come along, these guys you never seem to catch would have the merchandise right now, and you'd have nothing."

"Until we meet in Paris, then," he said. "I stay at—"

"The Hotel Saint-James, on Avenue Bugeaud," Pruett said, fairly smirking. "It'll be a day or two before the package gets there. We'll need to discuss our next move. I'll be in touch."

"I DIDN'T THINK I'd hear from you so soon," Barbara Price said, uncertain whether she should feel relieved and glad or worried and afraid.

"The play's unraveling," Bolan stated. "It may already be too late to save it, but we have to try."

She was inordinately pleased by Bolan's use of the collective pronoun, but she didn't know which *we* he had in mind, and didn't press her luck by asking him. Instead, she simply asked, "What's going on?"

"We tried to grab the warhead, but I messed it up," he answered. It was Bolan's style to take responsibility for anything that happened on a mission, even though she would have bet the Farm that someone else's error lay behind the failure. "If you have a chance, when this is over, tell the Company they've got two agents down."

An ID photo of the spook named Able Deckard flashed in Price's mind, but this time she imagined she could see the skull beneath the skin. She knew that number two would be the Russian contract agent, Rurik Something, but she couldn't give the second corpse a face.

"I'm sorry," Price told him.

"Not your fault. They picked the game and knew the rules." His brusque response unsettled her, but not at much as his next comment. "Anyway, that's not the bad news."

"Oh?" The sudden chill she felt couldn't be blamed on air-conditioning.

"Somebody grabbed the package while we had our hands full with the escorts."

"You mean a backup?"

"Not unless the guy was working blind," Bolan replied. "He came in out of nowhere. One of Krestyanov's torpedoes tried to tag him, and the stranger took him down without a second thought. The kid and I were already pinned down. I think I glimpsed his car, as he was burning rubber out of there, but it was too far off to see the make, much less the plate. Some kind of compact job, most likely swapped for something else by now. Dead end."

"They'll need to get it back," she said, thinking aloud.

"My thought, exactly," Bolan said. "The problem is, without connections or a way to reach them, we're deadweight in Moscow, going nowhere fast. If we can't get a lead from someone, somewhere, we may just as well pack up and leave."

And there it was: the challenge. If she turned him down or if Brognola turned her down, she guessed the warhead would inevitably find its way to Krestyanov again. The doomsday plot would be delayed, but that was all. A momentary breather on the road to Armageddon.

"I can ask around," she said, no question as to whom she would be asking when she placed the call. "We may come up with something on this end. You never know."

"The clock is running," Bolan said. "They probably won't try St. Petersburg again. For all I know, they may start looking outside Russia for a target. Any way it plays, they have to figure someone's breathing down their necks. They may get sloppy, but they're no less dangerous."

"I hear you."

"You've got that contact number," Bolan said, reminding her.

"I do," she said, confirming it, and knew what it had cost for him to trust her with the phone number, which could in turn produce a street address, send raiders to the spot where he and Johnny stood their lonely vigil now, alone. In fact, she hadn't shared that bit of news with Brognola, simply reporting back to Washington that Striker had checked in.

Now, it was time for her to make another call.

"I'll do my best," she promised him.

"That goes without saying," Bolan told her, even though it didn't. Not in this case.

"Watch your back."

"That's Johnny's job."

"Then, you watch his, okay?"

"Sounds like a plan."

"I'll be in touch."

"I hope to be here when you call."

And that was it. The man she knew as Striker, as her friend and so much more, was gone.

Damning the lump that made it suddenly impossible for her to swallow, Price started jabbing angrily at the buttons on the telephone.

"I'M LOOKING at my calendar," Hal Brognola said, "and this isn't April Fool's Day."

"You're so right," the sultry voice from Stony Man confirmed.

"So, I'm assuming this isn't somebody's half-assed notion of a joke."

"You're two for two," Barbara Price responded.

"Goddamn it!" Brognola exploded. "How could they let someone waltz in there, pick up the nuke and waltz back out again?"

"Excuse me, Hal? There must be something wrong with our connection."

"What?"

"Okay, so much for subtlety. I didn't want to say this, but to hell with it," she forged ahead. "We've frozen Striker out since this thing started. You don't want to tell me why, I'll live with that. It's your prerogative. But you will not sit there and blame these men for 'letting' anybody grab the nuke, when we've done everything within our power to withhold vital information and material assistance.''

She hesitated, caught her breath, and went ahead before the big Fed had recovered from his momentary shock, much less decided how he should respond. "Now, if you want me packed and out of here, that's fine," she said. "I may as well go, anyway, if you expect me to obstruct our people in the field. That wasn't in the job description, and I'm tired of having to avoid the bathroom mirror just because I don't like what I see."

"Nobody's asking you to leave," Brognola said, his stomach churning as if he had just consumed a quart of Tex-Mex chili, with a double shot of jalapeños. "And I'll be insulted if you do."

"Right now, you want to know the truth, I don't give a—"

"Can I get a word in edgewise, here?" he interrupted her. "You win, okay?"

"I say again, we seem to have a bad connection."

"You can expect it to improve," Brognola said. "I've had some problems on this end, not knowing who to trust—or, maybe I was trusting too damned much. That has to be a first. Without belaboring the point or getting into all the need-to-know bullshit, let's say I got some bad advice and maybe didn't ask the proper questions." Thinking better of it, he amended, "No, let's say I definitely didn't ask the proper questions, or at least I didn't keep on asking. There's a problem in the Company—what else is new?—and now I'm guessing it goes higher up. It's an embarrassing damned thing to be admitting at my age, but I apparently got suckered. I've been betting on the wrong damned team and hoping Striker wouldn't bitch their play."

The dead air on the line was like a vacuum, sucking at him, forcing him to say, "If anybody packs up after this, it should be me."

"Oh no, you don't!" the lady snapped at him. "You don't

make up for a mistake by throwing in the towel and leaving someone else to deal with it. You want to bail, at least hang in there long enough to try and put things right.''

"It's probably too late already," Brognola replied, "if someone else has grabbed the nuke, and we don't even know—"

"Enough!" Price cut him off. "If I'm not fired, I'm doing what I can to stop this thing from blowing up in everybody's face, and I can't do that sitting on my hands, complaining that it's too damned late. Now, either help or get the hell out of my way."

Brognola had to smile at that. "One question."

"Yes?"

"What are you wearing?"

Price's laughter seemed to take her by surprise, clearing the air between them like an industrial fan, sucking the rancid fumes away.

"So, what do we do now?" she asked him, sobering after a lapse of thirty seconds.

"I've got calls to make," the SOG director said, already thumbing through his Rolodex file.

"Would that include the folks who gave you bad advice, by any chance?" Price asked. "Because, if you want me to check them out—"

"We'll get to that," he promised her. "Right now, we can't afford to tip them off. It takes a gentle touch."

"Who's got a gentler touch than me?" she challenged him.

"I'd answer that," Brognola said, "but I'm afraid you'd come up here and kick my ass."

"So funny, I forgot to laugh," she groused.

"Okay. For now, just run a full-court press on Krestyanov, Valerik and that crowd. If either one of them is leaving Moscow, we need to know when, and where he's going. If they're taking company along, find out how many and identify the rest, if possible. Krestyanov wouldn't try a deal like this unless he was protected, up the line, and we don't gain much, slamming him, if we leave Mr. Big in place to shop around for other spooks.''

"I'm on it," Price said, and then added, "By implication, you could say the same thing here at home, I guess.''

Brognola felt the sour churning in his stomach once again. "You're guessing right," he said. "Don't worry. When the shit comes down, I'll tell you where to aim the fan.''

"I'm counting on it. 'Bye.''

It wasn't often that Brognola felt embarrassed, and less often that he felt ashamed. That morning, he felt both, and there was room to spare for an abiding rage that simmered in his gut and brought a flush of color to his face.

He still had one hand on the card file, his thumb flattened against a certain card, beside the name.

"I know you now, you bastard," he addressed the square of cardboard. "You're about to wish you'd never heard of me.''

"WHY PARIS?" It was a ridiculous suggestion, in the circumstances. If it hadn't been so dangerous, so deathly serious, Tolya Valerik might have laughed out loud. "Why me, for that matter?''

"Paris, because that's where the merchandise is going," Krestyanov replied without emotion. "You, because I paid you very handsomely to put the package in my hands, and now it's gone.''

Valerik did laugh then, a startled, barking sound. "You can't blame me for that goddammit! I delivered—and ahead of schedule, I'll remind you—to your circus freak. It's not my fault he lost the merchandise to someone else before the day was out. Complain to him, why don't you?''

"Nikolai is dead," the colonel told him, sipping vodka over ice. "My other men are dead, as well. All dead. Perhaps you'd like to join them?''

Staring hard at Krestyanov across his desk, Valerik found

it difficult to credit what the former spy was saying. Here, in Valerik's office, he had come alone to make death threats.

"I don't know whether you are arrogant, courageous or insane," Valerik told his guest. "You have no weapon on your person, while I have my finger on a button, here beneath my desk, which will immediately summon men with guns. Perhaps you doubt that they would kill you on my order and discard your body in the Moskva?"

"Not at all," Krestyanov answered, seeming singularly unimpressed. "I think your soldiers, most of them, are idiot enough to do most anything you say without a second thought. That helps explain why they will never rise above their present station, but will always be in thrall to someone like yourself."

"If you are wise—"

"You, on the other hand," Krestyanov interrupted him, "are not a total idiot. At least, I don't think you are, although I may be wrong."

"You play a risky game, Vassily."

"Not if you have half the brains I think you do," Krestyanov said. "If I were talking to an idiot, he would have pressed that button underneath the desk. I might be dead already. A wise man, though, must realize that while I have come here alone, I am not without friends in Moscow. Friends who would be less than thrilled to learn of my demise. In fact, they would most certainly retaliate with every means at their disposal—which, by no coincidence, include the Parliament, the courts, police and the military, the armed forces of the Motherland. Do you believe I am exaggerating, Tolya? If you do, by all means press the button…and prepare to see your world destroyed."

Valerik felt his face aflame with anger. "If you have such power at your fingertips," he said, "you don't need me in France."

"That is correct," Krestyanov said. "I don't *need* you in Paris, Tolya, but I *want* you there. You should be eager for the trip, in fact."

"How so?"

"You have a debt of honor to avenge—or, rather, many debts, by now. Your empire has been ravaged and your army decimated by a team of faceless enemies. You want revenge."

"Again, why Paris?" Valerik pressed.

"Because the men who tried to take the package from me are, I feel quite sure, the same men who have stalked you halfway round the world. Those who survive will be in Paris, trying to complete their mission. You will have a chance to face them there."

Valerik blinked and swallowed, looking for an out. He didn't want to face the bastards who had hounded him through the United States, to Canada and on from there to Europe. Valerik wanted someone else to kill them, at a healthy distance from himself, and then present him with the heads on silver platters.

Then, something came to him. "You said the men who hunt me *tried* to take the package, as if they did not succeed. And yet, the bomb is gone."

"It has been taken by another."

"And who told you this?"

"The master of the man responsible, in fact."

"This makes no sense," Valerik said.

"It makes a kind of sense," the colonel said. "One group set out to steal the package, but they failed. Lukasha and his soldiers fought them to a standstill on the highway. At the same time, an associate of ours was watching and he saw an opportunity to liberate the cargo, thereby making sure that it wasn't recovered by our enemies or the police."

"This friend of yours—"

"Associate," Krestyanov said, correcting him.

"Whatever. This associate of yours secured the package and he kept it safe, you say? If so, why must you go and look for it in Paris?"

"*We* are going, Tolya. The plan is to retrieve the warhead and find the perfect place to use it. The nuke is in France, or will be soon, because the watcher who retrieved it fears what may become of him if he returns it to us here, on Russian soil.''

''He won't return the goddamned thing to *us*, Vassily. You keep making that mistake. I found the thing for you. You paid me for it, on delivery. It's yours, not mine. I do not want and will not take it back, at any price.''

''No one has asked you to, my friend.'' The colonel's voice could be seductive, when he wanted something, but the razor's edge was always there, beneath the velvet. ''You are simply helping me, because my own men have been incapacitated.''

''Take policemen, soldiers, politicians,'' Valerik said. ''You've boasted here today that you can use them as you will. Let them accompany you to France on this fool's errand.''

''Tolya, if it pleases you to act as if you have a choice, by all means take a moment to enjoy yourself. But let us understand each other, here and now. If you do not join me in Paris, with sufficient force to guarantee safe conduct for the merchandise, you will be out of business by this time tomorrow. There are no holes for you to hide in, no bribes large enough to help you, if I make one phone call and report your uncooperative spirit. Are we clear?''

Valerik thought about it for a moment, frowning to himself, before he asked, ''When do we leave?''

11

Another wakeup call, this time at 3:19 a.m.

"If you can call this sleeping," Price muttered to herself.

She had been tossing in her bed for hours, dozing off for ten or fifteen minutes at a time, then waking with a start from some fresh nightmare. She remembered bits and pieces of them: no two scenes were ever quite the same, but while their settings and accessories were widely varied, each gut-wrenching dream was interrupted in some version of the same climactic moment.

Price kneeling in the mud or dust or sand or surf, Mack Bolan dying in her arms. And she was screaming, not so much from loss, as from the knowledge that his death was all her fault.

That she had failed him when he needed her the most.

She snared the telephone receiver on her second grab and said, "I'm up."

"The quote was, 'Any information, any time of day or night,'" Carmen Delahunt said.

"Affirmative. From which, I take it you have something that you'd like to share?"

"Indeed, I do. You've got a party leaving Moscow in…let's see…well, hey, they should be loading now, if everything's on time. The names are phony, but surveillance gave us confirmation on Vassily Krestyanov, Tolya Valerik, and at least a dozen of Valerik's soldiers flying out today. The colonel and the godfather are booked first-class. The shooters get to ride in coach."

Price wasn't concerned about their seating on the plane. "Where are they going, Carmen?"

"Paris," the former G-woman replied. "I've got arrival times, assuming nothing holds them up. As far as where they're staying, I've arranged to have some eyes on tap at Orly. They'll be covered."

"Thanks," Price said. "I owe you one."

"At least," Delahunt replied. "Oh, one more thing you might be interested in. I don't see any link to what we're working on, but hey, you never know."

"What's that."

"Some kind of four-star diplomatic thing is going down in Paris, as we speak. If you want me to, I can reach out and pin down the particulars. Some kind of East-West deal, is all I know right now. The Russians have all kinds of people there, and so do we. The Brits are in, along with everybody else from NATO. I think the President's supposed to stop by in a day or two, for handshakes and a photo op. It looks like mega-party time."

The clamor of alarm bells in her mind brought Price to her feet. "Oh, shit!" she blurted out, before she thought to stop herself.

"Is that a bad thing?"

"It is, if someone nukes the party," Price replied.

"'Oh, shit' is right."

"I need to find out where they're meeting," the mission controller said, "ASAP. And where the President is staying, if he spends the night. Throw in addresses for the U.S. and the Russian delegations, too, if they're available."

"State ought to have that kind of thing on file. And Barbara...?"

"Yeah?"

"This means you owe me three."

Delahunt was laughing when she cradled the receiver, but

whatever humor Price might have shared with her had drained out of her body at first mention of the Paris summit meeting. Could it be coincidence that Krestyanov, Valerik and their goons were heading off to Paris now, with the diplomatic shindig just warming up?

It was a possibility, of course, but Price didn't buy it.

Not this time.

There was a chance, of course, that Krestyanov and his illicit retinue had other business in France. The summit meeting would allow them greater access to assorted diplomats and politicians, some Americans included, than the Russians could hope for when their contacts—or their targets—were at home, perpetually under scrutiny from bodyguards and journalists. Perhaps they only meant to do some dirty business while they had a chance. The bomb might be headed off in a wholly different direction and it could vanish, lost beyond recall, while Price focused all her energy on Paris.

They might never find a better target, though, and that's what she was betting on.

She had two calls to make, and was debating which should be the first, when her phone rang again. This time, the switchboard operator told her it was Hal Brognola on the line.

"You're either working late or early," Price said by way of salutation.

"Take your pick," Brognola responded. Fatigue was audible, his deep voice even raspier than normal. "Either way, I got what I was looking for."

"Which was?"

"An ID on the mole inside the Company. It wouldn't stand in court, but it's enough for me. I'm satisfied."

"You want to share?" she asked.

"Guy's name is Noble Pruett. A career man, no spring chicken. He signed on a year or two before the big crackdown on oversight, just time enough to whet his appetite for black ops in the field and soak up lots of stories from old-timers who were at the Bay of Pigs, in Chile, Guatemala or Angola, pick your poison.''

"I don't recognize the name.''

"No reason why you should,'' Brognola replied. "He's middle management—assistant to the deputy associate director, or some such convoluted crap—in one of the Company's several divisions. He's topped out for life on promotions...unless, of course, there was some kind of shakeup, something that would clear the rungs above him.''

"Like a new cold war?''

"Bingo. In fact, he's been predicting it for years—hell, almost since the Berlin Wall came down. He's managed to convince some biggies here in Wonderland that Reds are on the rise again in Moscow. Just because they haven't surfaced yet, that doesn't mean they're not at work, like termites. When he's pissing in your ear, it's all about preparedness. The guy's a salesman.''

Price picked up on the sour tone and asked, "What did he sell you?''

"Is it that obvious?'' He sounded bitter.

"Only to a friend.''

"Well, let's just say he's got a line of patter, and he backs it up with hard proof if you question him. Most of the time, anyway. We've picked up half a dozen jobs, the past three years or so, from tips he's given me.''

"So, you had ample reason to believe him, then.''

"I thought so, anyway,'' Brognola said. "When Striker asked for help on this new deal, I ran the gist of it by Pruett. Russia is supposed to be his major area of expertise.''

"I'd say that's true.''

"Besides,'' Brognola said, "I was concerned about the thought of someone in the Company collaborating with the Russian Mob. We didn't know about the KGB connection then, and I was nervous about reaching out to anyone I didn't know.''

"And Pruett told you they were already on top of it. Some

kind of mole hunt going on, would be my guess. It would be best if no one rocked the boat.''

"And like an ass,'' Brognola said, "I swallowed it.''

"It's understandable.''

"I guess,'' he said. "If you're a total idiot.''

"You need to stop that, now, and finish with your story. I've got news that won't keep long.''

"Okay. Long story short, they got an ID on a dead American from Striker's dust-up, yesterday. His name was Able Deckard, and he worked for CIA.''

Striker's connection. "And?'' she pressed him.

"And, I pulled some strings, avoiding Pruett, and found out who Deckard worked for at the Company. We had a little chat last night. Most of the night, in fact. Turns out that Deckard had been working on the foreign angle of the mole hunt, and he eyeballed one of Pruett's people meeting with Krestyanov's team in Berlin.''

"So, they can pick him up now, right?''

"They're working on it,'' Brognola replied, "but Pruett took some time off, recently. It seems he's gone to—''

"Paris.'' Price was sure before she mouthed the word, her accuracy verified by sudden silence on Brognola's end of the line.

"How did you know that?'' he demanded.

"I was just about to phone you, when you called,'' she said. "The Moscow heavies are en route to Paris as we speak. Apparently, there's some big diplomatic sit-down starting up this weekend, too. I'm thinking, if they find a way to get the package out of Russia—and my gut keeps telling me they have—Paris could make a nifty target, with the summit on.''

"Have you told Striker, yet?''

"I was calling him as soon as I got done with you.''

"You're done with me. Tell him I'll make arrangements for a set of wings. He needs to be there yesterday.''

"I'm on it,'' she replied.

"And, Barbara?''

"Yes?"

"I'm sorry."

"Okay," she told him, "but I'm not the one who needs to hear it."

"Right."

The line went dead, on that note, and Price keyed the number for an outside line. Once she got a dial tone, there were ten more digits to connect with Bolan, in Moscow. Waiting for the link, she wondered whether it would be a cutout number, with an automatic switcher on the line, of maybe someone local picking up, to make the relay manually. The last thing she expected was the sound of Bolan's voice, without a go-between.

"Hello?"

"It's me," she told him, wondering if she would have to switch the scrambler off on her end to be understood.

"What have you got?" he asked her, answering one question, while his tone left others unresolved.

"Your folks are in the air," she told him, "bound for Paris. It's coincidental with some kind of major diplomatic bash. The Man's supposed to be there in a day or two. His counterpart from Russia's coming, plus all kinds of lesser lights from Stateside, most of Europe."

"What about the package?" Bolan asked.

"No word on that," she said. "It could be going anywhere, but if I had to bet, I'd put my two bucks on the main event."

"Makes sense," he said, sounding distracted now.

"There's one more thing."

"Which is?"

"We're scrambled here, I take it?"

"That's affirmative."

"Okay. I talked to Hal just now. Long story, and he needs to tell you most of it himself, I'd say. For now, you need to know we're all on board, and Hal thinks he's identified the Company connection to your people over there."

"Someone I know?" he asked.

"Doubtful. Guy's name is Noble Pruett. Middle management at Langley, and a Russian expert. I can fax you the particulars, maybe a mug shot, if you want."

"Sounds good." His voice had softened somewhat, adding, "Thanks. I'll try to look him up next time I'm in the neighborhood."

"No need to wait," she said. "He's on his way to Paris, too."

"Well, now," the Executioner replied, "it sounds like quite a party shaping up. I may just have to crash."

"BUT WE'RE NOT SURE about the bomb?" The problem nagged at Johnny, like a sharp stone in his shoe. "How can we split for Paris if we're still not sure about the bomb?"

"That's why we're going," his brother replied. "Krestyanov and Valerik will be there, and now this Pruett from the Company. It's old home week. I wouldn't miss it for the world."

"It's funny you should mention that," Johnny retorted, "since the world is just exactly what's at stake, here, if we drop the ball."

"I hear you, Johnny, but we've dropped the ball already. Hell, we've lost the ball, and as we speak, the only people in the world who may know where it is are on their way to Paris. Maybe they're expecting a delivery, or maybe not. If you can think of any better way to find out where the damned thing is, we'll drop my plan right now and follow yours."

Johnny considered it for thirty seconds, give or take, then shook his head. "I don't have squat," he said. "Let's see the Eiffel Tower while we've got the chance, before somebody melts it down."

His brother's smile was long on irony and short on mirth. "Okay," he said. "The Farm has wangled places for us on a diplomatic flight that leaves in—" glancing at his watch "—two hours and twenty-seven minutes. It's the quickest they could manage. No inspection of our bags at either end, so that's a plus.''

"I'm almost finished packing, now," Johnny said. "Can I make a call before we go?"

"Switzerland?" Bolan's smile was different, almost wistful.

"Not if it's a problem," Johnny said.

"I don't see any," his brother replied. "Just bear in mind that her end's not secure."

"No mention of our plans or destination, right," he said. "I just want to find out if she's all right."

"It couldn't hurt," he said, already on his feet and moving toward the bathroom. "I'll just catch a shower for the road and finish packing up the hardware."

"Thanks."

"Save that," his brother said, "until we see what's waiting for us at the other end."

Johnny felt vaguely nervous as he called up the Swiss number from memory and entered its nine digits on the keypad of his cellular phone. He had lied to his brother about his main reason for reaching out to Suzanne King, but since they both knew he was lying, and they both knew why, he reckoned that it really didn't count. Johnny had promised not to mention Paris, the potential bloodbath in the making, and he wouldn't. Personal security was part of it, but he was equally determined not to worry her unnecessarily.

Besides, if Suzanne knew where they were going, she would probably attempt to follow them and turn up in the middle, just when it hit the fan.

A hotel desk clerk answered, speaking German, shifting seamlessly to English after Johnny dropped the alias Suzanne had used to register and asked to speak with her.

"Of course, sir. Just a moment."

Okay, so it wasn't altogether seamless, after all.

He waited through some clicking sounds, a moment of dead silence, and the echo of what sounded like an auto horn, before Suzanne came on the line.

"Hello?"

"How are you?"

"Bored and lonely, up to now," she said. "Are you all right?"

"In transit," Johnny said, and left it there. "I wasn't sure when I'd have time to call again."

"Well, here you are." And then, without the smiling voice, "I hope you're being careful."

"It's my middle name," he told her. "Which explains why I don't put it on my business cards."

She laughed at that, an honest sound, but fraught with strain. "Wish you were here," she said.

"It shouldn't be much longer." Johnny skated right up to the line, before he stopped.

"I'll be here," Suzanne promised.

"Listen, one more thing..."

"Please, don't."

"If anything should happen—"

"I don't want to hear this. Please."

"You need to hear it," Johnny said. "If something happens—"

"No!"

"—someone will be along to take you home, or someplace else, if you prefer. It will be someone you can trust. You ask who sent them, and the answer should be 'Hal from Wonderland.' Got that?"

"Yes, dammit! Are you satisfied? Maybe you want to read me your last will and testament, to cheer me up?"

"Suzanne—"

"No, wait." Her voice cracked, balanced on the verge of tears. "I'm sorry. I just don't like thinking of...you know."

"No sweat," he said. "Most likely, this will be a milk run, anyway."

Liar.

"At least, I'm glad it's not about my brother any more," she said. "He wasn't worth all this, not half of it."

"He was, to you."

"I thought so, anyway. Is that a laugh, or what?"

"Nobody's laughing."

"Well, for what it's worth, I lost my rose-colored glasses somewhere between Tucson and Berlin. I don't think I'll be shopping for another pair."

"You know," he said, "you mostly find your happy endings on TV."

"I just might have one," Suzanne told him, "if you take care of yourself." When Johnny didn't instantly respond, she said, "Uh-oh. Three strikes in one. I push too fast, I sound too needy and my timing sucks."

"No, no, and just a bit," he said. "The timing thing, I mean. It's time for me to hit the highway. Miles to go before I sleep."

"Alone, I hope."

"Unless you're counting Mike," he said, reverting to the alias Bolan had used in all his dealings with Suzanne.

She laughed at that, a sound less fraught with worry. "No," she said, "but I'm relieved to know he's sticking close."

"It's cool," Johnny replied. "I told you that we go way back."

"That's something else for us to talk about, another time."

"Sure thing," he said. "And now, I'd better—"

"Go," she finished. "Right. I'll see you soon."

"Sounds like a plan."

She hung up then, and Johnny felt a sudden urge to call her back immediately, but he swallowed it and closed the cellular phone, slipped it back into his pocket. His brother was finished in the bathroom, just emerging with a towel around his waist.

"Any hot water left?"

"Plenty, by Moscow standards," he replied. "Back home, you'd call it lukewarm, going on room temperature."

"I'm not sure I can stand to give up all this luxury."

"Look on the bright side. Maybe they'll have lukewarm water when we get to Paris."

"Right. If we have time to wash our hands." He paused unbuttoning his shirt, and asked, "You really think they wan to smoke this diplomatic gig?"

"It obviously wasn't their first choice," his brother said "but it could be a fallback option. Maybe it's a blessing fo them in disguise, depending on who's there."

"The president, you said."

"Both presidents, ours and the Russians'," Bolan correcte him. "They're not participating in the meet per se, from wha I hear. More like a walk-on guest appearance, for morale."

"And if the meeting is ground zero, that would open up lot of vacancies, on both sides."

"Right. And change some attitudes at home, besides."

"A war?"

"If it was all one-sided, maybe," Bolan said, "but we'v got the heavies on both sides collaborating. My guess woul be they're thinking empire, not annihilation."

"So, they'll want a scapegoat," Johnny said.

"No problem, there. The world's full of fanatics. If the can't frame one group, chances are another one will try t claim the credit on its own."

"Meanwhile, a rumor here, a rumor there…"

"No matter which nuts take the rap," his brother said, "yo can expect some major changes, East and West alike."

"Unless we stop it."

"There's always that."

"How much time until that flight?"

"Two hours on the nose."

"Give me ten minutes," Johnny said, "and we'll be out c here."

THEY TAXIED to the airport, having ditched their bullet-riddle car the night before. It seemed to take forever, but when Bola checked his watch, around the midpoint of their drive, he sav that they were making decent time. Anxiety could skew pe ception, and he made a conscious effort to relax.

Good luck.

This trip wasn't the first time he had raced against disaster, with the smart odds riding with the other side, and while he had emerged victorious in each case heretofore, that only emphasized the possibility that something could go wrong this time.

No soldier's luck was iron-clad. No one always won. And if he lost this time, it wouldn't simply mean his death, or Johnny's, but a wholesale slaughter on a scale the planet hadn't seen since 1945, with aftershocks that might prove almost equally destructive for democracy in Russia and the States.

No pressure here, he thought.

His mind kept coming back, throughout the drive, to Brognola and Price. Their sudden shift from strict neutrality, or worse, to offering all possible assistance in the home stretch raised more questions in his mind, and answered none. Price had told him that Brognola would explain himself, when there was time and opportunity, but meanwhile, everything came down to trust—the one commodity that had been running short between them, from his first day on the present mission.

Now, despite the fact that they were both "on board," as Price had told him, offering material assistance to the best of their ability, he found that he couldn't stop wondering about the change, a part of Bolan's mind suspecting that the flight to France itself might prove to be a trap. Granted, they had their hardware with them on the flight, but it was stored as cargo. He and Johnny would be stepping off the plane unarmed at Orly Airport, easy marks for shooters or a raiding party of police.

He caught himself before the paranoia blossomed, told himself that Brognola would never do that, but the fact remained that Bolan simply wasn't as sure as he would have been two weeks before. So much had happened, much of it still unexplained, and doubts inevitably filled the gaping blanks.

He wondered if those doubts would ever be replaced by

certainty again—and, if they were, what would the final truth reveal?

Would he and Brognola be friends again or mortal enemies?

It was too much to think about, and Bolan concentrated on the job he had to do in Paris. First, he had to isolate his targets—Krestyanov, Valerik, and the new mark, Noble Pruett, out of Langley. If the three of them were confident enough to meet in Paris, and if Bolan somehow found a way to crash the party, it would make his work much easier.

But it wasn't enough to simply set up his targets and knock them down, he realized. Until he found out where the bomb was stashed, and either neutralized it or reported its location to a nuclear emergency response team, he couldn't afford to let the three top plotters die. In fact, not knowing which of them might hold the secret to the warhead's whereabouts, Bolan was cast in the peculiar role of having to protect them, even as he tracked them down.

Until he had them in his grasp, at least. From that point on, he could apply whatever pressure might be necessary, short of death, to jar loose any secrets they possessed.

Interrogation wasn't Bolan's specialty. In fact, during his Asian war, while he was known to many as "The Executioner," for his uncanny skill at infiltrating hostile lines and taking out high-ranking enemies—up close and personal, or from three-quarters of a mile away—he also earned the tag of "Sergeant Mercy," for the care he showed to wounded soldiers and civilians on both sides. On more than one occasion, he had interrupted military torture sessions, when it seemed to him that the interrogators either liked their work too much, or else were seeking information that was readily available through other, less barbaric means.

That facet of his personality aside, though, no one who had ever dealt with Bolan in the field presumed that he was soft. As a proficient sniper, with nearly a hundred registered kills in two years' time, he had mastered the art of slaying in cold blood. Conversely, when the icy calm gave way to rage—

always controlled, if only by the narrowest of margins—he became a one-man army.

And Bolan wouldn't shrink from rough interrogation, either, if it was required to save a life—much less the tens of thousands who would be incinerated or irradiated by a nuclear explosion in a major modern city. He would do what was required to find the bomb, and he would live with it, as he had lived with all the other ghosts, from the beginning of his long and often lonely war.

"Sorry?"

Johnny had made some comment, Bolan conscious of the sound, oblivious to any meaning in the words.

"I was just saying that I've always wanted to see Paris."

Bolan nodded. "There's a lot to see. I hope you get the chance."

"Is that supposed to cheer me up?" his brother asked.

"Sorry, again."

"Forget it. I was thinking, once we wrap this up, I may just stay in Europe for a while. Take two or three weeks off from paperwork and window peeping, see the sights, soak up some history and culture for a change."

"You should be able to afford it," Bolan said, thinking about the duffel bag of cash they carried with them, liberated from the Russian Mafia at several stops across two continents.

"My thoughts exactly," Johnny answered. "Maybe take a run at Monte Carlo, see if I have any better luck than when I go to Vegas."

Bolan had to smile at that. His brother gambled rarely, betting no more than the minimum allowed at any given time, and cashing out before the house could get its hooks into his bankroll. On the firing line, however, Johnny went for broke and played like there was no tomorrow, risking everything, trusting his older brother's skill and smarts the way some people put their faith in an omniscient, faceless higher power. At the gaming tables, he would never lose more than a few stray dollars; in the real world that the Executioner inhabited, he ran a daily, sometimes hourly risk of losing everything.

Bolan accepted Johnny's daredevil behavior as a fact of life he couldn't change, no matter how he would have liked to see his brother choose another course in life—becoming a librarian, perhaps, or hanging out his shingle as a lawyer, concentrating on the tedium of torts and contracts. It would never happen, Bolan knew, because the tragedy that stripped them of their parents and their sister had determined Johnny's course in life, just as it had the Executioner's.

Bolan was torn between two evils, hoping that the nuke was on its way to Paris, so the long, protracted game of hide-and-seek that he had played across the past two weeks could end at last, while simultaneously hoping it was hidden somewhere, anywhere, else. Maybe the near-miss on the highway north of Moscow had been frightening enough to make the plotters call a time-out, gather in the shadow of the Paris summit meeting to discuss their options, while the warhead sat in mothballs, hidden in some peasant's barn, or some street soldier's underground garage. Maybe…

Enough.

They were about to reach the airport, and he knew there would be time enough for fretting on the flight to Paris, while he was digesting rubber chicken from the microwave, or making one last effort to catch up on sleep, before he hit the line again.

Of one thing he was relatively confident: Paris was sitting on a powder keg, and Bolan was about to light the fuse.

12

"I'll miss all this."

Vassily Krestyanov was gazing out the tinted window of their limousine as they rolled along the Avenue des Champs-Elysées, past so much history and culture that it made Tolya Valerik vaguely ill. Ahead of them, he could already see the Arc de Triumphe, standing as a monument to French imperial ambitions which, though trodden under by the hobnailed march of history, had never really been renounced.

"I won't," Valerik told the colonel, fishing in his pockets for a pack of cigarettes.

"You don't like Paris, Tolya?" Krestyanov didn't appear surprised. Amused, perhaps, as if Valerik's little quirk was symptomatic of some deeper illness which, since it wasn't contagious, made a fitting subject for derision.

"It's nothing special," Valerik said, lighting his cigarette.

"You have a jaundiced view, perhaps."

Valerik shrugged. Why waste the effort needed to explain that he was virtually frozen out of Paris by the Corsicans, who dominated prostitution and narcotics in the city—and in most of France, for that matter—with ruthless tactics that impressed even the Russian godfather. The last time he had sent a scouting team to Paris, two of his envoys had disappeared; the third—or part of him, at least—came back to Valerik by express mail, stamped and labeled as prime cuts of veal. The giveaway had been the dead man's silk, hand-painted tie, included with the steaks. A quick report from Moscow's top forensics lab confirmed the flesh as human.

Valerik had never punished those responsible for the insult, primarily because he never managed to identify them. He wasn't afraid of them today—in fact, a simple gangland rivalry would have been a welcome diversion, just now—but he was conscious of a general uneasiness within himself, roughly equivalent to the sensation he experienced when he went boating on any body of water larger than the Moskva River.

"You should really try to see the Louvre," Krestyanov said. "It's truly exquisite…and, after all, you may not have another chance."

"I'll pass," Valerik said, watching the shops and colorfully attired pedestrians slip by his window. You could recognize the tourists, most of them Americans, because they smiled and had the look of people who bathed. "I just want to be done with all of this."

"To spend your money, yes?" Krestyanov nodded to himself, as if he had unveiled the secret of the universe. "But there is more at stake than profit, Tolya. I believe you understand that, too."

"I'm not an idiot," Valerik groused. He had grown sick to death of listening in silence, feigning rapt attention, while the one-time colonel spun his web of dreams about recapturing the "glory" of the old USSR. As far as Valerik could remember, things in Russia were immeasurably better now—even considering the high rate of inflation and the constant shortages—than they had ever been under the Communist regime. Except for the high-ranking Communists, of course.

Though he would never say it to Krestyanov's face, Valerik had the whole Red-comeback scheme marked down as a somewhat pedestrian, albeit grandiose, attempt to feather certain special nests, at the expense of Russia's masses. Not that he objected to the concept of a rich elite surviving on the toil and sweat of the pathetic proletariat. He was relieved, however, that his final deal with Krestyanov had put sufficient funds into his Swiss account for him to buy himself a scenic mountaintop, perhaps an island, and retire in peace.

The world could tear itself apart, for all he cared—as long as he had time to clear the line of fire.

The limousine was headed south, now, cruising like a shark among the pilot fish on Avenue Victor Hugo. More shops, boutiques and open-air cafés for the mobster to ignore. French motorists, he noted, were almost as rude and reckless as their counterparts in Moscow. He kept hoping for an accident, a little blood to brighten up his day, but none of them obliged Valerik, as the limo made another turn, this time westbound, on Avenue Bugeaud.

"I think you will enjoy the Saint-James, Tolya," Krestyanov said. "It is a magnificent hotel."

"I'm sure."

Valerik's soldiers, stiff and angry from flying coach, ignored the desultory dialogue, examining the city much as big-game hunters would regard an unfamiliar jungle, seeking prey. Their hardware had been checked through, riding in the swollen belly of the plane, but they had stolen several moments to rearm themselves, before boarding the limousine. Valerik pitied the gendarme who was naive enough to stop and frisk one of them on the streets. He could expect a beating for his trouble, and would be extremely fortunate if they allowed him to survive.

"When do we meet the others?" Valerik asked.

"Soon," Krestyanov said. "Perhaps tomorrow morning. There is certain business that I must transact this afternoon, but you need not concern yourself. I'll take one of your men along for company. You and the rest are free to see the city and amuse yourselves."

Dismissing him, as if he were a child—or, worse, a personal valet whose services weren't required until his master's shoes needed another coat of polish for the grand cotillion. It was tempting for the Russian godfather to say that *he* decided when and where he would amuse himself, but what would be the point? He was in Paris, even now, because Krestyanov had demanded that he come. It was too late to alter the embarrassing dynamic of their strained relationship.

Unless, of course, something should happen to Krestyanov while they were in France.

Would it be such a tragedy, Valerik wondered, if the terror bombing never came to pass? What if the hunters who had stalked him all the way from the United States, and who had also targeted Krestyanov in Berlin, should somehow find them here? Or, more specifically, what if it were believed that they had struck again, more fortunate this time, taking Krestyanov out before they fled? It should be relatively simple, then, for Valerik to locate and neutralize the warhead. Krestyanov's political supporters would be furious, of course—and they might try the plot again, another day—but in the meantime, there would be no evidence connecting Valerik or his men to the humiliating failure of their master plan. Why should the various conspirators retaliate against his Family when he had done his best to help them seize the government again, and he so plainly shard their mourning of Krestyanov's loss?

"What's funny, Tolya?"

"Funny?" Valerik realized he had been smiling to himself, embarrassed by the lapse, rushing to cover it. "Oh, nothing. I was just remembering the first time I saw Paris, many years ago. They had this brothel where—"

"I can imagine," Krestyanov assured him. "It's a great relief to know that you're not unaffected by the finer things in life."

"I have my moments," Valerik said, smiling again. And thought, in fact, I'm having one right now.

If Nikolai Lukasha had been still alive, Valerik might have scrapped his budding plan. The giant had intimidated him too much, although he dared not consciously admit it, even to himself. But Lukasha was dead, and good riddance to the hulking freak. Krestyanov trusted Valerik for his personal security in Paris, and that was the first mistake could remember his companion making since the two of them had known each other.

Never mind.

Depending on its nature and the circumstances, one mistake was all it took to kill a man.

THE LUXURIOUS GEORGE V Hotel, was famous for its antique furniture and art, the small "secret" salons that were discovered here and there by roving guests, and the impressive price tag on its rooms. Some of the hotel's classic charm was lost to renovations, in the 1980s, and its breakfast lounge, unfortunately, had become a magnet for French television personalities and hangers-on, but the George V was still *the* place to stay in Paris, if a person could afford the tab. Its clientele included Greek shipping magnates and petroleum tycoons, the CEOs of multinational conglomerates, plus the occasional film star.

And ranking diplomats, of course.

Vassily Krestyanov wasn't expected when he entered the George V that Saturday. He didn't know which floor Zhenya Romochka's suite was on, much less its number, and the clerks at the George V were so well known for their discretion, where the privacy of paying clients was concerned, that Meg Ryan once lampooned that very trait in one of her romantic comedies. It wouldn't do to simply ask. Instead, Krestyanov crossed the lobby to a bank of pastel-colored telephones that only worked inside of the hotel. He lifted the receiver, waited for a hotel operator to respond and asked to be connected to Monsieur Romochka's room.

A moment later, he was speaking to a bodyguard.

"Hello?"

"I need to speak with Zhenya. It's important."

"Who is this?" the bodyguard demanded, turning surly in an instant.

"Tell him his Uncle Josef needs a moment of his time before he gets back to his busy schedule."

"I don't know an Uncle Josef."

"That's because I'm not your uncle," Krestyanov replied. "Now, give Zhenya the message, if you please."

"Wait there," the guard commanded, as if Krestyanov might find some way to slither through the line and follow him. So stupid. So predictable.

He counted forty-seven seconds on his watch, before Romochka's voice came on the line. "Dear Uncle Josef!" he enthused, playacting for his stooges. "I'm so glad you called! Unfortunately, I don't have much time before the diplomatic banquet, and—"

"I'm in the lobby," Krestyanov informed him, cutting through the chatter. "I can either come up to your room, or you can choose another meeting place. In either case, we need to talk. Right now."

Romochka hesitated for a moment, but Krestyanov knew that he would not, could not, refuse. "Of course, dear Uncle. What a grand surprise that you are here in Paris. I should have time for a glass of vodka if you'll meet me in the third-floor lounge. It's near the elevators."

"All right. Leave the gorillas in their cage," Krestyanov said, and cradled the receiver, moving toward the bank of elevators with a measured stride.

The third-floor lounge was large enough to seat perhaps a dozen patrons, in an atmosphere designed for intimacy. Romochka was already there ahead of him, alone, when Krestyanov arrived. The politician's vague expression of uneasiness delighted him. This one would never be a problem to manipulate.

"My friend," Romochka said, when they had ordered and received their vodka over ice, "what brings you all the way to Paris at this time?"

"I wanted to inform you that our plans have changed," Krestyanov said.

The politician frowned, as if his vodka had a bitter taste. "Have changed? I'm not sure that I understand."

"You haven't heard, I take it, that the package never made it to St. Petersburg?"

The sour look intensified, but it was clearly not the vodka, since Romochka drained his glass in one long swallow and immediately signaled for another.

"What went wrong?"

"There was an effort to retrieve the merchandise," Krestyanov told him. "It wasn't successful, but the effort drew too much attention. There will be too many questions, as it is, once all the bodies are identified."

"Bodies? How many were there?"

"It's of no great consequence," Krestyanov said. "Except for Nikolai, of course. I'll miss his smiling face."

The politician clearly didn't know if he should laugh at that absurdity or not. Instead, he grimaced, his porcine features writhing for a moment in what could have been imagined either as a smile or an expression of condolence.

"Nikolai," he said. "The giant."

"Just another bag of fertilizer now," Krestyanov said, dismissing his lieutenant with a shrug. "In war, men die."

"Of course," Romochka said. "As for St. Petersburg, it will be there next month, even next year."

"And for a long time after that, I trust," the colonel said. "I've picked another target."

"Oh?" A sheen of perspiration was now visible across Romochka's forehead, though the lounge was air-conditioned to a constant seventy degrees. "And what...um, where... would that be, then?"

"What better than a summit meeting, when our common enemies are all together and the incident need not contaminate our Russian soil?"

"A summit meet—" It hit Romochka, then, the lag between reception and absorption of the data once again confirming Krestyanov's opinion that the man was nothing but a stooge. "You don't mean Paris, surely? Here? This summit meeting?"

"When else will we have another opportunity like this?"

Krestyanov asked. "In five years? Maybe ten? It's perfect for our needs, and I, for one, am not prepared to wait another moment."

"But, you can't just…this is…." Suddenly, behind the politician's eyes, another light went on. "For God's sake, man! I'm here!"

"And I have every confidence that you'll survive," Krestyanov said.

"But, how—?"

"The George V has a vault downstairs, if I am not mistaken, where the guests can leave their jewelry and other valuables?"

Romochka shrugged. "It may, but I don't see—"

"You will, of course, be warned well in advance of the event," Krestyanov told him. "At the proper time, you will present yourself to the concierge and tell him that you wish to place some item in the vault, for safety's sake."

"What should—"

"It makes no difference what the object is," Krestyanov cut him short. "Go out and buy some bauble, if you must. God knows you can afford it, with your sticky fingers in so many pies."

"Now, see here!"

"It will require some time for you to do the necessary paperwork, a bit more to obtain your key and have the concierge conduct you on a tour of the facility. While you are thus engaged, well insulated from the outside world, the incident will have occurred. When you emerge, you'll be a hero. A survivor. That's the next best thing to martyrdom."

"When I emerge?" Romochka was perspiring even more, as if to match the sweat beads on his vodka glass. "What makes you think I will emerge? A blast like that, in downtown Paris, will destroy the damned hotel and bury me alive, inside the goddamned vault. I would be better off holding the damned thing in my lap when it explodes!"

"Please, calm yourself," Krestyanov said, sipping his vodka slowly, in a demonstration of the proper attitude.

"You want me calm? All right, then. I'll fly back to Moscow on the first flight leaving Paris, shall I? You go the vault downstairs and wait for several thousand tons of stone and steel to fall on top of you."

"We have consulted experts, Zhenya, and their calculations are precise. The warhead is a small one, twenty kilotons at most. Destruction at the point of detonation will be absolute, of course, but the impact at longer ranges is dramatically reduced. In fact, I'm told that at three miles—roughly the distance from the conference center to this very spot, a structure like the George V should sustain no damage worse than broken windows."

"But the radiation—"

"A target standing in the open, three miles out, should suffer burns equivalent to first degree, with no long-term effects. Below street level, in the vault, you'll be completely safe."

"Until I step outside," Romochka muttered.

"In which case, since you're obviously wise enough to stay exactly where you are and wait for help, the experts will advise you whether there is any danger on the street. If there should be, they will supply you with protective gear."

"I don't like this, Vassily," the politician said. "I hope you understand that. I don't like this plan at all."

"In which case, you must simply do as you are told," the colonel responded, "because it really makes no difference what you think."

HARGUS WEBBER was relaxing in the sauna at the Royal Monceau Hotel, unwinding from another morning of forced smiles and handshakes, when a gust of cooler air disturbed the steam and drew him from the hinterlands of sleep. He squinted through the cloying atmosphere that looked like San Francisco when the fog was in and felt like Mississippi in the summertime. If Webber squinted through the mist, he could make out a human form, standing beside the brazier stacked with superheated stones, ladling water on the hot rocks to produce more steam.

"In case you didn't see the sign outside," the senator spoke up, "this sauna's occupied. If you don't mind—"

The man-shape turned to face him and responded in a deep, familiar voice. "You seem to have some spare room, Senator."

"Pruett?" A moment of confusion, spiked with dread, froze Webber's tongue, but he recovered swiftly, drawing on his long experience with rough-and-tumble arguments in Congress. "You're a long way off your range, I'd say."

"I had a few days of vacation coming," Pruett said, crossing the narrow room to find a seat against the wall, to Webber's left, a foot or so of space between them.

"Let me guess, you've always had a yen to visit Paris?"

"On the contrary. I've been here many times, though it was mostly business, I admit. The last time, eighteen months ago, I came to get a dying declaration from a Chinese dissident in exile. He'd been poisoned with..." The man from Langley seemed to catch himself. "But, you don't want to hear war stories, do you, Senator?"

"I'd rather find out what you're doing here. It's risky, dammit. If the two of us are seen together—"

"Not a problem, Senator. We won't be."

"Even so, you won't mind coming to the point, so we can cut this short."

"Ah, yes. The famous Southern hospitality."

"Bullshit. Is there a point to this, or not?"

"The point is that I've got some news I couldn't trust to telephones or couriers. It's critical. You might say, life-and-death."

"All right, I'm listening."

"There's been a problem with the trigger incident in Russia," Pruett said. "It won't be going down today, as planned."

"That's typical," Webber said, running sausage fingers

hrough his damp gray hair. "Those damned Russians could uck up a wet dream."

"It wasn't entirely their fault, Senator."

"Never is," Webber said sneering. "They've got scape-goats galore. So, what's happening, then? A postponement?"

"Minimal," Pruett replied. "A day or two."

"That's not so bad."

"One other thing—the incident will not take place in Rus-sia, as originally planned."

"Is that a fact? And where, exactly, do they plan on setting off the goddamned thing?"

"Paris."

"If you think that's amusing, Mr. Pruett, I assure you it is not."

"It wasn't meant to be," the spook replied. "This time tomorrow, give or take, a fair amount of Paris will be history."

"The hell you say!"

"I can assure you it's the truth," Pruett said. "If the war-head's not already here, it will be by tonight. It's perfect, when you think about it."

"Perfect? Jesus Christ, man!"

"Stop and think about it, sir. A blast on neutral territory takes out the incumbent leaders of the East and West. A small band of fanatics takes the blame, as planned, and while they're Russian nationals, they hate the Reds as much as they hate us. The demonstration of their power prompts a crackdown on the group, back home, and gives the Reds all the momentum they should need to sweep the next election. Meanwhile, Stateside, the vice president moves up the ladder, and the country gets a closer look at what a klutz he really is. You'll take him easily, come next election, with the specter of another Soviet regime to help you out. And since the Reds can't be connected to the bombing, there's no grounds for NATO to react. Both sides come out ahead, and all it cost us is some Frogs."

"That all sounds fine, in theory," Webber said, "but you're forgetting one small detail, Mr. Pruett."

"I don't think so, Senator."

"Then try this on for size—we're sitting here in Paris, wait ing to be vaporized when that damned thing goes off!"

"We won't be," Pruett told him. "You should know by now that I don't make a move without some kind of backup plan."

"And you've been needing them a lot," Webber replied "the way your big plans have a way of falling through."

"What matters is the end result."

"And I can promise you the end result of this will not be my ass getting blown to smithereens."

"Of course not, Senator. Now, would you like to hear about the crisis that will very soon require your personal attention back in Washington?"

"I'm listening," Webber said. "And you'd damn well bet ter make it good."

THERE WAS NO question of a flight to Paris, not unless he meant to leave the bomb behind, so Christian Keane had driven night and day, staying awake with coffee and amphet amines, until his nerves were fried and he had been reduced to wearing sunglasses around the clock. His cash was running low as he pulled into Paris, shortly after dusk on Saturday, but he had made it. That was all that counted.

He had seen the mission through.

Keane had contacted Pruett while several hours outside Paris, and his superior had related to him the plan to detonate the "merchandise" in France.

He had a number for a small hotel on Rue Van Gogh, close to the Seine, where Pruett was supposed to have a room, but touching base again could wait. Before he took the next step he was desperate to feel human once again. That meant a shower and a change of clothes, a decent meal, perhaps a little sleep. Pruett wasn't expecting him for two or three more hours, at the earliest.

So, let him wait.

As far as Keane could tell, it didn't matter if the heart of Paris went to hell at noon, or two o'clock, or half-past three. As long as the event took place, and all the crucial principals were well beyond the killzone, it was all the same.

Keane found a place on Rue Berbier du Mets, behind Le Manufacture des Gobelins, where tapestries had been produced for more than half a century before Columbus sailed for the New World. Keane knew that much about the place because there was a stack of tourist pamphlets in his room, and he glanced over one of them before he hit the shower, paranoid enough to take the metal suitcase with him to the bathroom, setting it beside the toilet after he had locked the bathroom door.

And if that made him paranoid, so what?

He made it through the steaming shower with no SWAT team to interrupt him, toweled off in the bedroom, and was dressed again before room service brought him up a double helping of Coquilles Saint-Jacques, the scallops cooked with mushrooms, in white wine and lemon, served on the half-shell with a bed of piped potatoes. Keane washed it down with white Bordeaux, then lay on the bed, still fully dressed, but sleep eluded him in spite of his fatigue, the alcohol and the delicious meal.

His mind was racing now, imagining his meet with Pruett, later that night, and then the wholesale carnage of the following day. He had only been to Paris twice before, and never felt a great attraction for the city. Still, imagining the heart of it in ruins, with as many as a fifth of its inhabitants reduced to ash or doomed to suffer through the final throes of radiation poisoning, he had to stop and wonder what had brought him here.

Any way he sliced it, when he turned the problem inside out or stood it on its head, the answer was the same: he was a patriot.

This sacrifice would help the U.S. find its way after a decade wasted floundering and kissing up to Russians and Chinese.

The very nations that had vowed to conquer or destroy America while Christian Keane was coming up through high school, moving on to college, now enjoyed "most favored nation" status, to the point that recent U.S. Presidents had shared the deepest, darkest secrets of national defense with diehard Communists or those ex-Reds so recently converted to "democracy." Instead of raising hell with China over the continuing suppression of minorities and dissidents, the spineless crowd in Washington had handed over missile guidance systems in return for fat political donations—bribes—and closed their eyes to daily torture, executions, the atrocities of the "reeducation" camps. Russia, meanwhile, had turned into a giant money pit that seemed to have no bottom, gulping U.S. foreign aid, advanced technology and medical supplies like there was no tomorrow.

Keane felt no qualms about his role in what would surely take place the following day. For one thing, he believed ends justified the means. And for another, he was confident that no one on the planet, other than his one immediate superior, would ever know the part that he had played. Pruett would never share that knowledge, for if Christian Keane were ever publicly identified, his own downfall wouldn't be far behind.

And how could Pruett hope to run an empire from a prison cell at Leavenworth?

As long as sleep eluded him, Keane decided that he might as well go on and make the call. He spent five minutes looking for the telephone, before he realized, to his chagrin, that there was none in his hotel room. Stepping into the hall, he found a public telephone midway between his room and the single elevator. Rummaging around in pockets for sufficient coins to make the call, he locked his door behind him, then thought better of it and went back to fetch the metal suitcase, taking it along to keep him company. That way, if someone came in through the fourth-floor window in his absence, there was nothing they cold steal except his clothes.

He read the telephone's instructions, printed in a jerky kind of pidgin-English, primed the slot with coins and dialed his number. Noble Pruett picked up on the second ring.

"Hello?"

"It's me," Keane said. "When's the meeting?"

13

The tip, this time, had come from Stony Man. Bolan was hesitant, at first, to take the information at face value, but as Johnny pointed out, their only two alternatives were sitting in the hotel room until their cash ran out or driving aimlessly around the streets of Paris, searching for an English-speaking Frenchman who could tell them "where the Russians are."

With that in mind, Bolan had memorized the address of a château on the southern outskirts of the city, where, he was informed, the heavies would be gathering that night to break bread and discuss their plans. There was no word as to the warhead, whether Bolan should expect to find it on the property or not.

"You still think it's a setup?" Johnny asked, as they were driving toward the target in a rented Citroën sedan.

"It could go either way," Bolan replied. "That's all I'm saying. Watch your back."

"Sounds like a plan."

The château was in fact, as Bolan had been told, impossible to miss. It stood alone on ten or fifteen acres, where the landscaping ran more to shrubs than trees of any size, except around the house itself, where they were plainly used for shade. Its broad front windows and its second-story balcony had a commanding view of the highway for close to a mile in either direction, until the hilly landscape intervened.

"Feel like a walk?" Bolan inquired.

"There doesn't seem to be much choice," Johnny replied.

The château was ablaze with lights as they drove past and on around the next curve in the highway, looking for a place to leave the car. Bolan could see no lookouts on patrol, but he would bet his life that there were gunners on the property, remaining out of sight from passersby, protecting those inside the house. There had been time for him to count five cars out front, parked on the curving drive, and while he couldn't name their makes with any certain, they looked like money, sleek and bright and powerful.

A quarter mile beyond the curve, he found a winding access road that branched off from the highway, climbing through the hills. He killed the rental car's headlights, navigating by the moon, until he satisfied himself that no one passing on the main road, down below, could see their vehicle. At that point, Bolan parked it on the shoulder of the one-lane track, leaving as much room as he could for any other vehicles, and switched off the engine.

"Last chance to veto," he informed his brother.

"Hey, we have to check it out, right? Otherwise, we could be screwed both ways."

And he was right, of course. The first way being that Krestyanov and his co-conspirators would have a chance to plot their strategy and blow the warhead at their leisure. The other screwing was what Bolan would be doing to himself, blowing what could turn out to be his last, best chance of finding out if he could still trust Brognola and Stony Man.

"Okay," he said, "let's get it done." As they were suiting up, smearing their hands and faces with the flat-black warpaint that would keep them from reflecting moonlight, Bolan said, "Remember, we still don't know where the warhead is, or if it's even here. You saw the suitcase back in Moscow, but they could have changed the bag a dozen times, by now."

"So, I won't shoot up any luggage," Johnny told him with a grin, "unless it's trying to escape."

"Seems reasonable."

Bolan wore his nightsuit under jet-black military webbing,

the Beretta 92 in its shoulder rig, while canvas pouches on his belt contained spare magazines for both the pistol and his AKSU. Beneath the skinsuit, Bolan wore a Kevlar vest, knowing that it would offer only limited protection from a torso shot, dead-on to front or back, from certain calibers of weapons. He would still be vulnerable to head shots, any hit below the waist, and shots fired from the side that found the gaps required to let him move his arms. Even a fair hit to the center of the vest could knock him down, meanwhile—stun him, perhaps, until the shooters had a chance to finish him—and he had no defense at all against explosions, fire, or even something as mundane as being clobbered with a baseball bat.

Better than nothing, Bolan told himself, and watched his brother touching up his warpaint in the mirror on his side of the sedan. Johnny wore forest camouflage, for all the good that it would do him when they hit the brightly lit château. He looked ferocious and immeasurably young.

"You know," Bolan said, "I was thinking—"

"If it's not about our strategy for the approach," his brother interrupted him, "we really don't have time. Remember, I was on this gig before you came aboard. I'm going in with you. No arguments."

"Your call," the Executioner replied, all business now. "Watch out for any kind of sensors from the time we see the house. I doubt they've wired the place, but it they spot us that far out, we're really screwed."

"Heads up, then," Johnny said. "Or, in this case, heads down."

"We have no word on servants or civilians in the grounds," Bolan went on. "We make it to the house, barring hard proof to the contrary, assume that anyone you meet is hostile."

"Slash and burn," Johnny replied, psyching himself up for a confrontation with the enemy.

"Scorched earth," Bolan replied. "Let's go."

The hilly countryside between the access road and their intended target was more difficult to navigate than Bolan had expected, but they still made decent time. When they were still at least two hundred yards from eyeball contact, they could see the château's lights glowing beyond the final hilltop, homing in on it like moths drawn toward a light.

At last, they stood in darkness, overlooking the château. From that angle, a swimming pool was visible, but there were still no guards in evidence.

"Could be a wash," Bolan suggested.

"Only one way to find out," his brother said.

To which, the soldier had no argument. "I'm ready if you are," he said.

"As ready as I'll ever be," Johnny replied.

And they went down the hill together, side by side, to keep a rendezvous with Fate.

"I WISH TO WELCOME all of you," Vassily Krestyanov proclaimed, raising his wineglass, "to the first and last occasion when we all sit together in the spirit of collegiality."

"Some of us shouldn't even be here," Zhenya Romochka said, his wine untouched. "Meeting like this is too damned risky. It could blow up in our faces."

"Still, you came," Krestyanov said.

"As if I had a choice," the politician retorted, sullenly.

"We all have choices," Noble Pruett noted, clearly irritated, even though his voice and was still low-key.

"It would be most unfortunate," Krestyanov interposed, before the politician could think of anything to say, "if we lost track of all we stand to gain, this late in the proceedings. We are on the very brink of changing history, restoring order to a planet that is slipping into anarchy and decadence. The hazards are as nothing, by comparison to the rewards."

It was apparent from Romochka's sour frown he didn't view the change in their initial plan as any kind of blessing in disguise. Krestyanov guessed that he could blame most of their discontent on cowardice. They didn't mind participating in the cold-blooded destruction of a major European capital, but neither of them wanted to be at or near the scene when it occurred.

"Our change in plans," Krestyanov once again reminded them, "was unavoidable. Now, as to the placement and the detonation of the nuclear device—"

Precisely at that moment, an explosion rocked the house, rattled the windows in their frames and prompted Christian Keane to spill his wine, the goblet halfway to his lips. Tolya Valerik bolted from his chair and started shouting for the guards, apparently not realizing that they had to be otherwise engaged. The mafioso's second in command, Anatoly Bogdashka, rose and took him by the elbow, tried to calm him, but Valerik shook him off.

Krestyanov couldn't understand, much less respond to, the barrage of questions being thrown at him by his assembled guests and co-conspirators. How could he know what the explosion meant? Did they suppose he had arranged it, as some kind of entertainment to accompany their meal and conversation? Did they think his sense of humor that refined or that outrageous?

"Calm yourselves!" he snapped at all of them, the order barely spoken when he heard the unmistakable staccato rattle of Kalashnikovs from somewhere on the grounds. The gunfire buried any hope he had, however flimsy, that the blast had been a natural phenomenon or the herald of some accidental mishap. With the shooting, there remained only one explanation: they had been discovered, somehow, and their meeting was under attack.

"Be quiet! All of you, shut up!" Krestyanov bellowed to the room at large. He was somewhat amazed when they stopped yammering and all of them, except Valerik and Bogdashka, went back to their seats around the dining table. From the outer grounds, a momentary lull in fighting gave way to another fusillade of automatic fire, some of Krestyanov's cronies flinching at the racket.

"Rest assured," Krestyanov told them, "that we have the

best security available, well armed, professional and able to defend the house. We shall, in any case, evacuate at once. There should be ample time. If Mr. Keane would kindly fetch his bag…?''

''Sure thing,'' the blond American replied. When he stood, Krestyanov saw the pistol in his hand and made a mental note to chastise any of the guards who might survive the night for failing to disarm his visitors.

The rest of them were on their feet again and milling near the exit, anxious to be gone, when Keane returned a moment later with his heavy bag. It should have been amusing, watching as the rest backed off, keeping their distance, but Krestyanov had forgotten how to laugh.

Another time, perhaps.

''If you will follow me,'' he said, and nodded to the two armed sentries hovering outside the exit from the dining room. ''An orderly retreat will help insure that everyone gets out alive.''

IF CHRISTIAN KEANE had been a superstitious man, he would have said the suitcase that he carried—or, perhaps, the goddamned plan itself—was cursed. That simply wouldn't fly, though, and it left him with two real-world possibilities: the first was plain old, everyday bad luck; the second was betrayal, someone at the heart of the conspiracy who maybe had cold feet and had decided he could save himself by selling out the rest.

And Christian Keane didn't believe in luck.

It never once occurred to him, forced to consider explanations in the heat of battle, as it were, that there could be a third, equally logical scenario for what was happening. It didn't cross his mind that someone from the Company—much less another agency, of which he had no knowledge whatsoever—might connect the dots, collate the data and dispatch a strike force to expunge the plotters when they least expected it. When they were something very close to sitting ducks.

And so it was that Keane examined each of his companions with a jaundiced eye, as they began evacuating the château. He kept the Walther P-5 automatic pistol in his right hand, while the suitcase did its best to drag the left side of his body down and out of line. Part of the weight was psychological, he thought. The bomb itself weighed only thirty-five or forty pounds, the metal suitcase with its lead shield twelve or fifteen more, the thick foam-rubber padding next to nothing. Call it sixty pounds and add another ten, just for the sake of argument. Keane bench-pressed nearly four times that amount on weekly visits to the gym. There had to be something more than simple gravity that made him feel as if the world itself was handcuffed to his wrist, slowing him down.

It wouldn't be much longer, though.

He concentrated on the man in front of him—coincidentally, the Russian politician—and decided that if things went sour for him, he could waste the whole damned party with a single magazine, and make his break alone. One round for each of them, including Pruett and the pair of grim-faced Russian riflemen, before he had to drop the bag and fumble for a second magazine. No double taps, but he could do it, if he kept his wits about him and remembered that he had to nail the shooters first.

It was the ultimate worst-case scenario, but if he had to run for it alone, uncertain who the sellout was, Keane knew that he couldn't afford to leave a wagging tongue behind. As for the nuke, well, that was something else entirely. If the plot was scrubbed, along with its participants, Keane didn't plan to carry on alone and make himself some kind of human sacrifice. What would have been the point?

He had been careful to touch no part of the metal suitcase but its sturdy handle, which could easily be wiped clean of his fingerprints in something like one second flat. That done, it wouldn't matter who retrieved the case or what they did with it, since nothing short of being caught red-handed could connect the bag to Christian Keane.

Not once the others had been permanently silenced.

It surprised him, at that moment, to discover that he was considering mass murder, as if it had been decided, nothing left to think about but the mechanics of the act. In truth, Keane hadn't decided anything yet. He was prepared to go ahead and plant the bomb in Paris, if it seemed the plan had any reasonable prospect for success—meaning coming out of it alive. He told himself that gunning down his comrades was a fallback option, not to be employed unless it was apparent that the group couldn't escape en masse, and he was forced to make a break for it alone.

Just wait and see.

But he would keep his finger on the Walther's trigger while he waited, taking up the slack.

There came another blast, outside the house, and this time windows broke, instead of simply rattling. Keane smelled cordite in the air, and flashed back to the last time he had fired his gun, when he retrieved the nuke from Krestyanov's outnumbered men.

He clenched the Walther's grip until his knuckles blanched.

The sounds of combat from outside were escalating, drawing closer to the house with every passing moment. Keane was moved to wonder if this might not be some kind of trap, a double cross, but he couldn't think of a reason for Krestyanov to betray the rest of them, when the conspiracy had been his brainchild to begin with.

Which presumed, of course, that Krestyanov was responsible for the attack.

Keane took another look around him, at the other faces, searching for a hint of anything that would betray a double agent, let him spot the traitor now before it was too late. Once they were in the open, possibly surrounded, it would be too late.

He gave no thought to who the outside shooters were. It made no difference to him whether they were Russians, Frenchmen or Americans. What mattered was that they were enemies, and Keane meant to evade them or destroy them if he could.

Above all else, the bearer of the bomb intended to survive.

JOHNNY HAD HOPED they would get closer to the house before the shooting started, but their luck ran out when they were still a hundred yards out, advancing from the east. He didn't see the sentry lurking in the shadow of a chest-high hedge until the guy stepped out in front of them and started blasting with some kind of compact submachine gun.

Maybe "blasting" wasn't quite the proper term, since their assailant's gun was fitted with a sound suppressor, reducing its report to something like the sound of heavy cardboard being torn. They caught a break, his first rounds high and wide, perhaps the product of a jerky trigger squeeze, and by the time he found his mark, the brothers had already gone to ground. He ducked back out of sight, and Johnny was about to strafe the hedge, when his brother reared back and lobbed a frag grenade across the leafy barrier.

Its blast, after the muted stutter of the SMG, sounded like thunder in the night. Johnny was on his feet and moving well before the echoes died away, rounding the corner of the hedge to find his target lying crumpled on the grass, one leg twisted beneath him at an angle that would certainly have made him gasp with pain if he had been alive.

There was no question of surprising anyone inside the château, now, and Johnny shrugged off any thoughts of stealth as he began to run in the direction of the house. He could hear his brother behind him—hoped it was his brother, anyway; then knew it, when he wasn't gunned down from behind—and concentrated on the well-lit ground in front of him. If there were more guards on the property, they should be coming—

Now!

Three riflemen came into view on Johnny's right, emerging from behind the northeast corner of the house, while four or five more troops immediately showed up on his left. They opened up on him at once, and he could hear their bullets cutting through the air around him, too damned close for comfort.

Johnny hit the deck, still critically exposed, but offering a lower profile to the gunners who were still advancing, firing as they came. Some of them may have thought that he was hit, already dead or dying. Either way, they were distracted by his brother, several of them swiveling to bring Bolan under fire, ignoring Johnny in their bid to make it two for two.

And in so doing, they condemned themselves.

Johnny sighted on the nearest of them first, the trio on his right, scooting around on close-cropped grass to frame them in his rifle sights. The nearest of the three was short, no more than five foot five or six, but he could just as easily have been a center for the Lakers, seen from Johnny's worm's-eye view. His automatic piece was tracking his brother across the lawn, orange muzzle-flashes winking on and off, when Johnny shot him in the chest, a short burst from twenty yards away, and slammed him backward on the lawn.

The two surviving members of the threesome didn't miss their friend immediately, focused as they were on nailing Bolan. Johnny had the second target lined up in his sights, until a burst of AK fire erupted from behind him, and the gunner's head exploded like a melon with a cherry bomb inside. The dead man kept his balance for another beat or two, blood pumping from the ruin of his shattered skull, but when he tried to take another forward step, his legs turned into rubber, and he toppled slowly forward, sprawling on the grass.

By that time, Johnny had acquired his final target, raked the sole survivor of the trio with a burst that whipped the AK-47 from his grasp and nearly took off one of his arms in the process, spinning him as if he were preparing for a game of blind man's bluff. He made it through three-quarters of a turn before another burst slammed into him and dropped him in his tracks, his legs thrashing on the grass before his blood spilled out through ragged, gaping wounds.

Incoming fire began to chew the turf around him, Johnny instantly reacting as he spun to face the gunners clustered near the southwest corner of the house. Unlike their late, lamented comrades, they weren't advancing in a rush, but had spread out to form a skirmish line, seeking to keep their distance while they filled the air with lead. It was a good move, minimizing the disturbance of their aim by forward motion, still allowing them to duck and weave as necessary to protect themselves.

And Johnny only hoped that it wasn't too good a move.

For he could feel that he and his brother were running out of time.

TOLYA VALERIK hesitated on the threshold of the exit from the house, feeling the others massed behind him, pressing forward, anxious to be out of there and gone. He shared that feeling, but he wouldn't let his fear grow into panic, driving him into the jaws of death, full-tilt, before he knew what he was doing.

"Hurry up, for Christ's sake!" one of the Americans demanded, sounding peevish, almost childlike, as the ringing sounds of combat dwarfed his voice. Valerik doggedly ignored him, made an effort to ignore them all, as he surveyed the killing ground outside.

He couldn't see the shooters, though from what he heard, if he wasn't mistaken, they were fighting somewhere to his left, around the east side of the house. The cars were parked off to his right, some fifty yards due west, and at the moment, the mobster thought it may as well have been a mile. The finest athletes he had ever seen couldn't outrun a bullet, and Valerik, for his part, had never been a track star on the best day that he ever had.

"What are we waiting for?" Romochka asked, whining in a tone unlike the voice that roared and ranted when he spoke in Parliament.

Valerik almost answered, "To save your worthless life,"

but he decided it would be a waste of precious breath and energy. His object was to reach the car that he had come in, with Krestyanov, Bogdashka and their escorts. Make it to the car alive, get in before a sniper tagged him from the darkness and stay low, trusting the sturdy bodywork of the Mercedes-Benz to keep him safe until they managed to get out of range.

It sounded easy, when he spelled it out that way, but seemed impossible, as he stood trembling on the threshold, one step from exposure to the deadly guns outside. Perhaps if he retreated, found someplace to hide, inside the house...

"We're wasting time," Krestyanov said, his lips close enough to Valerik's ear that his breath tickled like a lover's, raising goose bumps on the mafioso's flesh.

"We need more men," he told the colonel, hoping that he sounded logical, instead of craven and afraid.

"They're busy at the moment," Krestyanov replied. "They're buying time for us, if we don't waste it standing here, wetting our pants."

Valerik felt the angry color in his face, would almost certainly have struck out at Krestyanov for the insult under other circumstances, but survival was his first priority, just now. Simple embarrassment could be avenged some other time, if he was still alive. And if he wasn't...well, what difference did it make?

"All right!" he snapped at Krestyanov, at all of them. "All right, then, damn you! If you're all in such a hurry to be killed, let's get it over with!"

"No, wait!" Zhenya Romochka blurted out. "Perhaps he's right. Why don't we wait and—"

"Wait my ass!" one of the Americans said. This time, Valerik glanced around and saw it was the one called Keane, who bore the deadly suitcase in one hand, an automatic pistol in the other. "You want to stand around and argue all night, be my guest. But I suggest you get the fuck out of my way, and I mean now!"

Keane thumbed back the pistol's hammer, Valerik noting

that their two armed escorts made no move to stop him. They were Valerik's men, but both of them were watching Krestyanov, a clear sign that they understood who had the best chance of directing them toward life, instead of sudden death.

Valerik marked them both for future execution in his mind, uncertain at the moment whether he would live to see it through. With any luck...

Bogdashka stepped up close beside him, on his left, and said, "There's no more time, Tolya!"

He was moving, before his conscious mind could intervene and hold him back. Valerik heard the others rushing out behind him, wondered if the gunners he had marked for death had wits enough to watch their back and cover the retreat. Perhaps, if all else failed, the colonel could remind them of their duty, stiffen their resolve.

Ungrateful bastards! He had brought them from the peasant hovels where they spent their wasted childhoods mired in poverty, and he had given them a taste of power. For them to desert him now was nothing short of treachery, no matter that they did so in an effort to protect themselves.

Valerik swore their deaths wouldn't be either quick or clean. He meant to make them suffer for betraying him.

If only he could make it through this night alive.

14

The second clutch of gunners, five in number, didn't rush toward point-blank contact in the manner of their three late comrades, opting for a bit of distance as they formed a ragged line and started laying down a screen of automatic fire. It was a fairly safe approach toward covering two men, and Bolan knew that he had seconds, maybe less, in which to turn the odds around and claim them for his side.

Firing his short Kalashnikov left handed, the Executioner unclipped a frag grenade from his combat harness, yanked its safety pin and lobbed the bomb toward the middle of the skirmish line. The shooters either didn't see it coming or else they were so caught up in the chaotic moment that they didn't recognize the danger. Either way, they stood their ground and kept on firing, as if totally oblivious to hurtling death.

The frag grenade landed almost between the middle gunner's feet, and he had time to glance at the wobbling egg, frowning, before it went off in his face. The guy was shredded, nearly vaporized by shrapnel, while the four men flanking him were scattered, tumbling over scorched and bloodied grass, disarmed by force of impact, crimson streaming from their wounds.

There was a chance some of them would survive, and Bolan cared nothing about their future health, as long as they were out of action for the moment, no more threat to Johnny or himself. As he approached the spot where they had fallen, he observed one hardy gunner struggling to his feet, looking about him for a weapon, and a short burst from the AKSU put him down again, this time for good.

Johnny was close behind him as he reached the southwest corner of the house, spotlights positioned overhead making a false noon on the killing ground. Bolan took out the nearest sets of lights with two quick bursts from his Kalashnikov, then ditched the empty magazine and snapped a fresh one into the receiver.

He had no idea how many more defenders might be waiting for them on the grounds, perhaps inside the house itself, but they had taken care of nine and suffered nothing more than minor scrapes and bruises in the process. They were already ahead, on points, and it wasn't in Bolan's nature to retreat simply because he was uncertain of the path ahead.

"Two ways to go," he told his brother. "We can split up now and flank the house, or stick together and make sure we watch out backs."

"Last time I checked," Johnny replied, "divide-and-conquer mostly worked against the other guys. If it's a choice, I'll stick."

"Suits me," the Executioner replied.

"Besides," Johnny said, grinning, "I may get to save your bacon for a change."

The kid was joking, Bolan knew, and shared his smile. Johnny had saved his life on more than one occasion, and if the Executioner was ahead in that department, he couldn't have proved it, since he didn't bother keeping score. Johnny was Bolan's last surviving kin, and he would give his life without a second thought, without an instant of regret, to spare the kid from harm.

He risked a glance around the corner and saw nothing, drew no fire. "Looks clear," he said, "but be prepared for anything."

"Sounds fair."

He ducked around the corner, moving in a combat crouch, aware of lighted windows up ahead. No movement showing as he closed the gap, then dropped to scuttle underneath the first one on all fours.

Bolan had almost reached the second window, when he heard a crash of breaking glass behind him, followed by a snarl of anger and the rapid-fire explosions of a large-bore pistol. Pivoting, he was in time to see a hulking figure leaning halfway through the shattered window, firing point-blank into Johnny's chest with what appeared to be an old Colt .45, the standard semiautomatic side arm of the U.S. military.

The Executioner didn't have to aim at that range, squeezing off a 4-round burst that left the Russian shooter nearly headless, dangling from the window like a sad, unfinished scarecrow. Palming a grenade, he primed and lobbed it through the window, ducking as the blast within finished the shooter's sloppy job of clearing out the window glass. The dead man's jacket was on fire as Bolan passed him, kneeling at his brother's side.

By that time, Johnny was already sitting upright, grimacing in pain, but focused on the task of double-checking his AKSU. "Kevlar," he said, then thumped his chest like Tarzan, wincing at the contact with bruised flesh. "I ought to get some kind of an endorsement contract."

"I don't think they're big on public advertising," Bolan answered. "Can you stand?"

"Hell, yes. Let's get it done."

Bolan tried to suppress the dizzy feeling of relief. Any distraction in the middle of a firefight spelled potential death, regardless of the root emotion that inspired it. Grief, delight, shock, rage, bewilderment—all stood an equal chance of getting Bolan killed if he surrendered to their siren's song.

Celebrate later. Stay alive right now.

Beyond his line of sight, in the momentary stillness after so much gunfire, Bolan heard the sound of car doors slamming, unmistakable, first one and then another engine revving into life. He thought about the vehicles parked out in front of the château, and had a mental picture of his quarry slipping through his hands again, vanishing again to God knew where, perhaps beyond his reach.

The chase had gone on long enough, halfway around the world and back. Bolan was driven by a deep, compelling need to end it here and now, once and for all.

"They're splitting!" Johnny told him. "Jesus, let's get moving!"

And the kid was out of there, taking the point, with Bolan double-timing after, almost stepping on his heels. A few more yards, a few more seconds. It was all they needed.

And a little luck.

Let's not forget the luck, he thought, and plunged ahead to meet the enemy.

"Hold up a minute!" Noble Pruett said, wheezing, already sounding as if he were out of breath.

"We haven't got a fucking minute," Christian Keane shot back at him, wild-eyed beneath the floodlights, looking like some kind of stickup man, the shiny metal suitcase in his left hand, pistol in his right.

"We have to work out what we're doing, where we're going," Pruett told him.

"We can do that on the road, for Christ's sake! Are you crazy? This is no time to be standing in the middle of a goddamned shooting gallery and making small talk!"

As he spoke, Keane stretched to look behind Pruett, but seemed dissatisfied with what he saw. He sidestepped, moved a yard toward the house, as if expecting someone to emerge and challenge him at any moment.

It was all the edge that Noble Pruett needed.

Reaching underneath his jacket, Pruett palmed the double-action derringer that he had smuggled over in his check-through luggage, balled up in his socks. It held two .40-caliber Smith & Wesson rounds, in the classic over-and-under configuration, but at this range, Pruett only needed one.

He held the muzzle of the derringer an inch or so from

Keane's skull, behind one ear and angled slightly upward, toward the forehead. "Sorry," Pruett said, squeezing the trigger once before Keane had a chance to turn his head and spoil the perfect shot.

At nearly skin-touch range, the derringer kicked backward, driven by the force of its own muzzle-blast, but by the time the recoil rippled through his muscles Keane was down and twitching on the deck, blood spilling from his shattered skull to sketch a crimson halo on the driveway.

Pruett raised his eyes in time to find the Russians watching him. He couldn't tell if they were frightened, worried, or amused, and frankly he didn't give a damn.

"Deadweight," he told them, as he pocketed the derringer and stooped to claim the heavy suitcase and the Walther P-5 automatic pistol for himself. "Less to explain, this way. I stand a better chance of getting to our target with the package if I'm by myself."

"You're planning to proceed?" Krestyanov asked him, and the man from Langley knew that look. It was surprise. No doubt about it.

"Very well," Krestyanov said, glancing back toward the house. "We should be on our way."

"I'll take his car," Pruett replied. "You go ahead." He was compelled to set down the bag, then the pistol, as he crouched beside Keane's corpse and rifled through his pockets, grimacing at contact with the lifeless flesh before he found the car keys.

It struck him, as he rose and moved in the direction of Keane's rental car, while Krestyanov, Valerik and their cronies scrambled for their limousine, that there had been no sounds of gunfire or explosions from the south lawn for a while. How long? He couldn't say and cursed himself for not remaining more alert to his surroundings, saved another curse for the uncertainty of what the ringing silence meant.

The way he broke it down, still moving toward the rental car, there were three clear possibilities: the raiders could have taken out Valerik's soldiers, the defenders could have snuffed the raiding party, or the two sides could have wiped each other out. Two out of three scenarios put Pruett's side on top, with all the major players still intact, but he couldn't afford to gamble with his life against the underdogs. For one thing, they had beat the odds too often, too dramatically, in recent days, for him to count them out before he saw their bodies lined up on the lawn.

And for another, he was plain old, shit-assed scared.

That was a rare experience for Noble Pruett, at his present time of life. There wasn't much he feared, beyond exposure of his devious maneuvers with the Russians to remake the world and place himself atop the bureaucratic heap.

And death, of course.

Whatever else, he couldn't forget the Reaper.

Pruett didn't want to die just yet, and so he found a little extra energy, jogging instead of simply walking to the rental car. And then he heard the guns again, the bullets hissing past his head this time, and he was sprinting to save his life.

And save the merchandise, of course.

To keep his date with destiny.

THE TARGETS WERE already scattering when Johnny caught his first glimpse of them, half a dozen breaking toward a long black limo, while a seventh beat feet toward a plain sedan, parked in between two sports cars. On the driveway pavement, number eight lay facedown in pool of blood that spread and rippled even as he watched it, gravity continuing the work a lifeless heart had been unable to complete.

That told him all he had to know about the single shot he had heard a moment earlier—except, of course, for who the dead man was, and why the heavies had begun to kill one another. In regard to Question B, he got his answer, or a part of it, at any rate, when Johnny noted that the solitary runner clutched a heavy-looking metal suitcase in one hand.

"I see the package!" Johnny snapped, uncertain in that moment whether his brother had even heard him, much less registered the meaning of his words. There was no time to clarify, as Johnny took off in pursuit, already firing with the AKSU as he ran.

Nailing a target on the move was one thing; bringing down a runner while the shooter, himself, was in motion, took a special kind of skill. Johnny possessed that talent, but his haste betrayed him this time, and his first rounds missed the mark dramatically, smashing the windshield of a Lamborghini parked beside the plain sedan.

No good.

The Lamborghini's built-in theft alarm was whooping now, adding an extra note of chaos to the scene, as more guns started going off in close proximity. The runner with the suitcase spun and squeezed off a double tap at Johnny with the automatic he carried in his right hand. There was something shiny—looked like car keys—dangling from between his teeth, but Johnny didn't have a chance to check for details, as he ducked the bullets whizzing past his scalp.

More gunfire, then, as his brother cut loose, and two or three bodyguards in the limo party answered with Kalashnikovs, a couple others cutting loose with handguns, but without a great deal of conviction.

He fanned another burst at the zigzagging runner, being careful not to hit the bag his target carried, missing altogether in his caution. This time, he was wide and to the left, a black Porsche soaking up the hits, no car alarm engaged on this one to exacerbate the noise.

Slow down and mark your target, Johnny told himself. Or, better yet, stand still.

And make himself a stationary target, right. His chest and ribs still ached from the explosive impact of the .45 slugs that his Kevlar vest had stopped, the pain a grim reminder of the fact that he wasn't invincible, even with body armor covering a portion of his torso.

Still, if he allowed the runner with the bag to get away, how many thousands would die gruesome, agonizing deaths because he chose to save himself?

A sudden inspiration made him focus on the drab sedan that seemed to be the runner's destination. His target ducked between the Lamborghini and the driver's side of its plain cousin, almost seeming to present the metal bag between himself and Johnny as a shield.

He knew that this attacker didn't want to hit the warhead.

Johnny shifted focus to the vehicle itself, parked head-on toward the house, which meant that it was facing him, the headlights, grille, and bumper all reflecting pinpoints of the floodlights' glare.

Johnny kept moving, firing, but his target was a stationary object now, his slugs drilling the radiator and releasing gouts of water mixed with coolant, shattering the headlights, hammering around inside the cramped engine compartment, clipping wires and hoses, striking sparks on tempered steel.

The AKSU's slide locked open on an empty chamber, and he dumped the magazine, still moving, groping for a fresh one, ripping Velcro as he found it and reloaded on the run. His adversary stood beside the crippled vehicle, unmoving for a moment, hatred etched in furrows on his face before he raised his pistol, held it out at full arm's length and started squeezing off in rapid fire.

The guy was good, cool under fire, and Johnny had to hit the pavement, more pain flaring from the tender points of his near-death experience, before he came up firing from the hip. By that time, he discovered in a flash, his enemy had taken off across the lawn, hotfooting toward the highway and the vast, dark shelter of the night.

Cursing the bastard's speed, Johnny lurched to his feet and set off in pursuit.

"THEY'LL KILL US ALL!" Zhenya Romochka bleated, sounding like a frightened sheep, cringing as Krestyanov applied more pressure, forcing him inside the limousine.

"We're not dead yet," the colonel said, "but we will be, if you don't shut your mouth and move your ass."

"How dare you speak—"

Krestyanov slapped the man across his face, the impact sending ripples through Romochka's cheeks and chins. "Get in the car," Krestyanov ordered, leveling his side arm at the politician's face, "or I will leave you here."

It was apparent, even to a man of Romochka's limited mentality, that he wouldn't be left alive, and so he scrambled through the limo's open door, rushing to find a seat as far away from Krestyanov as possible. Tolya Valerik entered next, a headlong dive for cover, trusting in the limousine to cover him from sniper fire. His second in command, Bogdashka, hesitated long enough to squeeze off two more shots in the direction of the house before he ducked into the car.

That left Valerik's bodyguards, perhaps the last two left alive, both of them alternating bursts of gunfire toward the house with glances at the limousine, waiting their turn to climb aboard. Krestyanov watched their jaws drop as he blocked the doorway with his body, snapping orders.

"You two cover our retreat," he said. "We need a clear head start. When you've cleaned up here, take one of the other cars."

The shooters had arrived in several vehicles. Krestyanov didn't know or care where any of the keys were, any more than he cared whether these two made it off the property alive.

Before the soldiers had an opportunity to challenge him, Krestyanov ducked into the limousine and slammed the door behind him, locking it. His driver had the engine running, waiting for an order, and Krestyanov barked at him, "Get us out of here!"

The limo was taking hits as it began to pull away, accelerating. It wasn't equipped with armor-plating, but the bullets hadn't found their way inside. Not yet, at least. Krestyanov glanced back through the broad rear window, saw the soldiers he had just abandoned ducking, weaving, as if they were dodging hornets, their Kalashnikovs still spitting death toward the château. As he was turning back to face Romochka, a jerky movement on the dark lawn caught his eye and he leaned closer, his forehead pressed against the tinted glass.

The sight before him almost made Krestyanov laugh out loud, except that it could spell grim death for all of them inside the limousine. A solitary runner made his way across the château's gently rolling lawn, the stainless-steel suitcase banging against one leg with every second stride. Pruett's bland face was locked into a grimace from the pain and his exertion, swiveling to glare and mouth a curse in the direction of the limousine. Behind him, fifty yards back but gaining, ran a single gunman, his face in shadow, slowly but inexorably closing the gap between them.

"Driver!" Krestyanov called out. "We need to stop for the one with the suitcase!"

The driver cranked his wheel, the limo drifting leftward, off the pavement, rolling over grass.

"What are you doing?" Romochka cried. "You can't stop the car!"

"It will only take a moment," Krestyanov assured him.

"We don't have a moment, damn you!"

"Silence! We accomplish nothing if we lose the package."

Now, the others gaped at him in something close to shock.

"The package?" Romochka blurted out. "You want the warhead here, with us? Are you insane?"

"You know it's safe," Krestyanov told the politician, "but if you're afraid of it, get out and walk. In fact, if you don't shut your mouth, I'll throw you out myself!"

Romochka was about to answer back, but he thought better of it, bit his lower lip and slumped back in his seat to pout.

Meanwhile, the limousine was swerving on an interception course to meet the runner, Noble Pruett keeping up a decent pace, but still unable to outdistance his pursuer. In a few more moments, Krestyanov was sure, the hunter would decide that he was close enough to try a running shot and bring his target down.

Unless they got to Pruett and the precious suitcase first.

At first, the runner didn't seem to understand what he was seeing, as the limo cut across his path. Only when Krestyanov threw back the door and called for him to hurry, join them in the car, did Pruett crack a weary smile, hunch forward, reaching down inside himself to find more speed.

The armor-piercing bullets struck him, then, punched through his chest in gouts of crimson, hurtling on to strike the limousine and drill its bodywork, as Pruett went down on his face. The suitcase lay beside him, tantalizing Krestyanov, but hopelessly beyond his reach.

"Goddammit!" he exploded, reaching for the door to slam it shut. He rounded on the driver, snarling like a wounded animal. "What are you waiting for, you stupid bastard? Get us out of here!"

BOLAN HAD SEEN his first rounds strike the limo as it pulled away, knew that the wounds were superficial, and was forced to concentrate on the two goons his prey had left behind. Both of the gunners held Kalashnikovs, and both knew how to use them, but anxiety was playing with their reflexes, spoiling their aim. Not much, but just enough to buy him time for two short bursts that dropped the Russian soldiers in their tracks.

He took a precious moment, looked around for other targets, finding none at hand. The runner with the shiny suitcase was long-legging for the highway, God alone knew why, with Johnny trailing him in foot pursuit. As for the limousine, it was accelerating down the long driveway, and Bolan knew that he couldn't catch up to it on foot.

He hustled past the Lamborghini with its strident theft alarm and passed the plain sedan that dribbled coolant from its punctured radiator. Johnny's AK rounds had found the Porsche, as well, but there was no apparent fatal damage. Bolan prayed for keys in the ignition switch, found none and lunged beneath the dash, cursing the maddening delay, using the dome light to illuminate his search for two specific wires.

He found them seconds later, and the engine came to life. He slammed the driver's door behind him, AKSU in his lap as he ran through the gears, the speedster laying scratch as it responded like a hungry Thoroughbred. He whipped it through a tight U-turn and stood on the accelerator, shifting only when the tach began to redline, racing like a madman in the wake of the stretch limousine.

Bolan was gaining, when he saw the limo swerve off course, across the lawn, to intercept the runner with the suitcase. They were kissing-close to a successful rendezvous, when Johnny shot the marathon man from behind, dropping him on the grass, and the limo screeched off, gouging turf, swinging back toward the pavement and highway beyond.

Bolan already had the Porsche in fifth and kept it there, running arrow-straight along the driveway as the stretch came back to meet him, its driver seemingly oblivious to the pursuit. At this rate, if the wheelman didn't spot him soon, they would collide with stunning force in five...four...three...two...

One!

He braced himself for impact, cut the Porsche's steering wheel enough to keep from taking it head-on and slammed into the limo a yard or so behind the right-front wheel. The Porsche's engine sputtered once and died, its crumpled hood thrown back against the windshield, as it spun away from contact with the larger, heavier machine.

The stretch, meanwhile, had kept on rolling, barely slowing, until it slammed into the stout trunk of a massive weeping willow, stalled and died. Bolan was EVA by then and circling the limo's flank, where it protruded from beneath the willow's trailing branches, engine metal ticking loudly as it cooled.

A glance back toward the dead man with the suitcase showed him Johnny stooping to retrieve the warhead, moving cautiously to join him. Bolan focused on the limo, then, as first one door and then another opened, spilling passengers into the night.

He recognized Tolya Valerik, leaning on the shoulder of another man about his age and height, the second figure brandishing a pistol. Bolan shot them both, an 8-round burst that put them down on their backs, without a shot fired in return.

How many left inside the stretch?

He circled, caught a young man lurching through the open driver's door and punched him back inside with a short burst from ten yards out. The driver's legs thrashed briefly, through the open doorway, then were still.

"If you speak English," Bolan told the silent limousine, "you've got five seconds to clear out of there before I use grenades."

"We're coming," a male voice said, not as rattled as he would have liked. "Please, hold your fire."

He reckoned that the calm voice didn't issue from the first person who appeared, a sweating overweight man whose oily hair was hanging in his face, his teeth bared in an expression that denoted either terror or the onset of a heart attack. Behind the fat man, staying well behind him as he exited the limousine, a second man raised eyes to lock with Bolan's, and he recognized the stoic face at once.

Vassily Krestyanov.

"Be careful, please, with that Kalashnikov," Krestyanov said. "You do not want to kill a ranking member of the Russian Parliament."

"I don't?"

"It would be bad for international relations, don't you think?" the colonel asked him, almost smirking. As he spoke, he clamped his left hand on the fat man's corresponding shoulder, while the right fist raised a pistol, pressing it against the politician's temple.

"So, you want to do it for me?" Bolan asked Krestyanov.

"Only as a last resort," the former KGB man said. "I would prefer to walk away from this and take him with me."

"You can always dream," the Executioner replied.

"We are professionals," Krestyanov said. "I see it in your eyes. We are men of the world. We understand that such things as this messy business are not personal."

"You could be right," Bolan replied before he shot them both, holding the AKSU's trigger down until the magazine was empty and their twitching bodies lay at rest. "Or, then again, you could be wrong."

"All done?" his brother asked, trudging across the last few yards of grass, the heavy suitcase dragging down his left shoulder.

"All done," Bolan replied.

"We need to pass this off to someone," Johnny said. "It doesn't feel like something we can check through for the flight back home."

"I'm betting Hal knows someone who can take it off our hands. First thing, let's get the hell away from here. I need fresh air, ASAP."

"I'm right behind you, bro."

And so he was, throughout the long walk to their waiting rental car, through the dark.

EPILOGUE

"I have a feeling we missed someone," Bolan said. The sun was bright above him, Wednesday morning on the Mall, in Washington, past tourists lining up to enter the National Air and Space Museum.

"You did," Brognola said. "No way you could have known about him, though. He skipped the Russian's little party. Got cold feet and bailed before you had a chance to introduce yourself."

Brognola took a folded piece of newsprint from the inside pocket of his suit coat, opened it and handed it to Bolan. Beneath the headline Senator Committed Suicide, Investigators Say, he read about the "shocking" death of Hargus Webber, once considered a contender for the Oval Office, in his Georgetown home. The cause of death, according to police and FBI investigators, was a single self-inflicted gunshot to the temple, from a pistol found in Webber's lifeless hand. The clipping noted that a letter had been found on Webber's desk, a few feet from his body, but the contents of the letter were being kept under wraps "pending further investigation" by authorities.

"He copped out in the note?" Bolan asked.

"Webber didn't write the note," the Big Fed answered, reaching back inside his jacket for another folded piece of paper, handing it across. Bolan unfolded it and found it was a photocopy, two words printed in the middle of the page, in 36-point type, from a generic laser printer: PRUETT TALKED

"That's cute. Who sent it?"

Brognola responded with a shrug. "There were no fingerprints," he said. "They used a self-seal envelope, tap water on the stamp, so it's a wash on DNA. Postal inspectors traced it back as far as a mailbox on Constitution Avenue. The printer's probably a Hewlett-Packard, can't be more than ten or fifteen million of them in the country. Then again, it could have been an Apple."

Bolan handed back the clipping and the letter, with a weary smile. "What gave him up?"

"Your buddy Deckard got word back to Langley, about Pruett and his stooge. My best guess is, somebody worked it out from there. Maybe the senator had lunch with Pruett once too often. Maybe something showed up on the phone logs. Who's to say?"

Brognola obviously didn't feel like sharing details, and it didn't matter now. "At least it's over," Bolan said.

"I hope so."

"Meaning?"

"Listen, Striker...I don't know how to say this, but—"

"Then don't," Bolan suggested. He had spoken once again to Barbara Price, when they arranged the meet for him with Brognola in Washington. "Shit happens, right?"

"It's not supposed to," the big Fed replied, clearly disheartened. "Not like this."

"I think we ought to leave it in the rearview."

"Objects in the mirror may be closer than they seem," Brognola told him, with a rueful grin.

"You want to know the truth, I don't look back that often."

"Something might be gaining on you?"

"Something always is."

"Okay, if that's the way you want it. But I owe you—"

"Nothing," Bolan told him.

"Nothing, right." Brognola cleared his throat before he asked, "So, how's the kid?"

"I talked him into taking a vacation," Bolan said. "We had a few bucks left from Tolya's stash. He had some time."

"And company?" the big Fed asked. "I mean, from what I hear, it's not much fun to see the world alone."

"I've heard that too," Bolan said, smiling as he tilted back his head. And found that even with his eyes closed he could see the sun.

**A journey through the dangerous frontier
known as the future…**

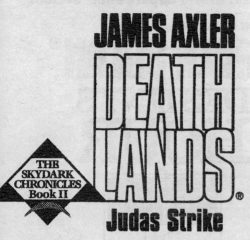

JAMES AXLER
DEATH LANDS®

THE SKYDARK CHRONICLES Book II

Judas Strike

A nuclear endgame played out among the superpowers created
a fiery cataclysm that turned America into a treacherous new
frontier. But an intrepid group of warrior survivalists roams the
wastelands, unlocking the secrets of a pre-dark world.
Ryan Cawdor and his band have become living legends in a
world of madness and death where savagery reigns, but the
human spirit endures….

Available in June 2001 at your favorite retail outlet.

James Axler

OUTLANDERS®

PURGATORY ROAD

The fate of humanity remains ever uncertain, dictated by the obscure forces that have commandeered mankind's destiny for thousands of years. The plenipotentiaries of these ancient oppressors—the nine barons who have controlled America in the two hundred years since the nukecaust—are now falling prey to their own rabid desire for power.

Book #3 of *The Imperator Wars* saga, a trilogy chronicling the introduction of a new child imperator—launching the baronies into war!